WHITE HAWK

WHITE HAWK

by Greg Redlin

ISBN: 9781651803066

The free bird thinks of another breeze
and the trade winds soft through the sighing trees
and the fat worms waiting on a dawn bright lawn
and he names the sky his own

But a caged bird stands on the grave of dreams
his shadow shouts on a nightmare scream
his wings are clipped and his feet are tied
so he opens his throat to sing.

>Maya Angelou's *Caged Bird*
>Etched on Tom White Hawk's gravestone
>Frank Clearwater Cemetery
>Rosebud Reservation
>South Dakota

My thanks to Lara and Ray for their editing expertise.

My appreciation to Barry, Tim, and Pete for reading the whole damn thing and providing valuable suggestions.

My deepest gratitude to my funny, sweet, and forgiving wife, Ro Ann. Thank you for the love, the loyalty, the children, and the Saturday-night dinners.

This novel makes a number of references to the Lakota people and life on the Rosebud Reservation in South Dakota. I apologize if anything I have written is false or misleading in that regard. I wrote this novel with the goal of inspiring empathy and justice for Native Americans in my state. The dominance and indifference of the invading culture has led to much suffering, not yet overcome.

PROLOGUE

For some living in this small Midwest college town, a newspaper headline unsealed a decades-old trauma they thought had lost its power over them.

**South Dakota Murderer Ends Up Dying Middle-Aged Death.
Thomas White Hawk's Passing Recalls Pain of
1960s Crime, Commutation Fight.**

The headline, brief and compressed as it was, carried a sense of relief. Tom had finally paid in full for his unspeakable crime. There is some justice in that sentiment, for the crime was brutal and impossible to understand. But retribution in this case had a hollow feel to it. In the rush to punish the criminal with an equally painful action, we had forgotten to ask about the root cause of his actions. What background influences and mental processes were at work in this gifted eighteen-year-old athlete and university student? Why did he, on an unseasonably warm Good Friday morning, slip into the side entrance of a modest home and murder a defenseless sixty-two-year-old man and rape his wife? Why did he remain at the murder scene, hiding out in the home all day, waiting for the sheriff to arrive?

Tom's parents died when he was young, eleven years old. He was placed in the Hare Home on the Rosebud Reservation, arriving "so lonely and so strong. All he had with him was a change of clothes in a little brown sack," recalled the boarding school principal. As Tom grew older, the melancholy he inherited from his father emerged, despite the awards and honors he received at a military academy he attended after boarding school. Extraordinary athlete that he was, it was the one thing he could not run away from.

After the military academy, Tom attended the University of South Dakota in Vermillion, where he lost his bearings, untethered from a boarding school or academy routine. Vermillion was a one-company college town built on a Missouri River bluff. The river current cut away that bluff, steep and high enough for the Nakota Sioux to convert it into a death trap, herding buffalo over it and slaughtering the injured. The river meanders by Vermillion, the shifting currents creating sandbars that the students sunbathe and party on. The town's elm-lined streets were named after Ivy League universities, Harvard and Yale, symbolizing the confidence Eastern educators had brought to the prairie when they came to teach in this higher-education outpost.

When Tom walked Vermillion's streets nearly a century later, the town's split personality was apparent: a broom factory, alfalfa processing plant, hardware store, locker plant, and lumber yard lent the town its rural background. The 3.2 beer joints, the jewelry stores, the stylish fashions in the clothing stores, and Old Main's tower on campus implied that the town's identity was more diverse and more complex than its rural context.

Vermillion was different. Democrats won local elections here. The Lutherans and Catholics claimed the majority of churchgoers, but it was the Congregational Church's towering colonial revival that drew the eye on Main Street. On campus, the Greek system siphoned off many of the students who spent four years in its arcane world. Fraternity-sorority exchanges, pledge life, hell weeks, ugly-man contests, insignia-stamped clothing, and a musical variety show called *Strollers* defined the college experience for the Greek students. The rest of the students, the "independents," watched the Greeks play with a mixture of envy, irony, and indifference.

Beneath the placid surface, prejudice swirled deep in Vermillion, as deceptive and treacherous as a Missouri River current. For Tom, the town was a strange place. Welcoming to his handsome face, it was suspicious of his background and color when he wasn't in the room. For me, college was the next step in my given trajectory. I was following my father's path: political science major, law school, law practice. Tom's tragedy changed all that.

Tom's crime took place five decades ago. Things have changed. The boarding schools Tom and thousands of others attended are no longer operating, their harsh methods and now-unthinkable goal of cultural disintegration condemned. University students have access to mental health services, regardless of skin color. Murder cases are assigned experienced, salaried counsel. A plea and death sentence in less than ten months would not be tolerated, regardless of how dreadful the crime or the race of the accused. And yet, despite the progress, whites and Native Americans face one another across an expanse as wide as the Missouri River in late spring.

PLEDGE

1

Tom White Hawk was the first Indian I'd ever met, and I grew up in South Dakota—Indian country.

I met Tom at a Sigma Alpha Epsilon fraternity smoker, which probably says more about me than it does about him. Tom had a quiet, confident bearing and thick, unruly hair tamed with Brylcreem. He was wary in this environment but not a bit nervous. His presence drew attention, although being the only Indian in the room didn't seem to bother him. Something told me he had plenty of experience with that.

Tom arrived early one fall evening with the other rushees, a raft of them meandering down Madison Street toward the fraternity house. It was the evening of the last smoker, the culmination of rush week. These rushees were the prized ones—mostly sure bets to pledge at that point—making their way single file through the receiving line and shaking hands with a greeting party of brothers, all earnest geniality. An SAE group played "Take Five"—not too badly, in fact—inside the house in the living room.

I stood watching the greeting party from the service entrance to the house. The evening air was humid, the cicadas singing on cue as the sunlight dimmed. The brothers were dressed semiformal, ignoring the muggy heat in striped shirts, jacquard cardigans, and the occasional turtleneck. We were kids pretending to be adults, untraveled but hardly naïve. Our mothers listened to Johnny Rivers tunes on the local AM stations, debated Ann Landers's marital advice with the other housewives on the block, and served dinner at 5:30 p.m. Our fathers ran hardware stores and pharmacies, sold office products and men's clothes, taught math and biology. Some were bankers, lawyers, and doctors, but the social and financial divides were like hairline fractures—you had to look hard to find them. We were neither the upper-class snobs of the stereotype nor the raucous *Animal House* characters of the movie. We fell in the center, data points at the top of the bell curve with no desire to explore the unknown on either end.

I took a final pull on my cigarette, flicked it into the street, and entered the house. Smitty, the house cook, had laid out shrimp, cocktail sauce, onion dip, and chips on dining tables for the guests. I copped a few shrimp, Smitty pretending to shoo me away, and walked through the French doors that led out to the catwalk overlooking the sunken living room. The brothers were hovering over the prospects—feigning interest in their backgrounds, solicitous and ready for the phony act to end and the humiliation, a.k.a. pledge training, to begin.

I hadn't been on campus long before I discovered Greeks ruled the university—literally. They held almost every student senate seat. The student body president and vice president were Greeks too. Conflict between the student leaders and the university administration was rare. The only controversy of any significance, documented by my research in the student newspaper's archives, occurred when the long-serving university president raided a student fund to finance the new student center. When his treachery was discovered, he was politely questioned for all of ten minutes at a student senate meeting, and then everyone left for *Strollers* practice.

Strollers was the annual musical variety show held in February. Sorority-fraternity teams practiced for months leading up to the big night. The event was held in Slagle Hall, the campus auditorium. The hall was packed with anxious parents and Greeks, many insanely drunk on Ever clear-and-juice concoctions. Though the first-place trophy never adorned the South Dakota Sigma chapter's display case, optimism always ran high during practices leading up to the big night. This was our year! In fact, the campus was so busy in those days, with *Strollers*, Greek exchanges, the annual Mother's Day Sing, and ugly-man contests, that it nearly missed the cultural revolution upending the country. Free speech, the Freedom Riders, and Dylan and Jimi Hendrix were obscure meteors that occasionally fell to our earth but didn't hit hard enough to make an impact.

By the end of the year, 1966, over five thousand American boys my age had died in Vietnam, leading to protests across the country. But the suffering and death in Vietnam hadn't quite registered with us. The draft lottery—where luck would determine whether one fought or stayed home, the course of a life forever altered—wouldn't be held for another three years.

Drugs? Sure, if you had a connection, but the news that you got high risked you getting beat up by the house drunk, a loathsome type bent on upholding the current order, until he too saw the light and traded beer and flavored vodka for pot and mescaline a few years later. By then, of course, most everybody in the house was getting high.

Why was Tom White Hawk at this university? Why was he going through fraternity rush that fall? What fate had led him into this all-white safety net of exchanges and formals, hell weeks and secret handshakes? What did I care? I was a captive of my youth and inexperience, like the rest of my brothers—dumb animals. Indians were a foreign species, stumbling in the alleys behind local bars and wandering aimlessly on highway shoulders in our hometowns. The Sunshine State had conquered, bullied, converted, and finally ignored its first residents, the mysterious Other.

Rich Zinner, SAE rush chairman, made his way toward me as I stood on the catwalk. "Your presence is most appreciated, *Sahib*," Zinner said sarcastically. Zinner had dark-brown hair combed Ivy League style and was wearing a navy polo and cream-colored khakis. He'd had the same sweet girlfriend throughout college, a blond, willowy Pi Phi who was also an SAE Little Sister. Zinner studied prodigiously during the week, partied cautiously on Friday and Saturday nights, and would be off to medical school next year. Rich tried hard to solve the world's problems too. He had a lot to do with Tom White Hawk's presence at this smoker.

"Sorry I missed the earlier smokers, Rich. I apologize. There's a lot to do at the paper this time of the year," I said.

"Paul's been here every night," Zinner said. He was referring to Paul Schurmanns, my roommate. Paul and I worked at the *Volante,* the student newspaper. Paul was the staff photographer, and I was one of a half dozen news writers. We'd moved out of the SAE house after our freshman year, tired of the late-night interruptions and social obligations but still clinging to the identity.

"You can make up for it by helping me out tonight. Roberts has been rushing this guy all week, but he has another prospect tonight. I need you to rush this guy. You're the perfect man for this job. Will you do it?"

"I want to know who this is before I say yes."

"Standing by the fireplace. That's Tom. We want him in the house."

I watched Tom for a few moments before turning back to Zinner.

"Why?"

"Tom went to high school at Shattuck Military Academy. He's premed. And he's an athlete. A very good one. All-conference football player. You know the drill. Keep him entertained while I take care of some other business. I'll close the deal with him before the smoker ends."

"Why me? I don't know him," I said.

"Because everybody else is tied up. I need your help," Zinner said. "Please, I'm begging you. I'm not asking you to be his best friend, just put the rush on. Harvey and I will talk to him later."

"Harvey wants him in the house?" I asked. Harvey Harrison was the fraternity president.

"Harvey went to a Jesuit high school in Wisconsin, remember? Campion's athletic teams played Shattuck. Harvey says Shattuck is a first-rate place. Lots of famous alumni. All the fraternities are rushing Tom."

"This is all a big joke, isn't it? This is a way of getting back at me for missing the other smokers."

Zinner looked disappointed in me. He had a right to be.

"Show some Phi Alpha, man. I'll be back, I promise," Zinner said. *Phi Alpha* was the SAE spirit cry.

I walked down the steps to the living room, working my way through the standing crowd. English Leather cologne and cigarette smoke thickened the air. The trio had just finished its last song as I introduced myself to Tom, the sudden silence adding to the awkwardness.

"My name is Craig Peters. Welcome to the SAE house."

Tom had a shy smile he was careful not to wear out, but he was generous with it that evening. He shook my hand, a light touch, and introduced himself. His eyes showed vulnerability, but his face was cast and hardened. His clothes were worn, cuffed pants riding too high. Months later he showed me his very serious Shattuck graduation picture, standing at attention in an officer's cap, epaulets, and dress uniform. Looking more closely at the picture, I would notice a hint of irony in those same eyes, as if to say, "How do you like my hard-ass imitation?"

Since Tom had already seen the house at previous smokers, I suggested we find an open room upstairs where we could talk. On our way up, we waited on the landing where the stairs turn, making room for Courtland Berry, who was coming down with a pledge in tow. Courtland passed behind Tom on the landing, mimed a war-whooping Indian, and then glanced back at me to make sure I had caught the joke as he continued down.

Courtland was in his early twenties, wound tight, a stickler for house traditions. He came from a prominent family. His grandfather, Tom Berry, had homesteaded in western South Dakota, leveraging 160 acres into a sprawling thirty-thousand-acre ranch near the Badlands, and he eventually became the state's governor in the midthirties. Courtland's father, Baxter Berry, was a melancholy man and a bit of brute, not the folksy Will Rogers persona his father was famous for. Perhaps his family experience explained why Courtland enlisted straight out of high school, spent three years as a grunt in the army, and was discharged before the run-up in Vietnam. Courtland's military career wasn't over, though. He returned to South Dakota and the university determined to earn the degree and an ROTC commission. He wanted back in the army, this time as a regular army officer.

For some reason, Courtland left me alone during pledge life, unlike many of my pledge brothers, who suffered under his relentless hazing. A half hour of pledge duty expanded into two hours of verbal and physical torture if you were so unlucky as to cross Courtland's path while cleaning the urinals or vacuuming the shag carpet in the living room.

I found an open four-man room on the upper floor, stuffy and too warm with the setting sun shining through the tall windows facing west. The window air-conditioning unit in the room wasn't working. We went to the back of the room, where it was darker and cooler, and sat down on opposite bunk beds. I offered Tom a cig, an Old Gold. He preferred Marlboros, he said. I went down to the living room and grabbed a handful from one of the trays placed throughout the house. He was still sitting on the bed, in the same position, when I returned. I gave him the Marlboros, spun the roller on my Zippo with my thumb, and lit our cigarettes.

"Where are you living, Tom?" I asked.

"Julian Hall."

"I lived there my first semester too. What a dump."

He smiled faintly, waiting for me to continue.

"Where are you from?"

"From Mission. On the Rosebud."

I knew Mission was on the other side of the state, west of the Missouri River, which divides the state in half, but could not have pointed to it on a map to save my life.

"What does your dad do?"

"He was an electrical engineer. But he's dead now. So is my mother. She was a nurse."

"I didn't know. Sorry about that, Tom."

Tom nodded.

"Do you have friends here at the university?"

"No one but Dottie, my girlfriend."

"Where's she from?"

"Springfield. We met a few years ago at a summer camp. She's a waitress at the Chimes Café downtown."

I didn't have the stomach to lay the SAE line on him, so I chose the safest route.

"Rich Zinner told me you were an athlete at Shattuck. Where's Shattuck, by the way?"

"Faribault, Minnesota. South of Minneapolis."

"What sports did you play?"

"Most all of them," he said softly, barely audible. I couldn't get anything else out of him. He wouldn't talk about it. Later, I discovered he was a fearless natural athlete who excelled at sports, especially track and field. He ran sprints and the middle distances, and he was a pole vaulter, breaking the Minnesota state record his junior year. On graduation day at Shattuck, he received several awards, both academic and athletic.

I was about to ask him if he planned on going out for track at the university when Zinner came into the room, dramatically waving the cigarette smoke away with one hand. He could be such a pussy.

"Sorry I couldn't be here earlier, Tom. Lots to do tonight," he said.

"We were talking about Tom's athletic career," I said.

"Tom's guardian, Phil, called me," Zinner said. "He told me a lot about Tom. About how well he did at Shattuck. Won a ton of awards. And he's premed. Studying to be a doctor."

"That's Phil's plan, not mine," Tom said, slightly offended at Zinner's patronizing tone.

"Have you been extolling the virtues of SAE?" Zinner asked me, concerned my attitude might be showing.

"We were getting around to that, Rich," I said.

"Okay. Let's go down to my room, and we'll talk some more. Harvey won't be able to join us. Perhaps he'll be free later," Zinner said.

Tom and I followed Zinner to the corner room he shared with Harvey Harrison. Zinner closed the door. There were pictures on the walls of Zinner and Harvey with their girlfriends at spring and fall formals. One picture had the two of them in ascot ties, sporting inebriated grins at an SAE Playboy party. Harvey had also hung his campus leadership and SAE award plaques on one wall for all to see.

Zinner gave Tom the usual sales pitch, how a few good men at the University of Alabama had organized the first chapter before the Civil War, how privileged SAEs were, what brotherhood means, how being an SAE could help Tom professionally one day. He pressed Tom when he finished, asking him whether he would be pledging SAE. It seemed more forced and uncomfortable than it usually did. Tom looked up, acting his part, and said yes, he was thinking about it. Zinner seemed happy with that. When we heard the music start to play downstairs, Zinner suggested we join everyone. The smoker was about over.

Everyone had gathered in the living room. Stepping out in front of the trio, Harvey signaled for quiet. Stick-thin and a heavy smoker, Harvey had authority written all over him. He was in his customary uniform: khakis, maroon penny loafers, and a white polo with his president's badge pinned above the pocket. He held a lit Camel in one hand, gesturing with it, smoke trailing in a zigzag trail, as he introduced himself. He said a few mushy words about his decision to pledge SAE and how it had changed his life. His inspirational message finished,

Harvey tossed it back to Zinner, who led the brothers in "Come Sing," the SAE fight song.

Across the room, Zinner caught my eye and nodded in Tom's direction. He was standing alone near the fireplace again. I didn't appreciate it at the time, but Zinner was a decent guy, something I hadn't yet learned how to be. I went over and accompanied Tom on his way out.

"Thanks for coming, Tom," I said, standing on the curb as he made his way down the street, which was milky white in the reflecting moonlight.

He glanced back, his head turned but his body moving forward, and said, "Yes, sir. Thanks for the cigs, sir."

I waved at him as he slipped into the night, realizing only then that I had forgotten to shake his hand and extract a firm pledge commitment. I turned and headed back into the house, recognizing Courtland's outline standing in the dark near the service entrance. He was a weird one, Courtland.

2

Caitlin was a news writer on the *Volante* staff. She was the only woman on the staff back then, standing out like Tom White Hawk at a fraternity smoker. She came to the *Volante* office one afternoon—a deadline day—dropped her books on a desk, and stormed over to where the other staff were working, or more likely wasting time. She was wearing a pullover sweater to keep warm in the cool fall weather, jeans, and tennis shoes. Her long hair was pulled back behind her ears, a gesture, I came to discover, that signaled frustration. I hadn't met her yet, but the guy who covered campus sports apparently had. She spoke to him while I pretended not to be listening.

"Hi. You're in the American lit course, right? Joe Basille's course."

"You are very observant," said the sportswriter.

"Fuck you, Beardsley. How did you do on the test we got back today?"

"Pretty well, as a matter of fact. I wrote about baseball as a literary metaphor. It wasn't that good, but Basille is a baseball geek. You gotta know your audience."

"What the fuck. I'm not going to pull that bullshit."

"Then prepare to stay unread, Caitlin. You are just average, like the rest of us."

"We'll see about that," she said, and went back to her desk without so much as a glance in my direction.

I had never heard a woman my age use the word "fuck" so naturally. Or use it in anger, for that matter. It was the sexiest use of the F-word I had ever heard.

After everyone had turned in their story copy to the editor, most of us went to the Grille, the student union coffee shop, where the staff hung out on deadline days. We sat down at a crowded table next to Caitlin's roommate, whom she introduced as Chris. Chris pushed aside some white institutional coffee cups and stacks of opened creamer packages to make room for us.

The conversation turned to the Vietnam War, but I paid little attention. Caitlin was still wearing makeup then, dark eye shadow and eyeliner that lent her a pouty, seductive Christine Keeler look. Her brown hair was long and straight, unlike the monotony of pageboy cuts in the sorority houses. Chris was a petite blonde with bright blue eyes and a husky voice. They were a study in physical and personality opposites. Caitlin seemed not to fully understand what sort of effect she had on men, a veneer of insecurity deepening the attraction. Chris knew very well the power of sex, and she flaunted it, teased and tormented men with it.

Later, when everyone rose to leave, I followed Caitlin and Chris. At the exit, I reached ahead and opened the door for them. They seemed embarrassed at the gesture, eyes rolling.

That Friday evening I ran into both of them again at the Varsity, a student pub. They were sitting at the bar. I joined them, taking the stool next to Caitlin. She was wearing a lemon-smelling fragrance. They ignored me.

"Hi. Remember me? At the *Volante* and the Grille this week?" I asked Caitlin when they had stopped talking.

"Oh, sure. Craig, right?" Caitlin said, turning her head but not her body toward me. Her hair fell below her shoulders, and she was wearing jeans and a dark T-shirt. They were drinking red beers in glass mugs.

"I remember you," Chris said, overhearing us. "The frat boy. The Dud or Delt or whatever."

"It's SAE, Sigma Alpha Epsilon," I said, feeling outed and sounding defensive.

"Oh," Chris said in a mockingly apologetic tone, "excuse me. I certainly didn't mean to offend."

"Forgiven. What are you two doing here? Cruising for frat boys?" I said, imagining that was funny.

"You're kidding, right?" Caitlin asked, but without malice.

"Of course. Do you know the band playing tonight?"

"Kid Sparrow. We're groupies," said Chris. "Caitlin's boyfriend Harlan is their sound manager. I'm here to get laid."

"I can help you with that."

"No, you can't. But nice try," Chris said, amused though clearly not interested.

They slid off their stools and made their way downstairs. Chris was the shorter of the two. Her hair was a sunny Scandinavian blond, and she wore it in the same flat style Caitlin wore hers, but Chris's jean skirt made her seem even shorter and a little pudgy.

"Come on down with us," Caitlin said, her hand on my arm, warm, inviting. "We'll get a table."

Surprisingly, Chris seemed as eager as Caitlin to have me along. A few weeks later, Caitlin told me they were high on mushrooms that night, having found Harlan's stash earlier that afternoon. They thought having a straight man along with them would be good for a few laughs. And that's the way it turned out. Chris and Caitlin were a kind of female company I had never experienced before, more like men in the way they talked about current politics and drank more than the first pitcher and told jokes about sex. Kid Sparrow played well enough—not the Fabulous Flippers, by any means, but they kept everyone on the dance floor most of the night.

I ran into Caitlin several times in the newspaper office over the next few weeks. She was friendlier after the night out but made no effort to acknowledge me unless it couldn't be avoided. I saw her outside the office, too, but at a distance, playing cards with a group of vets in the Grille or sitting in the dining hall with Chris and some other girls, eating lunch or dinner. Seeing Caitlin at a distance, with other people, hurt. It was obvious what was happening.

And then I got lucky. One Friday night Paul was on his way home for his uncle's funeral. I caught a ride with him downtown. He dropped me off near the Baptist church, which was on the same block as the Varsity. I walked down the block, the smell of spilled beer and pizza growing stronger the closer I got to the bar. A Greek exchange was breaking up, and sloshed Delts and Thetas were pairing up for some postexchange necking, entirely absorbed in themselves. Two Delt pledges were bent over, vomiting in the adjacent alley, streams of puke splashing on the gravel.

Inside, the place was packed with students who were there to listen to the band. Near the back, Caitlin and Chris sat at a table beneath a large wall mural. The mural was a throwback scene, with clownish 1950s fraternity men in V-neck sweaters and baggy pants stumbling from table to table and pawing the coeds, tiny bubbles hovering above their heads signifying how inebriated they were.

Grabbing a stool at the bar, I pretended not to see Caitlin and Chris. Harlan was probably at the table with them.

I was self-conscious, alone in a bar. And then Caitlin tapped me on the shoulder.

"Hey, frat boy, are you snubbing us?"

"I didn't see you. Where are you sitting?"

"Over in that far corner. Bring your beer and join us."

I followed Caitlin through the crowd. Her soft, straight hair fell down the back of her suede faux-leather jacket, the kind with fringes down the arms. She was wearing Loves Fresh Lemon again tonight. At the table, she introduced me to a couple of people. Chris was at the other end, spellbound by a guy with long hair parted down the middle and a well-trimmed beard, the replica of a beatific Jesus portrait.

I took the empty seat next to Caitlin, and she reached for a pitcher to refill my glass.

"You're left-handed."

"I was telling Chris how brilliant you are."

"No, I mean, there's something attractive about left-handed people. Especially women."

"I thought I had heard every pickup line in the book."

"I'll bet you have, but I'm not just any guy."

"Yeah, you are. Hey, where are your brothers tonight?" she asked, the customary sarcasm missing from her pronunciation of "brothers." And then she smiled. She favored her left when smiling too, her mouth opening a little wider on that side.

"Most are at an A-Phi exchange at Heck's."

If that told her anything about why I was at the bar, she didn't show it. Like most beautiful women, she was accustomed to and maybe expected men showing up without an invitation. We talked some more, mostly about the American lit course. She wanted to know what I thought of *The Sun Also Rises*. I thought the novel was moving and the language still fresh. She affected a disappointed, mocking look. She was not impressed. She couldn't get by the stylized prose and thought Jake Barnes was a phony tough guy, but she gave Hemingway credit for creating a female character in Lady Brett who made her own sexual choices, uninfluenced by society and damn the consequences.

The waitress brought another round of pitchers. I paid for them and then went to the head. Back at the table, I noticed the Jesus lookalike was no longer sitting with Chris.

"Is that Harlan who was sitting with Chris a few minutes ago?"

"Harlan's in Lincoln tonight. Kid Sparrow has a gig at a college hangout near the University of Nebraska campus. They're staying the night."

When Jesus returned to the table, Chris got up, and the two of them came over.

"We're going to Gunner's. Party there tonight. Want to ride with us?"

"Go ahead. I'll follow along. I know where he lives," Caitlin said.

Chris clenched her mouth, casting Caitlin a hard look, and then walked away.

The pair was no more than out the door of the Varsity when Caitlin suggested we leave. We walked out into the cold night, bracing after the warm, humid bar atmosphere. I followed Caitlin as she walked two blocks down to Center Street, where we turned north. We walked by the municipal liquor store, which was doing a brisk business. A man with a scowl and a marine buzz cut was standing at the door, carding customers as they entered. Another two blocks and we were standing on the sidewalk outside Gunner's, a trashed square-frame house needing paint. The screen door on the front porch was full of holes. The place was as packed as the Varsity and almost as loud. Drunks brushed past us, walking into the house without knocking on the door as we stood there.

Caitlin turned to me. She was shivering in her jacket, a frown on her face.

"You know what? Let's go over to my place. There are too many people here, most of whom are imbeciles," she said, rolling her eyes. I was falling for her, and in that moment the sarcasm she was sharing, as if we were old friends who wouldn't be offended regardless of what the other said, made her even sexier. She was fun to be with in a way I had never experienced with a woman.

Caitlin and Chris lived in an upstairs apartment next to a Sinclair station just off Main Street. We walked quickly to escape the cold. The apartment was a tiny student rental. They had decorated it with a braided rug on the living room floor and several fern and philodendron plants. A console TV with stereo speakers on either side and a turntable on top stood against one wall. LP album covers were stacked on a side table. We sat on the couch for a while, listening to *Rubber Soul* and drinking what was left of a bottle of Mateus in the refrigerator. When the wine was gone, Caitlin took my hand and led me into her bedroom, and she disappeared into the bathroom. She came back in her bathrobe. I was sitting on the edge of the bed, waiting for the next cue.

"You can take your clothes off now," Caitlin said.

Caitlin shed her bathrobe and sat up against the headboard of the bed. She had her panties on but nothing else. As I took my clothes off, she watched...well, *tenderly*, I think, is the right word, so different from the rushed and clumsy preludes of my prior experience.

But she caught herself and shape-shifted back into Caitlin, or the Caitlin I had known up to that point.

"Have you ever done this before?"

"Me? Sure. I've been around," I said, a little pissed.

"You're lying, aren't you? This is your first time, isn't it?" she said, amused.

If I had understood the attraction of inexperience, I would have said yes, but I had a lot to learn.

"It is not my first time. What do you think exchanges are? Sex education for Greeks."

"A fraternity man of the world."

"That might be a slight exaggeration."

"We'll see."

In the dark bedroom, Caitlin looked like a star in a noir movie, her straight bangs falling low across her forehead. She had large, full breasts, broad shoulders, and smooth arms, freckled and pale. I drew closer, wrapped my arms around her, and kissed her gently. She pushed me off playfully, claiming that my approach revealed what an amateur I was. I pushed back, and we started wrestling, relieving the tension. We lay there for some time afterward, our conversation trailing off. She fell asleep long before I did.

The next morning Caitlin poured orange juice into two glasses and made toast and coffee. We sat silently at a rickety table in the kitchen, the morning sun shining through the bay window. A green-and-white Sinclair sign advertising gas prices at $0.32 a gallon for regular was directly in the sight line of their window.

Caitlin was distracted, staring quietly at the sun's rays forming a pool of light on the kitchen floor. She held a coffee cup with both hands. Her fingernails were bitten down.

"Harlan will be home soon," she said. "And I've got laundry to do."

"Yeah, I've got to go too. I had fun. Thanks," I said and leaned over to kiss her. "Will I see you soon?"

"Not if I see you first," she said, holding the joke for a moment and then smiling. "Sure, maybe. We'll see."

I walked down the steep, creaky stairs on my way out, sensing that something was coming, something big, feeling how ready I was for it to begin.

I quit SAE cold turkey shortly after I met Caitlin. So I guess you could say there was a woman involved. Paul stayed active in the house, partying with the brothers at weekend exchanges, organizing the fall formal and the Playboy party, and attending the monthly chapter meetings. He was a cast member in the *Strollers* show too, requiring him to be at the house for rehearsals as the show date grew closer. Paul brought me house news, which is how I found out that Zinner and Harvey had turned Courtland, who had been dead set against allowing Tom White Hawk into the house. The quiet kid from Rosebud became SAE's first Indian pledge.

Tom won over his pledge brothers with his inscrutable stoicism. Hardened by his hazing experiences at Shattuck, he shrugged off the actives who tried to rattle him during pledge duties. Later in the semester, he was the hero in the intramural championship game against the Delts, SAE's bitter enemies. Tom bull-rushed the offensive linemen with a fury never before witnessed, caught three touchdown passes, and was carried off the field by the brothers after routing our hated rivals.

Toward the end of the semester, there was a blow-up between Tom and Courtland that changed everything. It happened during the culmination of hell week, where sleep-deprived pledges who have been prancing around the house in gunny sacks for three days, necklaces strung with onions hanging from their necks, are deceived into thinking they have successfully completed hell week. They're told it's time to celebrate, to get drunk. Everybody gets smashed. Blitzed.

Then, to the active chapter's feigned surprise, an official from SAE headquarters calls and announces that he will be arriving that afternoon to administer the national test to the pledges. After the pledges clean up the hell week mess in the house, they are separated, each one in an individual room. One at a time, blindfolded pledges are led into the living room and instructed to kneel in front of a table. The officer administering the test sits on the other side. The room is very dark. A candle burns on either side of the officer, and a copy of the pledge manual, the *Phoenix*, lies all Bible-like between the officer and pledge.

The officer asks the pledge test questions from the *Phoenix*. The brothers are seated behind the pledge, all but one of them cheering the test taker on. A single negative voice in the audience of brothers berates the pledge, advising him to quit now, proclaiming that the fraternity will be better off without this pathetic piece of shit. Every pledge flunks the test and is told that he will never become an SAE. Many of the pledges start crying. The brothers explode with anger at this outrageous development but are powerless to do anything, it seems.

It was all a ruse. All for a few laughs and the bonding effect. But this time, before Tom was let in on the joke, a fight broke out. Courtland had mercilessly badgered Tom the entire hell week and had assumed the role of the negative voice during

Tom's test, cackling with pleasure each time he gave a wrong answer. When Tom failed the test, he was led out of the room while Courtland followed him, pouring it on. Nobody thought he was being funny anymore, but no one in the house ever stood up to Courtland. Tom turned back, brushed off the two brothers who were consoling him, and went for Courtland. Tom decked him, knocking out two front teeth. Courtland lay there, bleeding heavily from the nose and mouth, but the son of a bitch called Tom a prairie nigger and started to get up as if to carry on with the fight. Tom stormed out of the house, never to return.

A week into the second semester, I was working in the *Volante* office when Courtland came to see me. I saw him at the far end where everyone entered, talking to the paper's editor. The editor turned and pointed in my direction. Courtland strode over to my desk, his head and chin tilted up a bit, as if he were a military courier bearing a message. He stood directly above me for a moment, looked for a chair and found one, then pulled it across the tile floor with a loud scraping sound and sat down.

"Well, what have we here?" Courtland asked sarcastically, as if he had caught me reading a *Playboy*.

"Writing a fascinating story about the quality of the food in the university cafeteria. It seems the students are unhappy with it. What brings you here?"

"I consider you a friend, Peters. In fact, I am here to help you. I have something of professional interest. Perhaps it will inspire you to write a truly important story."

Courtland had a file folder in his lap. The edges of a few mimeographed pages were sticking out of it.

"What is it? What have you got in the file?"

"It's a little something about our friend Tom White Hawk. It seems Mr. White Hawk went on a joyride over Thanksgiving vacation. He stole a car in Minneapolis and drove it back here to Vermillion. And then, in what might be the bonehead play of all time, he got caught running a stop sign with the car and got busted. A real Einstein, our brother Tomahawk."

"Is that a pledge name or your own personal pet name?"

"I call him whatever I please. But here, see for yourself," Courtland said, sliding the file folder slowly and with intended drama, like a smug detective who has the goods on someone.

The file folder contained a police report on Tom's traffic accident and arrest for interstate transportation of a stolen motor vehicle. Included in the file were some notes the sheriff took while interviewing Tom after his arrest. The notes said Tom was a member of the SAE fraternity. A friend of Courtland's who worked in the sheriff's office had given him a copy of the file.

"We haven't seen Tomahawk since the hell week fiasco," Courtland said. "Did you hear about that?" he asked, raising a suspicious eyebrow.

"Paul told me," I said.

"Now some weak-kneed brothers want to let him back in. We would have forgiven his outburst at the end of hell week, but this car theft business is serious. Tomahawk will not cross the SAE threshold again."

"Not sure why you're here, Courtland. I'm not in the house anymore. This isn't my business, serious or not."

"You care about this university, don't you? You work for its newspaper, don't you?"

"What is it about Tom that sets you off? What did he do to you?"

Courtland leaned back in his chair.

"I have to explain this to you? It's not obvious? Zinner and Harvey should not have allowed him to pledge. They thought he was a good one. It made them feel good. But our house isn't the right place for him."

"What do you want, Courtland?"

"I'm here as your friend. Tomahawk is a student here at the university. This is a real story, one people will actually read. They should know more about their fellow students, about their values."

"You want the *Volante* to write a story about the car theft?"

"Bingo," Courtland said, straight faced. "That's all I ask. But do it soon. We need to get this behind us. He's made a mockery of the house. Don't bother to see me out. I know the way."

"Why don't you give him another chance?"

Courtland shot me a look as if he had misjudged me somehow.

"He turned out like all the rest. He was sullen most of the time, didn't make friends."

"Like all the rest?"

"Come visit our ranch. I'll show you."

When he rose from his chair, he spotted Caitlin at her desk, rolled his eyes in her direction, and then looked back at me, nodding his approval.

I was slow to do the right thing. I put off going over to Julian Hall for a week before I finally worked up the courage. Several inches of snow had fallen the night before, covering the campus lawn in a soft white blanket. I walked over to Julian from the *Volante* offices, the bitter wind burning my cheeks. Despite the cold, most of the dorm room windows were cranked open to cool rooms overheated by the unregulated steam heat. Tom's room, 619, was on the top floor down a long hallway. Students were leaving for class. I had considered calling first, but I didn't think he'd remember me, or if he did, wouldn't want to talk. I knocked on the door.

Willie Stands opened it. Willie was a friend of Tom's, someone he'd met at the Wapaha Club, an Indian student organization. Willie couldn't have weighed more than a hundred pounds. He was wearing a white T-shirt and khakis. His belt was cinched to the last hole, and that still wasn't tight enough. He had a large head, with dark, shiny hair swept into a pompadour. His face, full of acne, betrayed no expression.

Tom was lying on the upper bunk, staring at the ceiling, shirtless. He had large sailor tattoos on one forearm that I had not noticed when I met him at the smoker. The room was very warm, with heat pouring out of their room register, steaming the window above it. Willie crawled into the bunk below Tom's. I discovered something about Tom at that meeting in his dorm room that always threw me off: his sudden openness, his life revealed and then shut down again as if you were caught prying.

"Hey, Tom. It's Craig. Remember me? We met last fall at the SAE house."

"I remember."

"Sorry for the intrusion. I need to talk to you."

"Doesn't everyone?"

"How are you? It's been a while."

"Been better. Been worse. I've had a lot of migraine headaches lately. I've got one today."

"Migraines are serious. Have you seen a doctor?"

"Many times, at Shattuck. I had an accident my sophomore year at a track meet. Got hit in the head by a shot put. The doctor said there was no neurological damage, but the headaches started after that. He gave me some pills, but they don't always work."

I was standing, leaning on his dresser, a battered old piece of institutional furniture. The top and sides were etched with the signatures and Greek affiliation of former occupants of the room. A picture of Tom and a middle-aged man in a western shirt and jeans in a horse corral was propped up on the dresser, along with Tom's hairbrush, a bottle of Brylcreem, some loose change, a billfold, and a prescription bottle of phenobarbital.

"Phenobarbital, huh? Never heard of it. Maybe a beer would be better. Want to go down to Thorsten's?" Thorsten's was a 3.2 beer joint downtown.

"No, thanks. I can hardly move my head, it hurts so much."

"What brings the headaches on?"

"I got into some trouble lately. Phil came to see me about it. We went at it pretty bad."

"Is that Phil?" I asked, pointing to the picture on the dresser.

"Yeah."

"What happened?"

"Nothing to worry about. Phil overreacts, you know what I mean?"

"Sure, like a parent. But then, I don't know Phil."

More uncomfortable silence.

"Was Phil here recently?"

"Yeah. He was worried I'd drop out of school. I want to. Maybe join the marines. Or get a job. He thinks I should stick it out, at least this year. He writes me these long letters full of dos and don'ts like I'm still a twelve-year-old orphan."

Tom abruptly stopped, pivoting inside somewhere, shifting into a darker corner.

"Why are you here?" he asked.

"There's something I need to talk to you about," I said. "I work at the *Volante*, as you may know. A few days ago, Courtland

Berry stopped by to see me. He has a file with your records. The stolen-car business."

Tom said nothing.

"Courtland wants me to write a story about it for the newspaper. I'm not going to do that, but he'll keep trying to embarrass you in whatever way he can. He's after you."

"It doesn't matter," Tom said. "I should never have pledged a fraternity. Phil's idea."

"It's more than that for Courtland."

"Maybe so. Fuck him. Thanks. Go now."

Willie, in the lower bunk, shrugged.

I went back to the *Volante* offices expecting to feel good about the effort, full of righteousness, but I couldn't shake the feeling that I had somehow let Tom down.

3

A false spring arrived in March that year, a warm spell the last week of Lent that melted most of the winter snow, leaving a few shrunken drifts in shaded spots. On Good Friday it reached eighty-three degrees, the summerlike heat weirdly depressing. I decided to stay in town rather than go home for the break. My parents were in California on their annual visit to my aunt who lived in San Diego. They liked San Diego and its predictably mild climate and escaped the South Dakota wind and cold for a few weeks each year.

I walked over to campus, which was deserted for the holiday. I entered the student center through a side door—the editor had given me a key—that opened into the *Volante* offices. I was killing time, reading through a stack of issues from the 1950s, when the phone in the editor's office rang. *What the hell,* I thought, *I might as well answer it.*

"Craig, hi. It's Rich Zinner. I thought I might find you at the newspaper. You are not going to believe what we just saw. Fucking unbelievable."

"What are you talking about?"

"Jan and I went to Whimp's for dinner this evening and came back to town on the low road along the bluff, then turned up the bluff at University Street."

Whimp's was a steakhouse a few miles outside town. It was popular with the local farmers and older students.

"Go on."

"Well, we reached the top of the hill and were driving down University, no traffic, nothing happening, until we saw about twenty or more cars, some of them police cars, parked outside a small two-story home. A crowd was gathered on the front lawn. The police had cordoned off a driveway and side entrance. The sheriff was escorting a man in handcuffs into a police car. The man was Tom White Hawk."

"What?"

"The guy in handcuffs was Tom White Hawk."

"How long ago was this?"

"A few minutes ago. I dropped Jan off and called you as soon as I got back to the house."

"Thanks. I'll go over there and see what's going on."

I ran back to my apartment and found the keys to my car, a 1948 navy Plymouth Coupe my father drove for many years and then gave to me when I graduated from high school. I was embarrassed to be seen in it. The overwrought grillwork on the front, the bloated fenders, the plush upholstered seat covers—everything about it said old lawyer's car. Tonight I gunned it, driving as fast as I could over to University Street, where the crowd was milling about, the warm setting sun casting skeletal shadows through the leafless trees.

Two policemen were standing guard outside the north side entrance to the home.

"I work for a newspaper. Can you tell me what's happened here?"

That introduction didn't impress. They looked at each other, and then the one with long sideburns, the bully type who graduates from high school and then joins the local police department to retry his grievances, said they were under strict orders not to talk to anybody. The other one said I might try the man standing with his girls at the neighbor's house.

The girls were twins, teenyboppers. They stood on either side of their father, one of them holding his hand. They were cute, skinny Olive Oyl look-alikes, their big eyes taking everything in. Their father was a high school science teacher, Mr. Hollman.

"I work for a newspaper. Can you tell me what happened?"

"Jim Yeado is dead. The gentlest man I have ever met. Wouldn't hurt a fly," he said, shaking his head in disbelief.

Yeado. The name was familiar. Then it occurred to me it might be the jeweler downtown.

"Any relation to Yeado Jeweler?" I asked.

"Jim's run that store for thirty years."

"The Indian boy," said one of the twins. "They left with him a while ago. Handcuffed. He's a university student."

"We live here, next door," Hollman said. "Some friends called the Yeados about a dinner party they had planned for this evening. When the Yeados didn't answer, they called us and asked if we'd check on them. I went over to the side entrance, the one the Yeados use, and noticed that a glass window in the door had been smashed in. It looked like someone had broken into the home. I wasn't about to go inside. As I was going back to our house to call the police, I saw someone inside the home closing the living room curtains. Then Loretta here saw Mrs. Yeado come out of the side entrance in her nightgown, acting strangely, especially for Dorthea, who is always so very proper. I went outside to see if I could help her."

"Did she tell you what happened? What did she say?"

"She didn't make any sense. She was in shock, talking gibberish, confused. She said she was looking for Jim. She needed to see him. She hadn't seen him all night. She didn't recognize me, looking right through me, as if I wasn't there. Said there were two Indians in the house, and one of them, the big one, had raped her. I held her hand until the police finally arrived. I noticed her wrists were burned, a band about two inches wide. When she got into the ambulance, the bottom edge of her robe slid up. She had the same reddish burn on her ankles."

"And the police arrived after that?"

"The police and Sheriff Wilson."

"What happened then?"

"Sheriff Wilson and the police chief went into the house through the side entrance. I want to tell you, everyone was frightened out of their wits. The neighbor on the other side of the Yeado home was on the lawn, poised with his shotgun. I made these two go inside the house until they brought out the Indian boy."

"And Mr. Yeado?"

"The county coroner arrived shortly after. Jim left on a stretcher, still wrapped in the rag rug they found him in."

I thanked Mr. Hollman for the information. I drove to the county courthouse on west Main Street, where the sheriff's office and jail were located. The sheriff's office was strangely quiet. A circular fan was rotating on the front desk, blowing warm air. The front desk was unoccupied, the secretary apparently having gone home. The dispatcher's office was at the end of a long hallway, where the public was not allowed. I heard voices leaking out from the office, but they weren't loud enough for me to make out what was being said.

I sat down on a bench opposite the front desk, confident I'd somehow convince the sheriff to talk to me once he showed up. A few minutes later, he arrived. With the sheriff was a tall man with a flat-top haircut and black frame glasses. He was in golf attire, probably taking advantage of the weather to play the first round of the season. Despite the golf wardrobe, he looked like an all-business kind of guy. They were heading toward the sheriff's office and didn't take notice of me until I raised my hand and called out the sheriff's name, as if I were in class.

"Sheriff Wilson. Sheriff Wilson. Can I have a word with you? I have a few questions."

They stopped and turned to me, sizing me up. The sheriff looked annoyed, the other man downright pissed.

"Who are you?" the sheriff asked.

"Craig Peters. I work for a newspaper. I'm writing a story about the murder this afternoon at the Yeado home."

"We're not talking to the press right now, son. And you'll have to wait in line when we do. Several newspapers have already called. Which one do you work for?"

"The *Volante*."

"Are you serious?" asked the other man. "Do you think we're going to stop this investigation, drop everything, to talk to the student newspaper?"

"I'm also a friend of Tom White Hawk's. I may be able to help. His parents are both dead. I have his guardian's name."

"We've got the guardian's name. Phil Zolbach. What did you say your name was? I don't think the prisoner mentioned you."

"Craig Peters."

"Nope. Didn't mention that name. Look, I can't make you leave, but we've got an investigation to conduct. We'll talk to the press tomorrow."

"And who are you?" I asked the taller one.

"Chuck Volesky, state's attorney."

"Thank you, Mr. Volesky and Sheriff Wilson. I'll be back tomorrow."

One flight up from the sheriff's office, a dozen or more law enforcement types and locals were milling around the rotunda of the courthouse, gossiping about the Yeado murder. Their voices echoed off the stone walls and terrazzo floor, voices of suppressed rage and shock. I approached two of them. One was a shrunken man in church clothes, short-sleeved white shirt and tie, the other a mechanic in coveralls, soiled with grease and oil, who looked as if he'd left work and rushed down to the courthouse when he heard the news. I asked them if they knew anything about the murder.

"Yeah, our friend is dead. Killed by those fucking Indians," the one in the coveralls replied.

"I thought the only person arrested was Tom White Hawk."

"He had an accomplice. They broke into the house together, but one of them left early. Headed back to the reservation, I hear. Hiding, like an Indian. The sheriff knows where he is. They'll have him in custody soon."

"What's his name?"

"William something. Maybe Billy. I don't fucking know. I do know they are gonna pay for this."

It must have been Willie. Willie Stands.

"Do you know what happened?"

"The big one shot Jim with a rifle, and then he scalped him and castrated him. Drained his blood like a savage. Then he raped Dorthea while Jim was dead or dying. Fucker doesn't deserve to live. He should die tonight."

The next morning I went down to the sheriff's office. This time I was prepared. I put on the only pair of slacks I had, leftovers from my SAE days, and brought along my reporter's notebook. I fantasized taking notes alongside other newspaper reporters at a news conference explaining the murder. But the sheriff's secretary was the only person in the office. I doubt she normally came in on Saturdays, especially on Easter weekend, but the murder had turned a lot of lives upside down in this town. She pushed herself away from the typewriter when I approached her desk, crossing her arms. The sheriff had no doubt coached her to say nothing about the murder.

I caught the title she'd typed in caps at the top of the paper in the typewriter when I approached her desk: "SHERIFF WILSON'S NOTES—MARCH 24, 1967." I held my glance a moment too long. She caught me looking at it. She pulled the paper out, turned the side with the typed letters face down on her desk, and looked suspiciously at me.

"What can I do for you, young man?"

"I'm a newspaper reporter. I'm here for the sheriff's meeting with the press. He's going to talk about the homicide last night."

She smiled, a triumphant look, as if I deserved what she was going to say next.

"Then you have a long wait on your hands. Sheriff Wilson will not be back for quite some time," she said.

"Where might he be?"

She thought about that for a moment, me the once-over, as if my appearance had a bearing on how she would answer, and then relented.

"He's on his way to one of the Indian reservations to pick up a suspect. Everybody else is over at municipal court with the murderer. He's being charged this morning."

"Where's municipal court?"

She sighed. "Downtown. City hall."

City hall was a block off Main Street in the center of town. It took me all of five minutes to drive the four blocks. All the street-side parking was taken near the building. Driving past the front entrance, I saw a knot of people emerging. A deputy sheriff, Volesky, and several other men, mostly uniformed police, were escorting the prisoner out. I stopped my car, double-parked, and rushed over to the scene. Tom was in the middle of the authorities, handcuffed, head down, following a deputy sheriff's lead. I was standing next to someone with a flash camera who yelled his name. "Hey, White Hawk, over here." Tom turned in the caller's direction. He saw me standing next to the caller but showed no hint of recognition before the caller snapped his picture. The expression the camera caught was unremorseful and demented. His hair was uncombed, his eyes narrowed and crazed—a killer. Another unsmiling Indian for the gallery.

The deputy sheriff guided Tom into the back seat of a squad car. I called out to Volesky, who was leaving in a separate car.

"Mr. Volesky. What happened in there? When will you talk to the press?"

"You missed your chance. You'll have to talk to your buddies over there," Volesky said, pointing to two men leaning against a car in front of city hall.

The two were newspaper reporters, the AP guy who took Tom's picture and a *Sioux City Journal* staff writer. I went over to them.

"Sorry to butt in, but I need some information for a story I'm writing for the *Volante*. What did Volesky say this morning about the homicide? What happened in the courtroom?"

"He didn't say much at all. Gave us the names of the victims and the accused. Otherwise, nothing. They ain't talking. The hearing was a joke."

"Did they charge White Hawk? Did they find his partner?"

"They charged him with premeditated murder and rape. I guess they found the other guy on the reservation and are bringing him back here."

"Willie? Willie Stands?"

"That's the name. I don't know about Jim, here," the AP newsman said, referring to the other reporter, "but I've got a lot of work to do and only a few hours before deadline. You can read about it in the *Argus Leader* afternoon edition. I've got to go."

Another dead end. I went back to my apartment, took a shower, and smoked a couple of cigarettes, thinking about the whole mess. I knew this was a story, unlike the car theft business, that the *Volante* should cover. And I had an angle no one else did. I knew Tom. I told myself I was concerned for Tom's welfare, but if I were honest, I was more interested in what this could mean for me than Tom. Tom was no stranger to that motivation, I thought. After a long nap—I hadn't slept well the night before—I dressed, a jacket and sweater since the temperature had dropped back down into the forties, and drove down to the Monogram News on Main Street.

The Monogram News sold cigarettes, chew, candy, home and garden magazines, *Playboy* and *Penthouse*, newspapers—those sorts of things. Tug, the proprietor, stood behind the counter, big half-circle bags under his eyes giving him a look of perpetual grimness. He was real chatty that day as I waited for the afternoon edition of the *Argus* to arrive, animatedly sharing an even bloodier version of the Yeado murder than the one I'd heard the night before. *Jesus Christ*, I thought, *Tom did that shit.*

Shortly after 3:00 p.m., the truck arrived. I wasn't the only one waiting for a paper. A long line had formed. The truck driver brought four bound stacks into the store, grunting as he hoisted them onto the counter near the cash register. Sure enough, there was Tom's headline on the front page.

USD Student Charged
with Rape, Murder

VERMILLION, S.D. (AP)—A University of South Dakota student from the Mission, S.D., area was charged with murder and rape Saturday in the slaying of a Vermillion jeweler and an attack on the jeweler's wife.

Thomas James White Hawk, about 20, obtained a continuance from Municipal Judge E. T. Michels to allow time to get an attorney. After a brief recess, White Hawk reappeared in court with Vermillion lawyer Lee McMillan as his counsel.

State's Attorney Charles Volesky and McMillan conferred, but no time for further proceedings was announced immediately.

Authorities were reportedly pursuing a theory that James Yeado, about 60, was killed in his home sometime Friday when he refused to give the combination to the safe at his jewelry store to a pair of burglars that broke into the Yeado home.

Yeado was found shot in the head in the basement of his house.

Mrs. Dorthea Yeado, in her 50s, was found tied up in an upstairs room of the house. She was hospitalized for medical attention, with symptoms including shock.

Shortly before White Hawk was brought into court, an aide to Sheriff Arnie Wilson said the sheriff had gone to Mission to bring back to Vermillion a second man who had been taken into custody on the Rosebud Indian Reservation for questioning. The man was reported to be about 20 years old.

The student directory at the University of South Dakota lists White Hawk as a freshman in arts and sciences, living in Julian Hall, a dormitory for USD men. The directory also indicates that he attended Shattuck Military School in Faribault, Minn., while in high school and is a member of the SAE fraternity.

The Vermillion chief of police said White Hawk had a record of having been arrested previously, in connection with a car theft.

Police said White Hawk was in the Yeado home when officers were summoned there Friday evening. He was reported to have surrendered without resistance.

The still incomplete investigation held evidence that Mrs. Yeado was a prisoner for hours and that her husband was killed long before authorities arrived at the home.

Both of the Yeados were in sleeping garments. Volesky said Mrs. Yeado was unable to talk much but that the dress of the Yeados indicated they were confronted in their home at an early hour Friday morning.

The murder of Yeado and the trussing of his wife was discovered about 5 p.m. Investigating officers said Yeado had been dead for several hours when he was discovered. Mrs. Yeado indicated too that she was tied up for hours.

The Yeados' store, one of two jewelry establishments in Vermillion, was not open all day Friday.

There was comment about it among other business owners, but there was no concern until Christie Hanson, a housemother at the University of South Dakota, telephoned the Yeado home and the store about 4:30 p.m. and received no answer.

She became worried because she had a dinner engagement for the evening at the Yeado home and couldn't understand why she could not reach them.

She telephoned a Yeado neighbor, Aike Hollman, a high school teacher, and asked him to determine whether the Yeados were home.

Hollman found a broken window at the back of the house and evidence that the door had been tampered with. He then went around to the front of the house and, on finding the door locked, returned home and called the police.

Police said the man arrested was in the house when they arrived.

Officials speculated that the men had planned to wait until dark and then force Mrs. Yeado to go to the store and open the safe.

It was not learned whether she was aware during the hours she was tied up that her husband had been killed.

TRIAL

1

Easter Monday was a joyless holiday for me growing up. Mom always made goldenrod toast out of the leftover colored eggs for breakfast, and by lunchtime, my brother and I were completely bored, missing our friends and the playground mayhem.

On the Easter Monday following the Yeado homicide, I woke longing for a simpler time like those uneventful Easter Mondays of the past, but there was no escaping the fear and confusion that had settled in my gut like a tumor, growing larger and more malignant the more I thought about what Tom was accused of.

I drove downtown and parked in front of the Monogram News, thinking Tug might have some information I could use. The store was closed. Deliveries were stacked outside the Monogram's locked front door: boxes of candy, three bundles of magazines, and a stack of *Minneapolis Tribune*s. An anonymous note hung on the door: "We are closed today in memory of our friend Jim Yeado."

I decided to look up Dottie, Tom's girlfriend and the only person in town with a connection to both his present and past.

She was a waitress at the Chimes Café. Perhaps she was there. The café was on Main Street, a few storefronts down from the Yeado jewelry store. The café's façade was covered with light-blue metal siding, a midcentury modernist touch out of sync with the small-town ambiance inside, with its booths along the wall, tables for larger groups in the center, and a counter with chrome stools capped by bright-red leather seats. Downtowners met in the Chimes for midmorning coffee and the daily lunch special. Faculty and students generally didn't patronize the Chimes.

The waitresses, blue-and-white restaurant hats bobby-pinned to their hair, outnumbered the few customers. One person was at the end of the counter, and a couple at a back booth was locked in a quiet argument. I sat down on a counter stool. A waitress came over to wait on me. She had shy but friendly eyes and very fine features that matched Tom's. If this was Dottie, I could see why Tom had fallen for her. I ordered two eggs sunny-side up, hash browns, toast, and grape jelly. After I handed the menu back to her, she acknowledged a call from the cook in the kitchen. He'd called for Dottie.

When Dottie returned with my order, I introduced myself as a friend of Tom's. She feigned not knowing him at first, but her eyes gave her away.

"Have you talked to him?" I asked.

"I can't. I can't talk about him after what he did. He bought a ring for me from Mr. Yeado. He called me while he was in their house. People look at me now as if I had something to do with it. Please leave me alone."

But she didn't walk away. She stood there, locked down, her emotions avalanching. A moment later she turned away and went back to the kitchen. When she came back, I was nearly finished with my breakfast.

"I want to help Tom," I said. That must have sounded as phony to her as it did to me. "I'm going to the courthouse after this to see him. Is there anything you want to say to him? Anything I should know? Do you know Philip Zolbach? He's Tom's guardian, right? How do I get ahold of him?"

"He's Tom's guardian. A couple of nights before the murder, Tom and I were supposed to go out. Tom wanted to introduce me to Phil and have dinner somewhere. Phil wouldn't hear of it. So they went off on their own. I knew Tom had some problems, but this is crazier than anything he's done before."

"What has he done before?"

"It doesn't matter. I'm leaving tomorrow. A lot of us are going home," she said.

"A lot of us?"

"My people. We can't stay here now."

"I can't tell you what to do, but leaving won't help Tom."

Dottie didn't appreciate the righteousness. She half smiled and walked back to the kitchen. She didn't come out again. Finished with breakfast, I wrote down my name and address on the bill in case she changed her mind, put two dollars and a tip on the counter, and left.

I parked the Plymouth in a Main Street parking space outside the courthouse and walked slowly toward the front entrance. The sun was shining in a clear sky, but a shifting, cold breeze blew dead leaves in erratic swirls on the sidewalk. March weather had returned. The warm interior of the courthouse was more welcoming. Sunrays shone down through the rotunda's skylight, reflecting off the terrazzo floor. The courthouse offices were closed for Easter Monday, except the sheriff's office.

The sheriff's secretary was at her desk behind the front counter, typing away, a pharmacy lamp lighting the material she was converting into typewritten pages. When she saw me approaching her desk, she covered the material with a file folder, as if I could read it from behind the counter.

"Good morning."

"Good morning. May I help you?" she asked, as if I were a complete stranger, not someone she had met and talked to last Saturday morning.

"Sheriff Wilson. I'd like to speak to the sheriff, please."

"I will have to check with him. He's been very busy, as you might know." She got up and started back toward the sheriff's office, until she realized she had left the sheriff's notes on her desk for me to read. She spun around, grabbed the notes, and took them with her into the office. She returned almost immediately.

"He'll see you now," she said, and went back to her typing without so much as looking at me.

Sheriff Wilson was a slight man who wore round, silver-rimmed eyeglasses and smoked unfiltered Camels. A bluish haze of cigarette smoke hung in the air above the pedestal chair he sat in, a swivel seat with three legs that squeaked when he sat down in it. His hair was short, but not in the intimidating flat-top style of the state's attorney, rather like a soft-bristled brush on his perfectly round head. He offered me a cigarette and then lit one for himself.

"How is it you know Tom White Hawk?"

"We were in the same fraternity."

"Do you know anything about the homicide last Friday? Had you seen Tom recently?"

"I haven't seen him for months. But I still care about him. I think he needs a friend right now."

"That's very big of you, Mister…what did you say your name was?"

"Craig Peters."

"I thought you said you were a reporter? Was that some kind of game you were playing?"

"I'm a reporter. For the *Volante*. But I am here today as a friend. I saw the sign announcing visiting hours. Am I allowed to see him?"

"He's in with his attorney right now. When he's done, I'll ask Tom if he'll see you. You had better be playing this straight. If Tom says he doesn't know you, it's the last time you'll be allowed in here and the last time you'll get any information from me, friend or reporter or whatever you are."

I waited another hour or so on the back bench in the sheriff's office with two reporters who were waiting to talk to the sheriff. I recognized the one wearing a tie as the reporter who took Tom's photo while he was being escorted out of city hall Saturday morning. He told me the sheriff had apprehended Willie on the Rosebud and brought him back here late Saturday. Willie was now in the county jail, a few cells down from Tom.

From the bench where we were sitting, I could see the door to the sheriff's office. The sheriff finally emerged from his office, glanced at the three of us as if hoping we had given up and left, and then walked down a long hallway to the cell block. He opened the reinforced door with his key and closed the door behind him. A few minutes later, another man opened the door and walked down the hall toward us. He was young, not that much older than me, with a London Fog trench coat draped over his left arm. He was carrying a large open satchel with legal pads poking out of it. He stopped to say something to the sheriff's secretary, who wrote down his request, and then he left without acknowledging the three of us.

"That's White Hawk's attorney," one of the reporters said. "Lee 'Mick' McMillan. He defended White Hawk on a car theft charge earlier this year. Mr. 'No Comment.' You won't get any information from him."

The sheriff came out a few minutes later, his wiry frame a faint shadow in the dark hall, and signaled for me to come with him.

"Tom said he would see you. You have fifteen minutes."

I suppressed a smile, glancing back to register the surprise on the reporters' faces.

The sheriff held the door to the jail unit open for me as I approached and then led me into a room immediately inside, where he had me sit down at a table. The sheriff and his wife, I discovered later, had the contract to make the prisoners' meals and serve them there. The room doubled as a visitor and inter-rogation room. A sheriff's deputy was there, standing outside the room while the sheriff went to retrieve Tom. The sheriff came back a few minutes later with Tom, his eyes acknowledg-ing but entirely indifferent to my presence. He sat down across from me. The sheriff had a deputy frisk me, confessing his embarrassment at not having done it sooner. The sheriff and deputy then left Tom and me alone in the room.

Tom looked distracted, high, soaring in his own mind. His hair was a mess, sticking out in all directions as if he had just gotten out of bed. He hung his head once seated, staring at the tabletop, his arms stretched out on the table. One of his tattoos was a mermaid with a white ribbon wound around her and "When love isn't madness, it isn't love" inscribed on it.

"Tom, how are you?"

"What do you think?" Tom said, barely above a whisper.

"Cigarette?"

He took one, and I lit it for him. He smoked, saying nothing. The room was so quiet you could hear the tobacco burn when he pulled on his cigarette.

"I hear Willie's in here with you."

"They brought him in late Saturday. He didn't get far, I guess," Tom said. I could barely hear him.

"I see you have a lawyer."

"He defended me on the car business."

"Do you need anything? Can I get you something?"

He looked at me, not seeming to comprehend my question.

"I saw Dottie before I came over here this morning. She's worried."

"We were going to get married this summer. That's off now."

"It'll work out somehow."

"No, it won't. It fucking won't. Don't bullshit me."

"Sorry."

"I didn't kill that old man on purpose. I don't remember much, but I know it was an accident. What am I going to do?" Tom asked. The features on his face, normally so inexpressive, turned into a look of sharp pain, and he started to cry. He cried for several more minutes without embarrassment.

"Have you told the sheriff what happened—the accident part?"

"I don't remember. I'm sure I did. The sheriff. The other men who questioned me. My lawyer. I told them all. Nobody believes me."

"Sheriff only gave me fifteen minutes. Is there anything I can get you?"

"Migraines are bad. Real bad. Stomach's bad too, twisted up. Puking a lot. The sheriff's deputies picked up my clothes and stuff in Julian this morning. Tell the sheriff the phenobarbital is for my headaches. Maybe he'll listen to you."

On my way out, I stopped in the hallway outside the sheriff's office, stuck my head in, and told him what I knew about Tom's headaches and medication. He said Mick had asked the same, but he'd have to wait until he saw the prescription before giving it to Tom. He said Tom's guardian might be able to help on that score. He was expecting Zolbach to visit Tom sometime that morning.

Philip Zolbach was crossing the rotunda, heading for the sheriff's office, as I was leaving. He had a strange bounce in his walk, rising up on the balls of his feet with each step. He was average size, maybe late forties, and wore thick glasses with an amber tint shade in the lenses. His rapidly advancing bald spot accentuated big ears. There was a practical air about him, efficient, no nonsense. He wore slacks and a white dress shirt. I recognized him from the picture on Tom's dresser.

"Mr. Zolbach? Philip Zolbach?" I asked.

He stopped, stepped back as if I were infectious, and then relaxed.

"I'm sorry. I'm a bundle of nerves today. I have so many things on my mind. Yes, I'm Philip Zolbach. To whom am I speaking?"

"I am a friend of Tom White Hawk's. He told me you are his guardian. Showed me a picture of the two of you standing in a horse corral at the Hare Home."

"Yes, of course. I remember now. You have something to do with the fraternity Tom joined."

"That's right."

"He said you were kind to him. More than I can say for some of those bullies."

"It's a long story."

"I'm sure it is. Why are you here? Have you seen Tom?"

"Yes. The sheriff gave me fifteen minutes with him."

"How is he? He must be devastated. I know I am. After all I did for him. I taught him so much when we were together at the Hare Home. All the time we spent hunting and fishing. Teaching him everything he knows about cars. The trips to the Black Hills and Minneapolis. All the sights. I was responsible for his admission to Shattuck. And the university here. O Lord, what I have done for him, and now this."

"What did you do at the Hare Home?"

"I was a counselor and maintenance supervisor. I know, a strange combination. I quit a job at Honeywell in Minneapolis and came to the reservation to make a difference, through the Episcopal Church. Sharing Christ's love with those in need. I was there when Tom arrived at Hare. Mrs. Artichoker, the headmaster's wife, and I were in the kitchen when we saw a car pull up out front. Tom's uncle Charles dropped him off. Poor Tom, he must have been eleven or twelve. His father and mother had died within the last year. His uncle left as soon as Tom was out of the car, leaving Tom to walk alone into the home, carrying all his possessions in a paper bag. Saddest sight I have ever seen. I have cared for him and loved him ever since."

"He's going to need you now. Have you met his lawyer?"

"No. I have an appointment with him this afternoon. Did Tom tell you anything about the murder? What kind of weapon he used?"

"We didn't talk about it. He's not very talkative right now. One of the deputies told me he used a rifle."

That seemed to upset Zolbach. He turned away for a moment to gather himself.

"Nice meeting you. I must go talk to Tom. This is so awful. So dreadfully awful."

Zolbach rushed off in his bouncy gait, making a beeline for the sheriff's office.

2

Tom White Hawk and Willie Stands entered the courtroom Thursday morning from a side door and were nearly seated before the spectators even realized the prisoners were in the room, having expected them to enter through the rear entrance. Sheriff Wilson and a uniformed policeman silently escorted them, without handcuffs, in through the judge's chambers, casually pointing out their places as if they were being seated for a theater performance. The sheriff was in his official best, a light-gray suit with narrow lapels and solid black tie. He could have passed for a colleague of the law school faculty who had come to watch the hearing.

Municipal court was held in a city hall conference room, where local attorneys took turns serving as judges for unpaid traffic fines, public intoxication, small claims, and various other misdemeanors. Charges for major crimes were initially filed here, and the defendants were subsequently bound over to the state court system. The judge sat at the front of the room behind a large wooden desk, a relic of some sort, with everyone else in rows of chairs facing him. There were no defense or prosecution tables, no witness stand, no judicial robes, no pictures of statesmen on the walls. It was all very informal and without pretense.

Willie and Tom were seated in the front row of chairs. Lee McMillan sat between the defendants. Ramon Roubideaux, Willie's lawyer, sat on the other side of Willie. Roubideaux was the first Indian lawyer to practice in South Dakota, a charming man with big, black glasses slightly magnifying playful eyes and the easy manner of a man accustomed to winning. Word was he had never lost a murder case.

Tom was composed, obediently attentive to McMillan, who was advising him on something, but otherwise ignoring everyone else. Tom wore a burgundy sport coat, a button-down oxford shirt, and a tan tie with brown stripes. Willie wore what appeared to be a new pair of khakis and a gray, long-sleeved shirt with an open collar. Willie's father sat immediately behind him, his lined face showing pain and his thick hair streaked with gray, a Hollywood-handsome man.

Volesky sat on the right side, radiating purpose. As the proceedings were about to begin, he approached the judge and whispered something to him. The judge nodded in agreement, and Volesky returned to his seat. A moment later a man in his late thirties escorted an older woman, her hair covered with a navy-and-white paisley scarf, along the side aisle and guided her to a chair near Volesky. I assumed, given how the audience hushed with her entrance, that Mrs. Yeado and her son, Robert, an attorney who practiced in Washington, DC, had just entered the room.

Judge Michels announced that the hearing would be divided into two parts. He would preside over the information being filed against Willie Stands but would subsequently recuse himself during the reading of the information on Thomas White Hawk because he and Lee McMillan were partners in the same law firm. Phil Crew, another local attorney appointed by the First Judicial Circuit earlier in the week, would hear the White Hawk charges.

Roubideaux rose and carried a paper with a motion to the judge's desk. The judge read it aloud. "The defense requests that the reading of the amended charges against the two defendants be waived and that the subsequent hearing be closed to the public with the exception of the witnesses." The spectators groaned with disappointment, but everyone dutifully filed out when the judge approved the motion.

Paul and I were sitting near the front of the room. Paul had come along to take pictures for the *Volante*. We rose to leave with the rest of the spectators on their way out, an odd mixture of small university town characters, law school faculty, reporters and photographers, Tug, Yeado neighbors and church friends, a few Julian Hall students, law enforcement officers, Courtland Berry, and Philip Zolbach. Dottie was not there.

The spectators lingered outside city hall, hungry for information or gossip of any kind, though most had given up hope of being allowed inside the conference room again today. I watched Courtland out of the corner of my eye. He was talking to one of the deputies, probably the fink who'd leaked Tom's theft arrest file to him. They weren't making small talk. Courtland was trying to make a point about something, and the deputy was buying it, judging by his body language.

I walked away when Courtland noticed I was within earshot and made my way toward Zolbach, who was talking to a couple, a man in a clerical collar and an attractive younger woman.

"Do you remember me, Mr. Zolbach?"

"Of course, you're Tom's friend. This is James and Deb Hubert. James is the Episcopal priest here in town. They know Tom. Tom was a member of their church," Zolbach said.

Hubert shook my hand as if we were old friends and introduced his wife. They were the perfect church-camp couple, cute and nonjudgmental. They wore sandals and were holding hands.

"Does anyone know what happens next?"

"We're not sure," Hubert said. "Mick said the charges filed against Tom last Saturday would be amended to first-degree murder. No premeditation. That's a big relief. I didn't think Volesky would bend, but apparently he has. It could make a difference. Half the people in this state want Tom to die for this."

"Who's Mick?" I asked.

"Tom's lawyer. Lee 'Mick' McMillan."

"What else?"

"Mick said he would submit a motion to have Tom evaluated, to determine whether he's competent to stand trial," Hubert said. "Frankly, I don't think he is now nor was he during the crime. He called me that morning while he was still in the Yeado home. So strange. He seemed perfectly rational, but wouldn't that be completely *irrational* behavior, given what had happened, what he had done? He asked about Good Friday services that afternoon. You know Tom, he's always hungry. He asked what we were having for dinner after the service. Said he would be there. He promised to bring Dottie too. I really didn't think much about it when he didn't show; he rarely came to services. I was stunned when I heard the news later that afternoon."

"Have you seen Tom since Saturday?" I asked.

"Twice. Sunday and yesterday. He's pretty down. I didn't know what to say to him. This is so out of character. I have never seen him raise his voice or threaten violence, and then this."

"James, we have to go. There are people waiting for us," Deb Hubert said, tugging on his hand.

"Okay. Phil, let us know if anything happens."

Zolbach wanted to talk some more, taking me to the side, away from the few remaining spectators. He was the nervous sort anyway, and that day he seemed about to explode with something that was troubling him.

"Did you hear?" he asked. "The murder weapon was a .22 magnum rifle. Do you know how he obtained that rifle?"

"No."

"I gave it to him when we were at the Hare Home. I kept it while he was at Shattuck. Cadets weren't allowed to have their own weapons. I had it until last week, when he asked me to bring it to him. Like a fool, I did. He said he wanted it for target practice. The sheriff asked me about it. I might be an accomplice. This is what I get for caring for him and loving him all those years. I had plans for Tom. He was my little boy. I was so proud of him."

"The sheriff will understand you had nothing to do with it. Tom will tell him."

"Tom's not talking to me. He wouldn't see me yesterday. He's acting as if this is all my fault."

"He'll come around. He's in shock."

"I'm the only adult in his life. He needs me now more than he ever has."

Willie's hearing lasted about an hour. The sheriff's deputies escorted him out of the courtroom, with his father trailing behind, a proud man crushed and humbled by his son's actions.

"He's a fucking killer and should die with White Hawk," someone called out.

Roubideaux, alongside Willie's father, raised his hand as if to shield the father from any other insults and walked with him to a parked car and drove him away.

While we waited for Tom's hearing to conclude, Zolbach told me about life at the Hare Home, where Tom spent his middle school years. The Hare Home was a functioning farm. The boys worked like hired hands, caring for the livestock—pigs, cattle, horses, and chickens. Tom was assigned the cattle chores, spending his afternoons after class feeding them, cleaning their stalls, attending to their medical needs. Tom and Zolbach rode the horses, often on overnight camping or fishing trips, just the two of them, the big reservation sky crowded with stars, the coyotes their only company. Tom was a loner who didn't mix well with the other boys, but he was always well behaved, a Boy Scout without the uniform and badges, anxious to please, as if he thought a single transgression of the rules would be cause for his eviction from Hare and transfer to another boarding school.

Zolbach could think of only a single instance when Tom had let his guard down. Tom and Zolbach had returned from Saint Paul, where they had spent the Christmas holiday. Mr. Artichoker, the principal, had appointed Tom head cattleman, and Tom delegated his responsibilities to his friend Henry while he was gone, asking Henry to be especially attentive to a cow that was about to calve. When Tom and Zolbach returned, Tom immediately went out to the barn and found the cow lying in her stall, afterbirth frozen to her hindquarters and the calf frozen and half eaten in the pig pen. Tom tracked down Henry in the dormitory. He slugged Henry in the stomach and face, pinned him to the floor, and kept punching him again and again until he was pulled off by the other boys.

The judge adjourned Tom's hearing for lunch. Lured by the smell of seared hamburger drifting from a diner across the street, Zolbach and I were about to cross the street when Tom emerged from city hall, handcuffed. Police officers quickly shuttled him out to a waiting police car. The same person who'd shouted at Willie and his father pushed his way through the crowd and yelled at Tom through the police car window that he was a killer and should fry in the electric chair. The sheriff gave instructions to the driver and guard before the car left. When the sheriff was done, he walked down past the city hall entrance and was starting to get in his car, an unmarked Chevy

Bel Air, when he saw us standing to the side, looking confused and needy. He didn't have to, but he shut the car door and came over to talk to us.

"You boys have been waiting for some time, haven't you? Look, I shouldn't say anything, but I don't see the harm. Mick asked that Tom be evaluated to see if he's competent to stand trial. The judge agreed, and so we're on our way to the Yankton hospital for the doctors over there to examine him. The court's in recess. We expect it will take a few hours. Once we have the doctor's evaluation on Tom, we'll know more."

"What about Willie?" I asked.

"Willie's been bound over to the state circuit court."

The Zip House had a narrow laminate counter, twelve stools with spinning seats, and a large grill close enough to splatter hot grease on the customers. The cook, his back to the customers, slapped and scraped a metal spatula on the grill while tossing hamburgers and onions.

We finished our cheeseburgers and the Zip House's famous spicy chili and stood in front of city hall, waiting for news. I remember thinking I had Zolbach figured out. He was a lonely bachelor who'd found a project in Tom, someone he could form into a perfect image of…exactly what, I didn't know, but something that matched what he wanted, or wished he had been. Zolbach was probably an only child, I thought, used to getting his way.

After a few minutes, the sheriff pulled his car into a parking space reserved for the police.

"I got word from the boys. They've completed the evaluation and will be back in less than an hour," he told us as he went back into city hall.

No one shared the evaluation with us, of course. All we knew was that Tom was deemed competent. The court resumed its session and adjourned in less than fifteen minutes. They led him out again. I found the evaluation later among the documents in his file at the courthouse. The superintendent of the hospital, Dr. L. G. Behan, conducted the examination: "There is little evidence of anxiety or depression and little show of feelings of guilt. His judgment regarding society is poor, but there is no evidence that he has ever had a psychotic episode. Impression: Sociopathic Personality Disturbance. Antisocial reaction."

I guess that meant Tom was only a little crazy, not so crazy he couldn't stand trial. He was bound over to state court on charges of first-degree murder and rape. The premeditation language was dropped, as Father Hubert had predicted.

I went back to my apartment and began writing my story, which was due Sunday evening for publication on Tuesday. The editor had promised me it would run on the front page of the *Volante* if I had it in by the deadline. The students would have something a whole lot more titillating than usual to read when they returned from Easter vacation.

3

The *Volante* editor kept his promise and ran my story on the front page. Several of Paul's pictures were published along-side the copy: a picture of the Yeado home, one of the Yeado Jeweler sign above the downtown store, and Tom's Shattuck graduation picture.

The morning the paper came out, Paul and I drove the Plymouth over to the Broadcaster Press, where the paper was printed. We had volunteered to pick up the papers and dis-tribute them on campus. It had rained the night before, a soft spring shower that left puddles of water on the Broadcaster's cratered parking lot. We found the papers in bales stacked on a pallet at the rear of the building. We broke open one of the bales as if opening the first Christmas gift, bursting with expectation, and took in the headline—"White Hawk Awaits Fate in Jail"—the byline, and photos like greedy kids. It felt really good.

We stuffed the bales into the trunk and back seat of the car and drove back to campus, where we distributed the papers to the kiosks at the entrances of the academic buildings. We nearly pissed our pants, we were so excited. The last kiosk was in the concourse of the student center near the pool tables. After loading it with papers, we sat down in red plastic chairs in the lounge area and watched the students pick up the paper, some even stopping to read the story after seeing the headline.

During that spring when so much was lost and gained, my relationship with Caitlin had faded into a confusing blend of friendship and occasional intimacy. We had worked out an arrangement—not the sophisticated kind the word implies— where she would decide what the tone would be when we were together. In other words, she was calling the shots. Harlan was still in the picture. He had a hold on her I didn't understand, and I stood little chance of breaking it. My only consolation was that he was no longer in school. He spent most of his time traveling with Kid Sparrow. When Harlan was out of town, as he was the day after my murder story ran in the *Volante,* she called.

"Hi, it's me, Caitlin."

"Yes, it is," I said officiously.

"Oh, come on, frat boy. I've been busy, you know, with everything. Tests and papers and *Volante* stories. I've been meaning to call."

I wanted to be with her all the time. These sporadic overtures hurt more than they helped.

"I've been busy, too, with the White Hawk story," I said.

"Are you doing anything tonight? Maybe go down to the Char?"

The Char was shorthand for the Charcoal Lounge, a step up from the Varsity. The Char served liquor.

"Sure, why not? What time?"

"I'll stop by your place about nine, okay?"

The next few hours went by slowly. I waited for her knock at the door, expecting her to change her mind, but she showed up.

I followed her outside to sit in the chairs on the front porch, an extra wide, old-fashioned one with a wooden balustrade. The night was warm and in high spring. An overgrown white lilac in the front yard was in full bloom, fragrant, its heavy flower heads drooping toward the ground. Students were strolling on the sidewalks, and townies were tending their gardens and lawns in the last light of the day.

Caitlin stretched out her legs, sitting in one of the chairs. She was wearing slacks and a blouse, an outfit that made her seem much older. She had spent the evening at the music museum on campus, covering its spring concert, Mozart's *Eine Kleine Nachtmusik*, for the *Volante*.

"How was the concert?" I asked.

"I don't know Mozart from Beethoven, but the piece tonight was beautiful. Now I know why people listen to classical music."

"The windows were open in our apartment tonight. I could hear the music."

"I read your story in the paper. I liked it. Pretty good."

"Good, but not great?"

"Settle down, puppy dog. It's a wild story, for sure. All happening right here in Vermillion. I wish you had introduced me to White Hawk. What's he like?"

"He's not what you would expect. He has very good manners. Speaks quietly, respectfully. Not outgoing, but friendly. He's not like most Indians."

"Oh, and how many Indians do you know, Mr. SAE?"

"As many as you do. And by the way, the SAE slur doesn't work anymore."

"Seriously, about White Hawk, did you think he was a killer and a rapist?"

"Not sure what to think. Who knows what his motives were, what was going on in his head? I understand robbing someone for money, but the killing and raping? Pretty fucking strange."

"I heard they found body parts in the kitchen stove."

"Hysterical rumors."

"Tell me more about what he's like."

"Quiet, but he's been around. Knows both worlds, white and Indian. He was a big athlete at Shattuck, where there were very few Indians, maybe two or three, and the rest white guys. Most of the guys in the house liked him until he got into a fight with one of them. Then they voted him out. Too bad. He was good for the house, and vice versa."

"Was he acting strange lately?"

"He'd lost interest in school. He had migraines, bad ones. Took some heavy drugs to relieve the pain."

"People are going to bed with knives and guns around here. The sorority houses are on lockdown."

"He's in jail, for Pete's sake. He had a friend with him, but this was an isolated incident."

"And the Indian thing. It makes it even scarier for a lot of people."

"Yeah, I know. Let's go to the Char Bar."

We walked two blocks down Dakota Street to where it intersects with Main. An attendant was filling up a car at the corner Sinclair Oil station next to Caitlin's apartment. Sinclair's big, green, happy dinosaur stood at the corner, that enigmatic smile on its face. The Charcoal Lounge, the Char Bar, was two more blocks to the west on Main Street. We walked slowly, our shoulders lightly brushing, my longing for her increasing each time. I wanted to hold her hand but knew she wouldn't let me.

The standing bar is on the left as you enter the Char Bar, with a massive rectangular mirror behind it that reflects your image as you enter and proceed toward the back to the tables and booths. The darker back room felt intimate. The piped-in lounge music was a welcome relief from the Beatles music playing on jukeboxes everywhere, all day long. It was the perfect setting, until someone called Caitlin's name from a crowded booth. It was Chris and her friends. They insisted we join them.

At the booth, Caitlin said something that made it seem as if it were a coincidence we had entered the bar together.

We slid into the booth next to each other, my leg pressing against hers. We drank bottled beer and ate beef chislic and talked about the Yeado murder and finals and everyone's summer plans.

After an hour I was ready to go. Caitlin looked at me curiously when I whispered to her I was leaving, as if there were no need for me to inform her. Chris, sitting across from us in the booth, was the only one who picked up on it. I got up and left, pausing for a moment outside on the sidewalk underneath the Char Bar's sign, a tall neon flame spiking upward into the night sky. Why hadn't I seen this coming?

4

A few weeks after my story ran in the *Volante*, the editor of the local semiweekly, the *Plain Talk*, called and asked me to stop by. Charles Bellman was a stuffy defender of the status quo, writing thunderous editorials on political subjects of local interest as well as news stories and features that reflected his allegiance to small-town life. Faded *Plain Talk*s were stacked on shelves in his office, with story drafts and the layout of next week's front page on his desk.

"Thanks for coming in, Peters. I read your story on the Yeado murder in the student newspaper. I've got a proposition for you. I need someone to cover this story. I can't write every damn story for the paper. If it were going to be one or two articles, fine, but this murder story will go on for some time. The hearings, trial, et cetera, et cetera."

"Probably right."

"I heard you know these two boys who killed Yeado."

"I know White Hawk. I don't know Stands."

"What is your relationship to him?"

"He was in my fraternity."

"Were you close friends?"

"No."

"How would you characterize your relationship?"

"I've talked to him a few times. We're friendly."

"Close enough that he'll see you in jail? He'll talk to you?"

"Yes. Some of the details in my story were based on my visit with him shortly after the murder."

"You have access. That's important. Here's my idea. You come to work for the *Plain Talk* this summer. Write stories for each edition, more if there is enough news to merit more coverage. The *Volante* doesn't publish in the summer, right? It's a good job for someone like you, inexperienced and all. I'll pay you by the story, twenty-five bucks a piece. When does your semester end?"

"The middle of May. Next week is finals week."

"Okay, you can start then. The week after next. We got a deal?"

"We've got a deal, Mr. Bellman."

"Okay. Remember, write about the locals involved, the people who are most affected by this. My readers are interested in White Hawk and his friend, Stands. But don't get carried away. Don't make them into heroes like Capote did with those two murderers, Hickock and Smith. People around here had great affection for Jim Yeado. He was everybody's gentle, lovable uncle. People hate White Hawk for killing Jim, and they don't want to be talked out of their anger at this Indian kid. You were trying to make people sorry for White Hawk in your *Volante* story. Leave the psychology stuff to the real writers. Get the facts straight. Add some description and comments from local people involved in the story."

"What about the Yeados?"

"Good question. We'll need a story about them. We buried Jim a few days ago, and all we ran was an obituary. A nice sympathetic piece would be good."

"What about an interview with Mrs. Yeado? Have her talk about what happened that day. The gory details."

"Not from her. It's beyond the pale, you know. It would turn people off. She probably doesn't remember much of it anyway. But the sheriff and the lawyers will talk about it. They'll want to project an image of someone in control of this terrible situation. People in Vermillion are still going to bed with weapons. Joan Holter told me she moves her living room furniture in front of her door every night to barricade the Indians out. I'll call Arnie and the two lawyers, Chuck and Mick, and tell them you'll be calling soon for an interview."

The *Volante* crowd, myself included, had often made fun of the motto that ran on the masthead of the *Plain Talk*: "The NEWSPAPER with the Best Advertising Coverage of Any Weekly or Semiweekly in South Dakota." It wasn't funny now. I felt as if *The New York Times* had offered me an assignment. Paul's parents were sending him to a photography program at the University of New Mexico for the summer, and now I had something other than construction or bartending to occupy my summer. Maybe I'd take a class. I had the apartment to myself, a job at the *Plain Talk*, and enough time to take summer-school courses, compliments of the old man, who'd agreed to help me out with the bills.

I knew the wire service reporters would be working the sheriff and attorneys hard for details on the murder scene, but no follow-up stories had run in the newspapers since the day after the murder. Nobody in authority was talking. Bellman said he'd open doors for me, so I went down to the sheriff's office the day after my last final exam.

I entered the courthouse through the side doors on the east wing of the building. The sheriff's offices were on the left.

Down the hall, behind a reinforced door with a prison window, Tom and Willie were locked in their cells. The sheriff was chatting amiably with a deputy, both leaning against the counter separating the staff from the entering public.

"Look what the cat drug in," Sheriff Wilson noted to his deputy. "Our friend from the *Volante*." The sheriff seemed to be in a better mood now that the stress of the murder and its aftermath were a few weeks behind him.

"Sheriff Wilson, you remember me. I'm flattered. One correction, though. I'm covering the Yeado murder for the *Plain Talk* now. The *Volante* doesn't publish in the summer."

"That's a shame," the sheriff said, deadpan, and then grinned. "What can I do you for?"

"Do you have a few minutes? I have some questions."

Sheriff Wilson gestured in the direction of his office. I followed him. His office was thick with stale tobacco smell. He circled behind his desk and sat down on his tripod chair. It squeaked as he sat down. He reached for a pack of Camels and a lighter on his desk. Behind him, Venetian blinds in a south-facing window blocked the midmorning sun. A picture of the sheriff kissing his wife in what looked like their living room on election night stood behind him on a credenza. He was a Democrat in his third term as sheriff in a university town and district where the Democrats easily outnumbered the Republicans. He was ordinary-looking and had an oversized, flat nose and eyes that assessed but didn't judge. His fingers were yellowed with cigarette smoke. The sheriff wasn't wearing a badge or uniform.

"How's Tom doing, Sheriff?"

"He's settled down some. Not so flighty, but he still has migraines. I don't think he's sleeping very well. When he does sleep, his dreams linger, haunting him, reminding him how alone he is. He says he doesn't dream about the murder, though."

"What makes you think it was a murder?"

"Okay. The night of March twenty-fourth."

"What does he do all day?"

"He asked for the books in his dorm room. And a friend brought him a psychology book. I've never seen anything like it before. He wants to know what happened that night. Wants to know why he did it. Most criminals don't ask that question."

"What else?"

"He's a painter. He asked for some supplies. Leonard, my deputy, called the university's art department, and they brought down some used brushes and paint, paper, canvas. They were happy to help. He's painted a few pictures for me and my deputies."

"I know he has stomach problems. Is he eating?"

"He sure is. My wife and I cook for the prisoners. Quite the glamour job, being sheriff. Scalloped-potato-and-ham casserole tonight."

"And Willie?"

"He's quiet. Doesn't talk much. Different backgrounds, you know. More like what we're accustomed to."

"Are they getting along? Still friends?"

"They're separated right now. In the same cell block, but three cells between them. We let them out to exercise at different times. For the time being, they eat in their individual cells."

"Can you tell me more about the scene that night? You know, for background. What did you find inside the house that day?"

Sheriff Wilson reached for a cigarette. He put it in his mouth, pulled a sliver of tobacco from his bottom lip, and looked directly at me. "The *Plain Talk* has been real fair to me and my department, but this is still an active investigation. I'd better not get into it. The state's attorney is the one calling the shots here. You never know about Chuck. Try him. He may tell you everything you want to know. Then again, he might kick you in the butt and toss you out of his office."

Chuck Volesky had been elected Clay County state's attorney and also had a successful practice on the side. He operated out of his office a block down from the courthouse. His secretary was out running an errand that day as I entered his reception area, furnished modestly but with an eye toward creating an air of competence. The door to his inner office was half-open. When I called out his name, his drill-sergeant voice boomed back, "Enter." I poked my head inside his office. His expression drooped when he saw who it was. He let out a short, exasperated sigh.

"Mr. Volesky, do you remember me? I'm a writer for the *Volante* and the *Plain Talk*. I'd like to interview you about the Yeado homicide. Do you have some time?"

He didn't answer immediately. He started to arrange the papers on his desk and then looked up at me again, as if having a second thought.

"I can't right now. If you want to wait a few minutes, I'll try to find some time. Not making any promises, though. Close the door on the way out."

I closed the door and stood waiting for a while, then sat in a chair in his reception room. The secretary's desk was new and matched the other décor. She was a neat freak. Everything had its place on her desk. The courthouse was visible through the window in the reception room, the smooth-cut white limestone of the old building luminous in the morning sun. An hour had nearly passed when his office door opened and he waved me in.

"I have fifteen minutes, half an hour at most. Come on in."

Volesky's office was spare too. His undergraduate and law school diplomas hung on the wall behind him, along with two black-and-white photos, one of him taking a jump shot in a basketball game and the other with his teammates, North Dakota 1952 state champions.

"Mr. Volesky, perhaps you saw the *Volante* story I wrote on White Hawk."

"I read it. You had some details wrong. So did the AP story in the Sioux Falls paper."

"That's what I am here for. To get the details straight."

"I hope so. Well, sit down," he said, gesturing to a chair in front of his desk.

Volesky sat behind his desk. He laid his big hands palmside down, like oversized meat hooks. His flat-top looked even more menacing close up, the front edge stiff with butch wax. He had puffy lips, his face frozen in a sullen pout.

"My story is going to include background information on you and Mr. McMillan. Do you mind telling me a few things about yourself?"

Volesky's bottom lip withdrew slightly.

"I don't mean to be falsely modest, but there isn't much to say. Grew up on a farm outside Grand Forks on the eastern border of the state. Parents were farmers, Norwegian Lutherans. Two brothers. Went to the University of North Dakota. Applied here, South Dakota, to law school and got in. Did pretty well too."

"Did you ever see yourself as a prosecutor when you were in law school?"

"Always."

"Even so, this couldn't be what you expected, Mr. Volesky. A high-profile death in a quiet university town?"

Volesky's eyes narrowed a sliver at the word "death."

"You don't get to pick your cases in this job."

"So tell me, why did Tom White Hawk break into the Yeado home?"

"He needed the money. He didn't have a plan. Two fuck-ups, these Indians."

"Tom's not stupid. He wouldn't kill someone for whatever was in a jeweler's safe. Isn't it more complicated than that?"

"You've come to the wrong place if you think I'm going to answer a question like that. I don't care why he did it so much as whether he intended to. And he did it. In this case that's pretty clear. This Indian boy killed a defenseless old man and raped his wife. He's a vicious killer, period."

"But White Hawk had a lot to lose."

"You might as well ask me why the earth revolves around the sun. I don't know what was going on in his head. I don't know why he raped an old woman after shooting her husband either. But I do know he is going to pay for it."

"Can you help me with some of the details of the crime? I know you went inside the house after the arrest. What did you find there?"

"The sheriff and chief of police found Mr. Yeado in the basement, wrapped in a braided rag rug, a pillow under his head. The coroner had removed the body by the time I got there."

"Was he shot in the head?"

"No. One of the stories had that wrong. He was shot in the chest area, twice. He had a blow to the head. White Hawk hit Mr. Yeado in the head with a cast-iron skillet. So hard he broke the handle."

"What else?"

"Upstairs in the living room, there wasn't much. Oh, he had turned all the hanging pictures toward the wall. Who knows why? The Yeados slept in separate bedrooms. Both beds were torn apart. White Hawk had tied and gagged her with nylon stockings. The stockings were still hanging from the bedframe. The closet was piled with clothes, the Indian hiding under them. That's where the sheriff and chief found him. What a joke. The stud athlete and Indian hero, quivering in the closet. Probably pissed his pants too."

"There's a rumor they found body parts in the stove. Did he castrate Yeado?"

"That's a new one on me. No, but they did find a pan of blood. He told us he cleaned up the blood in Mr. Yeado's bedroom and collected it in the pan."

"Anything else?"

"White Hawk said some pretty sick things to Mrs. Yeado before he raped her. I can't say what they were, but take my word for it, they show him to be a cold-blooded and calculating killer."

"Like what?"

"I've already told you more than I should. This is off the record, but I want people to know how shocked and angry I am. This son of a bitch is going away for a long, long time. The one in a thousand Indians that leads a privileged life, and this is the gratitude he shows?"

Volesky played at state's attorney like he probably did at basketball, elbows to the ribs. I left his office feeling bullied but with the information I needed for a story.

Lee McMillan's office was a couple blocks from Volesky's on the second floor of a turn-of-the-century commercial building on Main Street. A sign inside a second-floor window, "McMillan & Michels, Attorneys-at-Law," marked the location of the office. A shoe store had occupied the first floor for many years, but now the Whoopti Do, a beauty parlor, was in the space. The Zip House diner, where Zolbach and I had eaten cheeseburgers and chili, was right behind McMillan's building.

The stairway up to McMillan's office was dark. The air in the stairway smelled toxic, a brew of the Whoopti Do's shampoo, burnt hair, and pedicure products seeping through the wall.

McMillan & Michels's secretary greeted me pleasantly. She asked me to take a seat after I introduced myself and told her why I wanted to see McMillan. He would be right with me, she said. McMillan came out a few minutes later and invited me into his office. Volesky's clothes were purely functional and chosen to exude power and confidence, but McMillan chose his, or his wife did, with an instinct for what a client expected in their lawyer: tweed sport coat, pressed wool pants, and a deep-yellow silk handkerchief in his coat pocket. He had a phony smile that slid off his face immediately as we exited the reception area. He took off his sport coat before sitting down behind his desk. His silver cuff links gave off a sparkle of light as he crossed his arms and looked at me as if he hadn't quite made up his mind whether to talk to me.

"So, tell me. Why you are here this morning, Mr. Peters? It's Peters, right?"

"Yes, it is. I am covering the Yeado story for the *Plain Talk.* Looking for some background on you and Mr. Volesky. People want to read about you now."

"Why would anyone care to read about Volesky or me?"

"The *Plain Talk* is the town's news source. You're major actors in the White Hawk tragedy."

McMillan snorted with disbelief.

"Are you the one who wrote the story on Tom last month?" he asked, switching topics.

"Yes, I am."

"I didn't like it. Too much bullshit. Why don't you stick to the facts? You're going to make it harder to defend Tom. I'll tell his story in court, where it'll make a difference. You'll end up making him look unsympathetic, and that will complicate things for me."

"I'll try harder next time. But back to the story I'm writing now. How long have you been practicing law?"

"Not long. I graduated two years ago and then clerked for a state judge. Michels and I moved into this space a few months ago. Grand, isn't it?"

I thought so, but maybe I didn't understand what he meant. He was hard to read.

"Where did you grow up?"

"I don't know if I have yet."

"Seriously. Are you from around here?"

"I grew up in Sioux Falls. Came to the university as an undergraduate. Law school here too. Met my wife, Elaine, here at the university. She teaches French and English literature. That's about it."

"Have you been involved in a murder trial before?"

"I observed one while clerking."

"How did you come to represent Tom on the car theft business?"

"That was pure coincidence. The day he was busted, a Sunday evening, the sheriff called me and told me there was an Indian boy needing counsel at the jail. I went down there and took the case. Tom wasn't like any reservation Indian I had ever met. He looked me in the eye. Told me everything in clear language about the crime. An isolated incident, or so I thought, until this happened. Anyway, I got him off with probation. He asked for me when he got into this recent trouble."

"How will you defend Tom?"

"I was born at night, but not last night. I will tell you this much. I am working on a number of defense strategies. No murder case is the same, but there are some elements of previous cases and how they were defended that will help. I need money to do the research, though. A lot of money. There isn't enough out there for my expenses, to say nothing of the legwork needed. Tom has twenty-one dollars and eight cents in his bank account. No other assets. He's broke. He still owes me money for the car theft case. His parents are dead. The only people who have come forward with financial support are Phil Zolbach, his guardian, and Sam Deloria, an Indian man who works at the university."

"What are Tom's chances?"

McMillan pushed back into his office chair, raising his arms and stretching. A stuffed pheasant hung on the knotty pine wall behind him, its wings spread wide as if it had just been flushed from cover, bulging black eyes centered in a yellow eyeball.

"Who knows? It's not an easy case. But we'll find a way. I promised Tom I would."

I left McMillan's office confident I had enough information for a story. That was all I was confident of.

5

I filed my first story with Bellman a few days later. I sat in his outer office while he read the copy, listening to the girls take phone calls placing farm auction sales, rototilling services, and wedding announcements in the paper. I was surprised it took him so long. He finally came out of his office, a resigned if not grim expression on his face.

"I guess we'll have to go with it as is," he said, handing it to me. "I made a few changes. We don't have time for a rewrite. We go to press in a few hours."

"What's the matter with it?"

"Too much description and not enough information—like what are the charges and the penalties if convicted? What are people on the street saying? When is the next hearing? Your story was missing all those important details. But you'll get the hang of it. You'll have another opportunity in a few days."

Bellman ran my story on the front page of the *Plain Talk*, along with two others, one about the annual Masonic Lodge's Past Masters' night and the other recognizing the winners of the Clay County Rural Electric essay contest.

The following Thursday afternoon, a bright but cool day in late May, I pulled into a parking place in front of the courthouse. Clouds scudded across the sky above. The wind blew strong and erratically, whipping the treetops back and forth. The courtroom was on the third floor. The door was already open when I arrived at 12:30 p.m. for the 2:00 hearing. The courtroom was nearly empty. A court reporter was setting up his equipment on a desk between the jury box and the judge's bench. A janitor dusted the wooden benches. The furniture polish he was using had a lemon smell, reminding me of Caitlin.

I sat in the front row behind the balustrade and gate in an area reserved for the press. The public sat behind the press. Photos of territorial and state judges hung on the walls, all serious, aging men, not a smile among them. Zolbach came in, looking exhausted and anxious. The Huberts, James and Deb, were with Zolbach. Father James greeted several people as they made their way to the back row. Deb, head cast slightly down, drew attention in her peasant dress and long, curly red hair, which spread out over her shoulders and down her back. Courtland Berry showed up at the last minute, casting an eye over the spectators for an empty seat and finding one in the third row behind the defense table.

A few minutes before 2:00 p.m., Chuck Volesky and another attorney came in through a side door. Volesky glanced at the people waiting for the hearing to begin, making a kind of salute to someone, and then took his place at the prosecutor's table, facing the judge's bench. From the back, his flat-top looked like a stiff brush. Lee McMillan and Tom made their entrance a few minutes later, quieting the room. Tom was wearing the same burgundy-colored sport coat and striped brown tie he had had on at the municipal court hearing. I caught a glimpse of his face before he sat down at the defense table. His eyes were buried in his head, his mouth pinched shut. My guess was that he had another migraine. McMillan didn't look up, guiding Tom to his chair and then sitting down. I thought an inexperienced lawyer would be nervous, but he wasn't showing it. He fished out a yellow legal pad and a red South Dakota law book from his briefcase and started chatting amiably with Volesky.

Judge James Brady entered the courtroom through the door to his chambers. He was a tall man, so tall that his judicial robe ran high up his calves, like a long skirt. He quickly stepped up to the judge's bench and sat down in his chair. He arranged his papers on his desk and then looked directly at the expectant crowd, his square jaw jutting slightly to his right. His cat-eye glasses reflected light from the chandelier dangling above the bench. Sitting as tall as he was in his chair, he looked compromised, his authority undermined by a hint of farce. The AP reporter sitting next to me had covered a murder trial presided over by Brady a few years ago. He said the judge was a control freak, a real stickler for process and detail. He especially hated pushy lawyers. Shut them down immediately.

I expected some kind of introduction or explanation of what would take place, but Brady, after itching his mustache with the side of an index finger, announced that he had denied an earlier motion by the state's attorney to move Tom and Willie to the state penitentiary. Without any pause, Brady then proceeded to read another order, this one requiring the state to share its records and investigative materials with the defense.

The judge noted that Volesky had withdrawn the preliminary charges filed against Tom in municipal court and replaced them with felony murder and rape. McMillan moved that the new charges be dismissed for lack of evidence, and the judge said he would take it under advisement, as if it were a serious motion and he would actually think about it seriously. The judge then spoke directly to the attorneys but loud enough for everyone to hear, explaining that he would set the date for Tom's formal arraignment before the end of the day. With that the judge looked about the courtroom, signaled that the proceeding was over, banged the gavel firmly, and left the courtroom through the door to his chambers. Two sheriff's deputies, seeing Volesky nod to them, escorted Tom out before anyone had risen from their seats.

I stayed in my seat while the crowd exited the courtroom. Tom walked back to his cell, returning to the shame and fear I imagined would not let go of him, growing in strength when he least expected it. Tom surely knew he had disappointed both Indians and whites, opened old wounds, and confirmed stereotypes, exchanging white pity for white fear. Yeado's son, Robert, said Tom deserved a permanent hell of pain and sorrow to match his own grief. Who could blame Robert? Who could fault Volesky, the community avenger with a job to do? The homeless athlete had become a grotesque stereotype—the bloodthirsty savage, inspiring fantasies of violence in this collective nightmare.

I left the courtroom after finishing my notes. Outside, people were clustered together in groups, their conversations bouncing off the white-and-gray terrazzo rotunda floor, much louder than the night Tom was charged and jailed. The sun shone through a skylight directly above. Zolbach and the Huberts were off to one side, apart from the locals. I recognized a few of the law school professors, the same group that had attended the first hearing, and some Julian Hall friends of Tom's. Courtland was there too. He was standing near a watercooler. He waved me over and, when I was closer, thrust his hand out and gave me the SAE grip, grinning with malice as he squeezed my hand, hard.

"Brother Peters, the truth teller. The intrepid journalist. How goes it?"

"I'm fine, Courtland. I'm surprised to see you, though. Why aren't you at ROTC summer camp, saving the world? Jumping out of helicopters, all James Bond–like?"

"I leave for Fort Riley next week. I'm here on some unfinished business before I leave."

"What would that be?"

"I want to know whether your Indian friend castrated the jeweler before or after he killed him. I don't recall seeing anything in your recent story on that matter. Perhaps you'll include it in your next one."

"You're disgusting, Courtland."

"You've got it turned around, my friend. The killer is the disgusting one."

The last person I wanted to see at that moment was Phil Zolbach, but he was walking toward Courtland and me, with the Huberts in tow. They were all smiles, thinking they were in friendly territory. I knew, or had a good idea, of what Courtland would think of them.

"Craig, you remember the Huberts, don't you? Reverend James and Deb?" Zolbach asked.

"Of course," I said.

I noticed for the first time that Father James was much older than Deb. He was easily in his late thirties. His thick black glasses accented a hairline advancing in the wrong direction. Deb wasn't much older than me. Close up, her freckled pale skin and green eyes struck me as unreal, as close-up beauty can.

I had no choice. Courtland wouldn't leave. I introduced him to everyone.

"Well," said Zolbach, "if we have anything to be thankful for today, it would be that the state's attorney has dropped the premeditation language in the charges."

"And why would that be something to be thankful for?" Courtland asked, again with a malevolent smile, as if he knew what the answer would be and had his response ready.

"I've known Tom for nearly ten years. He's a loving, gentle boy, a God-fearing boy. He's not capable of planning someone's murder," said Zolbach.

Courtland blinked. His mouth was drawn tightly shut, forming a straight line above his square jaw.

"But isn't that exactly what he did in this case? Why else would he enter a home at five in the morning with a loaded rifle? He knew he was going to kill the jeweler once he had the combination to the safe. Otherwise he'd be picked up and thrown in jail the next day. He didn't intend on leaving any witnesses," Courtland said, then made an about-face and walked away.

"How do you know that man?" Deb asked. "What arrogance."

"Among other things. Ignore him. He's always been on Tom's case," I said.

"You must know him," Zolbach stated.

"In the same fraternity."

"Courtland. The name sounds familiar. I remember now. He's the one who didn't want Tom in the fraternity. He's the one who harassed Tom so terribly."

"What could he have against Tom?" Father James asked.

"Tom's an Indian. That was enough for Courtland. And now Tom has made it even easier. And he isn't the only one who thinks that way since the murder. The only difference is the rest have better Midwest manners," I said.

"We shouldn't allow this incident to legitimize hate and prejudice," said Father James.

Zolbach sighed. "Too late for that. I've known Tom for many years. It's different for the Indian, even someone as handsome and light-skinned as Tom. I know; I've seen the suspicion cloud the eyes of clerks and waitresses and gas attendants when we travel. It's so unfair."

Father James invited Zolbach and me over for coffee or an adult beverage, but I declined. I had a story to write with a next-morning deadline. Zolbach awkwardly thrust out his hand to shake mine. His hands were large for his wiry frame and rough with wear. He'd doubled as a maintenance man as well as a counselor at the Hare Home, and he was doing some of the same work at a boys' school in Faribault, Minnesota, where he had moved when Tom went to Shattuck. The Huberts were not hand shakers; they were huggers. Each hugged me for an uncomfortable amount of time. Deb smelled of fresh soap and patchouli.

"God bless you," all three chimed together, clustered together in the courthouse rotunda.

6

The next morning, a Friday, I drove over to the *Plain Talk* to drop off my story and pick up my paycheck. Bellman was out, so I left my story with one of the girls. She told me paychecks were written Friday afternoons and were usually available by 4:00 p.m.

I went back to my apartment and called the Clerk of Courts office. The person who answered asked me several questions about who I was and why I wanted the information. Apparently, one needed to pass a background check before public information was released in Clay County. She finally told me Judge Brady had scheduled Tom's arraignment hearing to begin in July. There would be no more court hearings to write about for several weeks, freeing me up to take a summer-school class.

I didn't have a summer schedule, but I knew where Paul had left his. I felt a little sheepish entering his bedroom, but I wasn't about to go all the way over to campus. The curtains in his bedroom were drawn to keep the hot summer sun out. His bed was made. On a desk in one corner he had stacked several spiral-bound notebooks, one for each class he took last semester. No textbooks. He had apparently sold them after finals. I didn't see a class schedule on the desk. I opened the first drawer, thinking I'd find one there. What I found were several *Playboy* magazines. We'd passed around dog-eared, ancient issues of *Playboy* in the house, and the sexiest layouts were always torn out, but these editions were in pristine condition. I took the top three out and opened the centerfolds on his bed. The best was Kim Farber, Miss February 1967, lying on a Murphy bed covered with a white tiger-striped blanket, caramel-brown breasts, hard nipples.

When I'd finished my solo tryst with Kim, I stretched out on Paul's bed and read two *Playboy* interviews, one with Fidel Castro and the other with Mark Lane, the author of a book on the Kennedy assassination we had read in Contemporary Politics last semester. I eventually found a class schedule. In it, there were several survey courses I needed for graduation. I chose a history course, Western Civilization, and registered for it that afternoon before going back out to the *Plain Talk*.

I saw Bellman standing at the window in his office as I pulled into the parking lot. When I walked into the office, the girls all looked up from what they were doing, bored with answering dumb questions about ads in the paper. One of the girls, a cute townie with hair pulled back and wrapped in a blue bandanna, wearing very short shorts that showed smooth, muscular legs, leafed through a stack of pay envelopes on her desk. She found one with my name, held it up above her head, and waved it back and forth a couple of times.

"Is someone looking for this?" she asked. When I reached for it, she pulled it back. "Is it true what they're saying about White Hawk? About the rape?" she asked. The other girls snickered.

"I give. What are they saying?"

"Remember how hot it was that day? The two neighbor girls, Roberta and Loretta, were sunbathing in their new bikinis in their backyard. White Hawk saw them and got all hot and bothered and raped Mrs. Yeado."

The other girls pretended to be disgusted.

"I'll be sure to follow up on that theory," I said.

She handed me the check. I thanked her and knocked on Bellman's half-open door.

"I read your story. Not bad," he said. "Still too long on description and a little short on essential facts, but you're getting better. I took some liberties with the final version."

"What do you want me to do next?"

"We've got to do something on Jim Yeado, something more than an obituary. This may sound cynical, but getting murdered has made him into an interesting person. People want to know more about what he did the day of the murder, what his relationship with White Hawk was, his Catholic faith, those kinds of things."

"You told me his wife wasn't talking. What other sources are there? His two kids don't live here."

"Your problem. You'll think of something."

"Do you have a copy of the obituary? I'll start there."

Bellman pushed the sliding lock on a green metal file drawer behind him and opened it. He reached in and pulled out the Yeado obituary. "One of the girls will make a copy for you. I wish I had more personal knowledge, but I wasn't that close to him. I took my business to Dallas Jewelry across the street. I went to the funeral out of civic duty. The funeral was sad, like they all are, but this one was different. The predominant emotion was anger at those two Indian boys, White Hawk especially. Manny Marshall, one of the pallbearers, was supposed to be eulogizing Jim, but all he talked about was the murder and how White Hawk deserved to die for it. It's all anybody could think and talk about. Jim Yeado was in the background most of his life, even at his own funeral. And then the strangest thing of all," he said.

"What was that?"

"The family buried him in Oregon. Yeah, after thirty years living here, thirty years of running a business and raising a family, they had the body shipped to Oregon, where his daughter lives. I don't think Jim had ever set foot in Oregon. Now he'll lie there forever. I heard that Dorthea will be moving out there too. They auctioned off her household items the other day. A friend of my wife's bought their china. A jeweler's set, very nice."

"In the path of the storm."

"What?"

"Nothing. Something I've been thinking about. Yeado and his wife. In the wrong place at the wrong time."

"This is Friday, Peters. I'll need your story by next Tuesday afternoon, no later than five, for next Thursday's edition."

"Okay."

"Hey," he said, his face brightening. "I almost forgot. Jim's best friend, Fred Barton, was one of the pallbearers. He lives across from the courthouse, on the same street as Meisenholder Motors. He told me he was with Jim on Thursday, the day before the murder. He'll have something to say, I'm sure."

I thanked him and took the obituary to get copied, then began reading it on my way out the door.

James Yeado Services Held
Burial in Oregon

VERMILLION, N.D.—Funeral services for James A. Yeado, 62, were held at 10 a.m. Tuesday in St. Agnes Catholic Church. Father Leonard Stanton officiated. Burial will be Monday in Mount Calvary Cemetery, Portland, Ore.

Yeado, a jeweler in Vermillion for 30 years, was found dead in his home at 315 S. University on Friday. Two university students have been charged with his death.

Yeado was born Sept. 14, 1904, at LeRoy, N.D. He married Dorthea McMahan Aug. 31, 1931, at Bird Island, Minn. They lived at Hector, Minn., and moved to Vermillion in 1937. Yeado was a member of the Father Flood Council, Knights of Columbus; the Fraternal Order of Eagles; and the Vermillion Chamber of Commerce.

Survivors include his widow, Mrs. Dorthea Yeado; a daughter, Mrs. Ivan (Lavaune) LaHale of Portland, Ore.; a son, Robert J. of Washington, D.C.; three grandchildren; and a sister, Mrs. Sadie St. Martin of Tacoma, Wash.

Rosaries on Monday evening at the Wagner-Iverson Funeral Home were conducted by members of the St. Agnes Parish and the Father Flood Council, Knights of Columbus.

Pallbearers were Fred Barton, Manny Marshall, Aike Hollman, Ernest Michael, James Donavon, and Lyman Heathcliff.

I took Bellman's advice and called Fred Barton. I can't say that he welcomed the opportunity to talk about his dead friend so soon, but he agreed to meet the next morning. Barton's white, four-square home was two houses down from the Pontiac and Chevrolet dealer in town, Meisenholder Motors. A breezeway ran between Barton's home and a large garage, out of which Barton ran a small-engine repair business.

A withered man, his face heavily creased, wearing a pair of clean mechanic overalls, the kind with two straps sliding on metal buttons in the front, answered the door. He apologized for not being ready. Something had come up that morning, preventing him from opening his business at the usual hour. He led me into the kitchen and through the wainscoted knotty pine breezeway that led to the garage. He struggled lifting the double-stall garage door but finally raised it high enough for the counterweight to do the rest of the work. Directly across the street stood the courthouse, the jail cellblock windows framed by the pink quartzite stone that banded the first floor. Barton found two metal folding chairs and handed one to me. We sat on the concrete garage driveway, the morning sun warming us.

"What did you want to know about Jim Yeado?" he asked.

"I understand you were one of his closest friends. Perhaps you could tell me something about his life? What kind of a man he was?"

"What you saw was what you got, you know? Jim went to Mass every morning. Went to communion and then had his breakfast at the Chimes Café. Sometimes we'd have him over here for breakfast. St. Agnes is just three blocks away. His day was very predictable, precise, like the watches he worked on. He went home for lunch, back to work at one, and then home again at five. Everybody knew his schedule, including the police. When he didn't open the store that morning, they should've called him. If they had, they might have saved his life," Barton said, fighting back a surge of grief.

We were both quiet for a few moments. I stood up and pretended to be interested in the contents of the garage. An extra-long workbench was covered with tools and solvents. A transmission belt lay on the workbench, and below it several five-gallon cans were overflowing with screws, bolts, nuts, and washers. The smell of gas and oil permeated the place. No pinups on the walls.

Barton was wearing a railroad engineer's cap. He removed it, revealing thinning hair matted on his head, aging abruptly without the cap. After he lit a cigarette, I started in again.

"Did you see him the day before—the day before the murder?"

"Briefly. At Holy Thursday services that night. We stood outside the church and talked. Made plans to play cribbage on Sunday afternoon after dinner. I think we invited them over for coffee, but Dorthea had some baking to do for a dinner party they were hosting the next night. She had a beautiful set of china she loved to show off."

"Had Mr. Yeado mentioned White Hawk to you? Did he say anything about the ring he sold White Hawk?"

"I was in the store once when White Hawk came in. I was downtown to pick up some medication at Davis Drug—I've got heart problems, not supposed to be smoking," he said, raising his cigarette in resignation. "Davis Drug is right next to the jewelry store. So I went over to see Jim and was standing at the counter talking with him when the Indian kid came in. He was somebody you'd notice. Big, strong-looking kid. Stiff, thick hair, real fine features. I wouldn't have thought he was an Indian but for his clothes. Worn-out khakis. Frayed shirt. And the tattoos. They're always a warning sign. But he was real polite. Soft-spoken. He was dropping off a payment for the ring he had bought for his girlfriend. Jim knew her too. I think she was why he was willing to sell White Hawk the ring on time. Dottie was her name. She worked as a waitress at the Chimes. Anyway, he dropped his payment off with Jim and left."

"Did Mr. Yeado say anything to you about White Hawk after he left the store?"

"Some kind words about what a cute pair those two Indians were. Jim wanted the best for them, and what did that son of a bitch do?" he asked, gesturing toward the courthouse cell windows across the street. "He broke into his home at night, shot him, and raped his wife. If there's a hell, he's going to burn in it. Problem is, I am not so sure there even is one."

Before I left, Barton went inside his house and came back out with a photograph in his hand, a picture of Yeado sitting at a desk peering at a stone of some kind through a jeweler's eyepiece. Yeado's salt-and-pepper hair, worn down to his collar, was swept back. In the background, glass cabinets were filled with boxed sets of rings mounted in velvet beds.

"I'm not even sure how I got the picture. It's all Jim ever wanted to do. Work quietly at his desk, sell enough jewelry to make a living, and go home at night to have dinner with his wife. That's what White Hawk destroyed—a life more valuable than his."

7

Barton gave me a few more Yeado vignettes for my story. I called two more pallbearers who turned me down for interviews before Aike Hollman, the high school science teacher and Yeado's neighbor, agreed to talk to me. I arrived at the Hollman home early in the evening. The ash and hackberry trees in front of the Yeado home had leafed out. The lawn was green now, with volunteer weeds poking above the grass like sentries. The house was dark, the curtains pulled shut. The ornamental evergreens on either side of the front entrance needed pruning.

I sat on the couch in Mr. Hollman's living room while he smoked a pipe and recalled what sort of neighbors Jim and Dorthea Yeado had been, reiterating their saintly life. I could hear the twins upstairs in their bedroom, playing the same song over and over on a forty-five-rpm record player—the Turtles' "Happy Together." When I was ready to leave, Mr. Hollman walked me out. We were standing on his driveway when a thought came to him.

"The murder occurred on a Friday morning, but I don't think it was the first time the boys were here. Someone sneaked into the Yeado garage on Tuesday and caused the rafters, filled with stored items and whatnot, to collapse. It created a huge, dusty mess. I helped Jim clean it up. I'll bet it was those two boys, hiding out in the rafters, waiting to jump Jim when he came home from work. They must have lost their nerve and left."

"So they had been planning to rob him before Friday?"

"Apparently so."

When I finished writing my Yeado profile, I drove over to the *Plain Talk* office and gave Bellman three typed pages on yellow legal paper. I waited outside his office and chatted with the payroll girl while he read it. She had shy, inquisitive eyes and likely had dreams of a life outside this tiny university town.

When Bellman was finished, he came out and handed the story back to me. He had added an anecdote about Yeado speaking at a chamber of commerce meeting, deleted several adjectives, and corrected a run-on sentence. He stood over me while I read the changes, his arms folded in a take-it-or-leave-it position.

"Looks good, Mr. Bellman."

"I thought so too. The family will appreciate it."

"The clerk of courts told me that Judge Brady has scheduled the arraignment hearing in July. That gives me time to interview White Hawk. How about it?"

"As long as you understand the rules. One story, and the rest of the time we cover it like any other crime. He's the perpetrator, the killer, and responsible for what he did. Nobody else is at fault. Did you see the letter to the editor in Monday's edition and my response?"

"No."

"A lady from Minnetonka who had had White Hawk as a guest in her home—her son was friends with him at Shattuck—wrote to tell us about what a fine boy he was and how there must be something in the water here that inspired him to kill Jim Yeado. Pardon my French, but that's bullshit. White Hawk's crime is on trial here, not his past, his parents, or how the white man treated the red man in the nineteenth century."

"I still want to write a story about Tom."

"Have at it, then."

I sat at a table, waiting for the deputy to escort Tom into the jail kitchen. The remnants of Tom and Willie's lunch were strewn on the kitchen countertop: leftover crusts of grilled cheese sandwiches, an empty can of Pringle's New-Fangled Potato Chips, and a half-full pitcher of cherry Kool-Aid. A warm frying pan on a stove burner left a homey kitchen smell. I couldn't see the cells from where I was sitting, but I could hear the din of what sounded like construction workers jackhammering concrete in one of them.

The deputy brought Tom out. He appeared much better than he had the last time. He looked directly at me as he entered, which I interpreted as being glad to have a visitor. The deputy left us alone.

"What's all the racket about back there? How long have they been working?" I asked.

"They started two days ago. They're replacing the bars in the cell windows with reinforced glass. Volesky wanted to send Willie and me up to the pen right away, before the trial, but the judge said no. So Volesky's taking no chances, escape threats that we are. You know, slip out and kill a few more white people and then flee to the reservation," he said, raising his eyebrows, his face contorted in a mock-terrified look.

"Seriously?"

"You white boys are too easy."

"I suppose so."

"Our cell windows are right at ground level, looking out to the west. The sidewalk isn't that far away. The car dealership and gas station, Meisenholder Motors, is across the street. We watch the cars go in and out all day long. The only danger we pose is to the girls who sneak up to the cell windows when they think no one is looking so they can talk to the famous killers. If I had known this was how to attract girls, I would have done something about it long ago."

The jackhammering stopped. I lowered my voice. The deputy was standing outside the room, within earshot.

"You're a lot better, Tom. Happy to see it."

"I need to talk to Dottie. Have you seen her?"

"Not since the day after."

"Tell her I need to see her right away. I miss her. Why hasn't she visited me?"

"I don't know. Has Phil been to see you?"

"Twice. He writes too. I've gotten three letters from him. We've patched things up. I feel bad about how I've let him down. I've let everybody down. I don't understand how any of this happened. A Shattuck friend gave me a psychology book, but that hasn't helped much. What the fuck is the matter with me?"

"I don't know. What did the Yankton hospital doctor say when you saw him?"

"He had made up his mind before he asked his first question. I was with him maybe fifteen minutes. They had me take a test, too, multiple choice. The doctor wrote up his report while I was taking it. He gave it to one of the deputies, and we were back on the road to Vermillion in no time. I sat in the back of the car, handcuffed, staring at the bluffs on the Nebraska side of the river. I felt my whole body rise out of the car and disappear into those distant draws and ravines, away with my relatives. Dream ended. Only one way I'm getting out of here."

"You have a lawyer."

"Yeah. Lee. He represented me on the car theft thing. I haven't seen much of him. Phil's worried. Thinks I need a new lawyer. Lee doesn't respond to Phil's calls and letters."

"Are your headaches still bothering you?"

"Not as much. They let me exercise every day outside. Not with Willie though. They let us out at different times. We can't be trusted. It would give us a chance to plan our escape, keep our stories straight," he said, straight faced. I couldn't tell if he meant it or not.

"What else are you doing to pass the time?"

"Painting. The sheriff got me some supplies. I painted some pictures of one of the deputy's kids. A few scenes from my own life."

"Who else has come to see you?"

"A couple of guys from my pledge class. But they quit coming. The Huberts visit quite often. Father James is a good guy. Deb and I are on the same wavelength. She comes more often than he does."

"Family?"

"I haven't seen any of them for a long time now. They were adopted out or went to foster families when we were very young. I've got an uncle. His name is Charles. He came once. He doesn't know what to think."

"Your parents are both dead, right? What do you remember about them?"

"Dad was a big, strong man. A marine. Went to Korea. Worked as an electrical engineer."

"How did your father die?"

"Car accident."

"What about your mother?"

"She was a beautiful woman, long black hair to her waist. She had French and German blood. She was a nurse."

He paused, the memory of his mother seemingly moving him.

"I was eleven when Dad died. Hey, why are you writing this down?"

"Taking some notes is all. In case somebody asks me to write a story about this."

"About what? About me?"

"A newspaper story. For the local newspaper. They hired me for the summer."

"You're no better than the rest, you know. You're my friend now that there's something in it for you."

"It's not like that at all. I want your side of the story. I can help. I'm sorry, Tom, I should have told you," I said.

Tom was looking away, to his right, his cheekbone clenching, something rising in him, a bitter anger at those who took and took from him and returned empty promises in trade.

"My side of the story is that I killed that old man and raped his wife. This isn't a mystery. Look, if you write anything about me, write about what I did at Shattuck. The awards I got there. I was a premed major. I was an SAE, right? Doesn't that mean something? I was doing pretty well until my headaches came back."

"Sure, I'll write about that stuff."

"And one more thing. Don't do that again. Don't trick me, man. Remember what happened to Courtland?" he said, somber as hell.

And then we both laughed.

"How is that spook, anyway?"

"Still around. He's been at both of your court hearings, snooping around, looking for skins to massacre."

"Tell him I said, 'Phi Alpha,'" he said, raising his fist, flipping the bird.

"Is there anything I can get you? What do you need?"

"I need stamps. I memorized a Shakespeare sonnet in a literature class at Shattuck and wrote it down in a letter to Phil. The Old English in the plays was too hard for me, but the sonnets were different—personal, you know. I had to recite number twenty-nine in class. I can still do it," he said, standing up from his chair, his eyes unmoving.

> When, in disgrace with Fortune and men's eyes,
> I all alone beweep my outcast state,
> And trouble deaf heaven with my bootless cries,
> And look upon myself and curse my fate...

Tom paused, thinking about the words or reaching deeper into his memory to find them, I couldn't tell. And then he went on.

> Wishing me like to one more rich in hope,
> Featured like him, like him with friends possessed,
> Desiring this man's art, and that man's scope,
> With what I most enjoy, contented least,
> Yet in these thoughts myself almost despising,
> Haply I think on thee, and then my state,
> Like to the lark at break of day arising
> From sullen earth sings hymns at heaven's gate;
> For thy sweet love rememb'red such wealth brings
> That then I scorn to change my state with kings.

Tom sat back down in his chair, the pain and loneliness he dwelt in each day, without the wealth of a sweet love, buried deep behind those dark, unmoving eyes.

8

Vermillion had a small-island vibe in the summer. Townies woke but did not stir much, weeding the garden, hanging out the wash, reading on the front porch. Lilacs, spirea, and tiger lilies flowered in nature's unbreakable order throughout May and June. Downtown, cars gathered outside the Chimes Café, leaving the rest of the street empty until late morning. The IGA butcher walked down the street in his apron to the Monogram News to pick up a paper. Traffic, what little there was of it, took its time. Most of the students were gone, working or traveling. Faculty were more anchored to the town back then, tolerating the local rural culture if not adopting it, arriving at the office late in the morning only to chat with the bored department secretary rather than work on their research projects.

I went to class each morning, three straight hours of Western Civilization Monday through Thursday, from mid-June until mid-July. After class I often went over to the Grille and looked for a table to join. There were a few SAEs who had enrolled in classes, usually to boost their sagging grade points, but I avoided them. I didn't go over to the house either, knowing what the scene would be like. The brothers who had stayed for the summer would sleep late each morning in the quiet and dark house, watch *Rifleman* reruns in the recreation room all afternoon, and then head downtown to one of the bars, which felt shabby and depressing in the summer when not crowded with loud and horny coeds.

After coffee at the Grille, I'd go back to the apartment, shut the windows and close the drapes to keep the cool air trapped inside, and study or work on my background article. I eventually finished it over the Fourth of July and delivered it to Bellman. He read it; cut out, in his words, the "fluff"; and declared it ready for publication. Before I left his office, he reminded me that Tom's arraignment hearing would be held Tuesday. I assured him I would be there.

When I got back to the apartment, Caitlin called. She was home in Sioux City for the summer, working at the Johnson Biscuit Company. She stood all day in an assembly line, packing oatmeal and sugar cookies in boxes with cellophane windows, the only woman under forty on the floor. Her father, Dutch Connors, a schoolteacher and track coach, had found her the job at the cookie factory. Dutch drove her across town each morning to the factory, grumpy, chain-smoking, staring ahead wordlessly but willing to do it because Caitlin's paychecks would finance her college tuition in the fall. Caitlin asked if I would come rescue her. The cookie factory was retooling her line, and she had the week off. She wanted to go to Tom's hearing.

I drove the Plymouth down to Sioux City the next morning, a Saturday. Sioux City was a meat-packing town, and the retching smell of rendered cowhide hung in the air, fouling a warm, cloudless day. The smell had lifted by the time I reached Morningside, where her family lived. Dutch sold tickets at the dog races in North Sioux City and painted houses during the summer. He had recently painted their house too, judging from the fresh paint smell. I knocked on the front door, and Caitlin answered it immediately. She had a bag packed, ready to go. Her parents were out, and her younger brothers and sisters were playing in the living room. Framed black-and-white photographs hung on the wall of the entryway, one of them a

classic pose with the six kids standing in a row, oldest to youngest, the four girls in jumpers and white socks, the two boys in
buttoned-up plaid coats. Each had a unique expression, not all
smiley-happy, all blended images of their handsome parents.

Caitlin wore cut-off jeans, a summer top, and sandals, white
as an envelope from working inside all day. A weary smile was
all she could muster. She was impatient to leave the scene,
aware that the ordinariness of her family life was out of sync
with the imperious, alluring woman I had gladly driven an
hour to pick up.

"Let's go," she said. "I have to get out of here. They're driving me nuts."

I reached for her suitcase, a cloth traveler with a lot of miles,
probably her mother's bag, but she pulled it back.

"I told them you are a friend, someone who was in town
running an errand and offered to give me a ride to Vermillion.
It would look weird if you carried my bag. You are a friend,
aren't you?"

"I came all the way down here to get you, didn't I?"

"You did, and I won't forget it. Come on," she said, tossing
her bag in the back. "I want to go to High Line today."

I didn't know where she was going to stay, nor for how long,
and I didn't ask, afraid the answer might be at Chris's, or with
Harlan, for that matter. When we arrived in Vermillion, I drove
over to my apartment and asked her if she wanted to come in.
She did, but she left her suitcase in the car. I found a bottle of
Coke in the refrigerator and filled two glasses with ice cubes.
When I handed her one, she kissed me.

"Thanks again for saving me."

"I was surprised when you called. After what happened last
time, I didn't know what to expect."

"You're too serious. Don't talk it to death. Go with it, and we'll see what happens. Hey," she said, nonchalant, pulling a joint out of her purse, "wanna smoke some dope?"

We sat on the overstuffed couch in the living room and passed the joint back and forth. The smoke grated and stabbed deeper into my lungs than cigarette smoke. I took several more hits, hoping to pass the loyalty test. Caitlin kept watching me as if there were some telltale reaction that signaled I was high.

"Sorry, I don't feel a thing. Maybe a little dizzy. Is that what being stoned is like?"

"Maybe it doesn't work on Republicans or SAEs. They don't have the gene."

"That could be. What I really need is a cigarette. Is that allowed?"

"I'll have one too."

The cigarette tasted delicious. Caitlin found a *Playboy* on the coffee table. I had forgotten to put them away. She opened it to the magazine's signature cartoon, the decrepit old lady with sagging tits and unflagging libido mounting a twenty-one-year-old stud. We couldn't stop laughing. No wonder people smoked the stuff.

Caitlin wanted to go to High Line, a remote landing on the Missouri River a few miles from town. She ran out to the car to get her swimsuit while I changed. I brought along a six-pack of Grain Belt and the Thursday edition of the *Plain Talk*. We drove downtown, stopping at the IGA for snack food. The battered floorboards in the store squeaked beneath our feet as we made our way back to the meat counter. I struck up a conversation with the two butchers in aprons behind the counter. Stoned, everyone's backstory took on an air of mystery and interest. Back in the car, Caitlin asked what she should do with the S&H green stamps they had given her when she paid for the groceries. I couldn't explain why that question was so funny, but we laughed uncontrollably for another five minutes before feeling sane enough to drive.

High Line was a neglected boat landing and a crude mini-beach of jagged riprap a mile or so off Timber Road. There were other parks and landings on the river more attractive to swimmers and recreational boaters, leaving High Line to high school and college kids looking for privacy. We waded through the shallow water out to the sandbars near the main channel, where the current ran stronger, shifting and swirling ominously. We spread our blankets out on the sand over the tiny bird tracks that were everywhere. No boats, no sign of a human presence on or off the water. The wooded bluffs on either side of the river enclosed us, adding to the sense we were in a sanctuary.

"This is a beautiful place," Caitlin said, slipping out of her shorts and top, exposing her swimsuit underneath. "So quiet, but for the wildlife."

"It's one of the last stretches of the Missouri not channelized. This part of the river looks pretty much like what Lewis and Clark saw when they came through. Imagine how difficult it must have been to pull their keelboats upriver."

"I thought they sailed up the river."

"Not on the first leg of their journey, against the current. They pulled the boats upriver from the shore."

"I wonder what Tom's people thought when they saw the boats?"

"We're fucked."

We drank the beer and talked for a while, and then both of us fell asleep in the warm sun. A horsefly sting woke me. Caitlin was already up and sitting in a lawn chair, reading my *Plain Talk* story. When she finished, she folded the paper up and handed it to me.

"Well, what do you think?"

"I don't get your point here. What are you trying to say?"

"That there's more to Tom than the cold-blooded killer everyone makes him out to be. He's an athlete and a pretty good student. He's funny too. More aware of who and what he is than you might think."

"If he's such a Boy Scout, why did he do it? Your story doesn't make that clear. The stuff about him being a star athlete and all makes him seem ungrateful. Psycho and scary, because he and his family seem normal and, well, white. And then he kills somebody and rapes a woman—not a young woman, either, an old woman."

"Now I know why Bellman made so few changes in the story. Fuck."

"Why didn't you write about his childhood? If he went to boarding school, it must have been difficult."

"Bellman didn't want that angle in the story. He made that pretty clear."

"And so you caved. Wrote the story he wanted?"

"Not that simple, but he does have final editorial approval."

"Okay. The end of all that, then," she said sardonically, as if lost opportunities were typical of me. "Let's go for a swim."

After we had our swim—more of a wade in the fast current—we dried off and opened another beer. Caitlin reached into her purse and pulled out the last of the joint we had started in the apartment. We smoked the rest of it. When the sun fell below the tree line on the Nebraska side of the river, shading the sand bars, we packed up and returned to the apartment.

The apartment was cool inside. Caitlin took my hand and guided me into my bedroom. We undressed and I moved on top, sliding into her easily. She came shortly after I did, her arms wrapped around me, holding me as tightly as she could, intensifying the moment. When she shook me awake toward evening, the afternoon's sunburn tightening my skin to her touch, I was dreaming. I was in jail. The details dissolved as soon as I woke, but the claustrophobic dream-fear lingered with me the rest of the night.

9

Caitlin stayed at my apartment. On Tuesday we went down to the courthouse an hour before the arraignment hearing began. It was another hot, humid day. Maintenance workers had covered the third-floor skylight to block the sun, keeping the rotunda area inside the courthouse cooler for the anticipated crowd. A few people had already gathered outside the courtroom. Everyone wore bright-colored summer clothes and glowed with weekend tans.

I saw Zolbach standing alone next to a window, his back to everyone else, watching some playful squirrels in a sugar maple tree on the courthouse lawn. "You've got to meet this guy," I told Caitlin, tugging at her blouse.

"Mr. Zolbach," I called out.

"Yes," he said, turning around, "what is it?" He looked older than I remembered and was frowning sourly. He was wearing a plaid shirt and slacks, a church outfit. The amber lenses in his eyeglasses made him look slightly odd, just off a bit.

"Hi, Mr. Zolbach."

"Oh, yes, of course. How are you?" he asked, his voice flat, emotionless.

"I'm fine. This is Caitlin. She's a friend. She also works at the student newspaper."

"Hello, Caitlin," he said, but turned back to me. "In his last letter, Tom said you came to see him. I thank you so much for remaining his friend. He has so few now."

"Have you seen him recently?"

"No. I drove in from Faribault this morning. I dropped by the jail, but the sheriff wouldn't let me see him. Some silly rule about no visitation on court days. Sheriff Wilson has given me trouble ever since this started. I'll have to stay overnight if I'm to see Tom. I called my lawyer. He's going to call Wilson. How was Tom when you saw him?"

"He was much better. Not as depressed. Jumped from one thing to another, shifting gears quickly. His sense of humor is back. We laughed a few times."

"I didn't know Tom to have a sense of humor," Zolbach said dismissively.

"Have you talked to McMillan about Tom's case?"

"Let me count the times. I've sent him letters, money for his expenses, a letter from Dr. Rumpf explaining Tom's shot put accident, but he doesn't respond. I know Lee was in a car accident and had an appendix operation, so I shouldn't be so pushy, but Tom's life is on the line here. Volesky wants the death sentence."

"So does most everyone I've talked to here in town."

Caitlin drifted away from our conversation, peering through the diamond-shaped windows in the courtroom doors, standing on her tiptoes. The muscles in her legs rippled like an athlete's, the legacy she so hated. She turned to look back and signaled me to come. The area reserved for the press was filling up. There were no court rules requiring credentials to sit in the press area, but a female reporter was an unusual species. My colleagues looked skeptical as they slid down the bench to make room for us.

We sat directly behind the prosecution table. Neither the prosecution nor the defense had arrived yet, but the spectator seats were nearly full. Zolbach must have been waiting for the

Huberts. He came in with them, Father James leading the way, with Deb following in a sundress and braids, holding James's hand as he guided her to a back row. To my surprise, Bellman came in with Fred Barton. Bellman was outfitted like the stereotypical small-town newspaper publisher—straw hat in hand, cream-colored linen suit, a comb-over failing to disguise his bald spot. He stubbed out a cigar in an urn outside the doors before entering the courtroom. He came straight to the press row, caught my eye, and signaled me to come talk to him.

"You're here, thank God," he said, a bead of sweat trickling down his left temple. His alcoholic cheeks blossomed in the light of the courtroom.

"Where else would I be? I said I would cover the hearing."

"I've been calling your apartment for several days. No answer. I didn't know what happened. I've discovered your last story has some serious flaws. That fairy-tale stuff about White Hawk's father being an electrical engineer is bunk. He was the town drunk and a wife beater. He did die in a car accident, but he was driving ninety-plus miles an hour on a dirt road on the rez, drunk, and careened off the road. He was a tough old warrior, I'll give him that. He crawled over two miles for help but died three days later. And his mother. She was never a nurse—far from it—and was known for selling her favors for booze. She was a melancholy woman, totally dependent on the old man, who beat her mercilessly. They found her dead, lying in bed, of a brain aneurysm."

Bellman looked at me as if I had an answer to his harangue.

"Anyway," he finally said, "I have news. Volesky told me he's amending the charges to premeditated murder. He's going for the death penalty."

"I know," I said, as if it were old news.

"Well, make sure you include that angle in the story. It's critical, a new development," he said, nodding his head and locking eyes with me, as if I needed a sign emphasizing its importance and the need to get this one straight.

As I was talking to Bellman, Courtland came in. He gave me a mock salute and went on, the smug bastard.

The defense and prosecution arrived, Volesky with the attorney who assisted him at the May hearing. Volesky gave a nod again to the crowd and sat down at the prosecutor's table. Tom and McMillan came in behind them. Neither looked up; Tom stared down at the floor, McMillan straight ahead. Tom wasn't wearing the sport coat and tie he'd worn at previous hearings, dropping any pretense, and was in the same open-collar shirt and ragged khakis he had on when I last saw him in jail. McMillan turned and asked Tom something once they were seated. Tom thought about it for a moment, his countenance in doubt, and then shook his head.

The clerk of courts announced Judge Brady, and we all rose. Not many judges are embarrassed by the entrance formality. Brady certainly wasn't, entering the courtroom with his face locked in serious-judge mode. His expansive robe fluffed like a hoop skirt as he sat down, momentarily shaking his dignity.

Once everyone was seated, Brady wasted no time, requesting Volesky to read the new charges into the record. Volesky rose, slowly for effect, holding his notes with both hands as if they were in danger of someone snatching them away or the wind blowing them out of those large claws. He read the charges.

"The said defendant did willfully, unlawfully, and feloniously, with malice aforethought, and without authority of law, *and with premeditated design*, and during the commission of a felony, and without justifiable or excusable cause, perpetrate and effect the death of James Yeado…"

McMillan must have known Volesky was going to include the premeditated language in the charges, but he pretended to be surprised. Several of the reporters made a note of the language change. When Volesky was finished, McMillan rose from his seat.

"Your Honor, if I might, I have an objection to the charges read by the state. May I explain?"

"Yes, of course."

"At the time the original charges were filed on March twenty-fifth in municipal court, they included premeditation language similar to what the state just read. However, at a subsequent hearing on March thirtieth, that language was withdrawn by the state. The defense in good faith assumed the matter was settled. Today that faith has been violated. That is my objection. I move that the language be struck from the charges before my client is asked to plead today."

"Very well. I need a few moments with the defense and the state before I rule on the motion. The court will take a ten-minute recess," Brady said.

A few people left the courtroom during the recess, but most stayed in their seats, not willing to forfeit them to the crowd that had gathered outside.

Caitlin leaned over and whispered in my ear, "Is Volesky always this full of himself?"

"Only on Tuesdays and Thursdays. The rest of the time he's a real asshole," I said.

One of the sheriff's deputies told me that Volesky, who drove a Cadillac, roared up the Yeado driveway the night of the murder and stormed over to the sheriff, who was standing on the front lawn, demanding to know why hadn't he been notified earlier. When the sheriff told him the perpetrator was still inside the house, Volesky dropped to the ground and crawled back to his car, which he drove quickly off to safety.

"Tom doesn't look like the glory boy you made him out to be in your article. He looks defeated, ashamed," Caitlin said, whispering in my ear. Her hair brushed against my cheek when she leaned in. I held back an urge to kiss her neck.

"That ain't the half of it. I'll explain later. But consider his circumstances. This has got to be difficult. He's let everyone down."

The meeting in the judge's chambers broke up. McMillan and Tom were the first through the door, followed by the two prosecutors and Judge Brady. We were close enough in the first row to smell the fresh cigarette smoke on the attorneys and judge.

"Mr. Volesky, I believe you have amended information ready to be read for the record, do you not?" said the judge, pushing back in his chair, apparently satisfied with the compromise agreed on in his chambers.

Volesky read the murder charge, this time without the premeditation language.

"Very well. Are there any objections to the charge as read by the state's attorney, Mr. McMillan?"

"We have none, Your Honor."

"Are there other charges to be filed today, Mr. Volesky?" the judge asked.

"Yes, Your Honor. One more, if it please the court."

"You may proceed."

Volesky read the rape charge. All eyes were fixed on Tom at that moment, the nineteen-year-old Indian boy. I looked up at the judge, for no reason in particular. His face was settled in a determined manner.

"Now, Mr. McMillan, is the defendant ready to plead at this time?" the judge asked.

"He is, Your Honor."

"Will the prisoner please stand," the judge ordered Tom. He stood. "Mr. White Hawk, by the charges in writing, filed by the state's attorney, you have been charged with the crime of murder. You have examined a copy of the charges, and the court states to you at this time that the offense with which you are charged is what is known as a capital offense and carries with it, in the event of your conviction upon trial or in the event of a plea of guilty, a possible penalty of death by electrocution.

"Now, that might be taken in the sense that, if you were to at this time enter a plea of guilty to that charge, it would be in my sole discretion as to whether to impose the death penalty or up to life imprisonment.

"In the event that you do stand trial before a jury, and a jury shall find you guilty as charged, and shall additionally recommend the death penalty, it would then be under the discretion of the trial judge as to whether to impose the death penalty or not.

"I make this full explanation not expecting you to enter a plea of guilty, but so that you will fully understand what is involved in this matter.

"Now, Mr. White Hawk, how do you at this time plead— guilty or not guilty?" the judge asked.

"I plead not guilty," Tom said. "Not guilty by reason of insanity."

"And as to the rape charge, Mr. White Hawk, how do you plead?" the judge asked.

"Not guilty by reason of insanity."

The courtroom was dead quiet but for two rotating metal fans mounted on pedestals blowing warm air in the direction of the audience.

"Very well," the judge said, and directed the state to transport Tom back to the Yankton State Hospital for a psychiatric exam, given his insanity plea. The judge turned to McMillan and allowed that the defense would likely desire an independent evaluation of Tom's mental health. He asked him for the names of two professionals he wished to have examine the defendant. McMillan gave the judge two names.

The court's business was finished for the day. Sheriff Wilson, sitting in the front row opposite the press, stood, walked through the gate at the center of the bar, and placed his hand gently on Tom's shoulder, gesturing for him to follow, back to his jail cell. The crowd followed suit, rising from their seats. Two of the reporters brushed quickly past us, Caitlin mocking their pompous behavior. The judge stepped down from the bench, reached inside his robe, and pulled out a pack of Camels, lighting one before he disappeared into his chambers.

Caitlin and I waited for the crowd to make its way out of the courtroom before leaving. Courtland was standing off to our right in the rotunda area, on the other side of the railing directly below the skylight. When he saw us exiting the courtroom, he came over.

"Interesting day in court, wouldn't you say?" Courtland asked.

"Are you talking about Volesky's clumsy attempt to slip the premeditation language into the charges?"

Courtland assumed his disbelief pose, the mocking contempt he usually reserved for a pledge who had failed to recite the "True Gentleman" or who couldn't remember all six SAE founding members.

"I'm talking about your Indian friend's new disguise. His not-guilty-by-insanity plea. You know, the crazy Indian defense?" Courtland said.

"You don't know what you're talking about, Courtland," I said. "What is the matter with you?"

"That's rich. Something's the matter with me. You and I both know it's an act. The Indian's playing a trick on us. He knows what he's doing; he'll play crazy until he gets off. The other stuff about being a good Indian, the white Indian—that's all an act too."

"And why is this so obvious to you?"

"He's been given so much by everybody his whole life. You said as much in your article about him. All the awards and the white people so proud of him. He's a cynical liar who's got you and a lot of other people fooled. I saw that from the beginning."

"Good for you, Courtland."

"And you know what? Your friend is going to fry. You heard the judge. He's a dead man."

As soon as Caitlin and I got back, we put on more comfortable clothes and went down to the front porch to escape the baking heat in my apartment. The porch on the old Victorian had several mismatched but comfortable rockers in it, facing east, shaded and cool in the late afternoon. With all the dry weather, the cicadas were already out, screeching in the big Dutch elm in the yard.

"Is Courtland right about Tom?" I asked her.

"That there is another Tom, one hidden from everyone?"

"Yeah."

"That could be said about everyone, couldn't it? Whites too. Courtland is a strange one. Why is he so obsessed with Tom and this case?"

"He was on Tom's case as soon as he pledged. He and Tom got in a fight during hell week. Tom got the best of Courtland. Beat him up pretty bad."

"Well, that explains some of it. Crushed male ego. But why did he have it in for Tom in the first place?"

"Indians here are always down on their luck. Worn clothes, no vehicle, hungry. Wandering along the roadsides, homeless. Their desperation scares you when you're young. Everybody makes fun of them and despises them, so you do too. Out where Courtland grew up, West River, it's worse. They're your neighbors, but on the other side of a very tall fence. Courtland's family has probably been at odds with the Indians for generations."

"That's so fucked up."

"So you don't think Tom is faking it?"

"Did you watch him in court today? If it's an act, it's a good one. He can work in Hollywood when this is all over."

10

I drove Caitlin back to Sioux City on a warm and humid afternoon. We had sex often during that hot summer week, usually twice a day, lying in bed or on the couch or on a sandbar, sweaty and giddy. She was quiet on the ride back, staring out her window, the faded yellow sundress she was wearing pulled up high above her knees to cool her muscular, shapely legs. She left her window open, since the Plymouth didn't have air-conditioning, the wind whipping her hair across that inscrutable face. I had learned not to force my hand, so I said nothing about seeing her again before classes started in September. Standing on the steps of her home, I bent down, and she gave me a light kiss on my lips. Behind her, two of her brothers were peeking through the picture-window curtains.

They kept Tom at the Yankton State Hospital for several weeks. I called the sheriff's office a number of times for news of his release, but they either didn't know or weren't telling. During the last week of August, I ran into McMillan at the Monogram News. He had a newspaper tucked under one arm and was discussing baseball with Tug. Tug always had the Twins game on in the store, the genial Herb Carneal calling the play-by-play, his sidekick Halsey Hall always ready with a dumb joke. That summer the Twins were on a great run, bewildering Tug. When I picked up my *Argus* each morning, he would complain about the manager's poor decisions, predicting that the Twins' winning record wouldn't last much longer, Labor Day at the latest. His favorite pitcher, and mine, too, was Dean Chance, who pitched in the all-star game and won twenty games that year. I waited for McMillan outside the store as Tug went on and on. Finally, McMillan cut Tug off and left the store.

"Lee, good morning," I greeted him as he left the store.

McMillan made out as if I were a stranger, then recognized me but failed to offer a handshake. "How goes it?" he asked. He was wearing a short-sleeved sport shirt with a window-pane print and a solid brown tie. He had walked the half block from his law office, coming down to the Monogram News for a stroll and, I imagined, a break from his tireless pursuit of justice for Tom.

"I haven't heard from Tom. Do you know when he's getting back from the hospital?"

"They brought him back middle of last week. I haven't seen him yet, if that's what you're getting at."

"Any news on his case?"

"It's slowed down some. Nothing on the docket until November, now that Judge Brady is on his way to Ireland for his honeymoon. The old boy's full of piss and vinegar for a sixty-eight-year-old, huh?"

McMillan seemed to have a habit of changing the topic.

"Have you seen the hospital report?"

"Nope. Judge hasn't released it."

"Any idea what's in it?"

"Nope. But I can almost guarantee you the state's doctors will say Tom knew right from wrong."

"What does that mean for Tom?"

"This state uses the M'Naghten rule, the test of whether the defendant knew right from wrong when the crime was committed. If the psychiatrists conclude Tom knew right from wrong when he killed Yeado, and the jury agrees, they may recommend a death sentence."

"What about the defendant's doctors? What will they say?"

"Don't know. They haven't examined him yet. I'm working on that."

"Will Brady give him a death sentence if the jury recommends one?"

"Don't know. I drove all the way over to the judge's home in Armour a few weeks ago to talk to him about it. He wouldn't say what he'd do if the jury convicts and recommends the death penalty. He's a talker, the judge is. He talked around the subject for about an hour on his back porch, sipping lemonade, me hanging on every word of that old gasbag, but I couldn't get a straight answer out of him. He did tell me about a case before him where a man had kidnapped a seven-year-old girl, raped her a number of times, killed her, and stuffed her down a well. He gave that guy life in prison."

"Would Volesky reduce the charges if Tom agreed to plead guilty?"

"Yeah, and pigs will fly that day too. Chuck wants the chair. Nothing will change his mind. Our only chance, and it's a slim one, is a change of venue. I need a petition for that. It's circulating right now. James and Deb Hubert are out drumming up signatures. There's not much else anybody can do. I've talked to some people, Indian people sympathetic to Tom's case, on and off the reservation. They want to know what happened, why he did it. As if I knew the answer to that one."

"So what do you think?"

"We need a diagnosis that convinces the jury Tom was sick, insane, when he did it. Short of that, the state has a strong case," McMillan said. He sighed and glanced quickly to see if he had convinced me of the futility of Tom's predicament, and then he turned in the direction of his law office and walked away without a word.

That afternoon I went to see Tom, intending to talk to him about the lies about his family he'd told me. He'd played me, like I supposed he'd played a lot of people growing up on the reservation and at Shattuck, but I was still pissed. I entered the courthouse through the east side entrance leading to the sheriff's office. Neither the sheriff nor Leonard was there. A deputy I didn't know was reading a magazine at his desk. He was happy to have someone to talk to.

"You bet," he said when I asked to see Tom. "I'll go down and ask him." The deputy walked bowlegged down the hall toward the jail. He was back in a few minutes. "He'll see you," the deputy said. When we were about halfway there, he stopped and looked around to see if anyone was listening.

"You might need to know this," he said, speaking softly. "Yesterday Tom had a visitor, his girlfriend, Dottie. Her first visit. She's fine-looking, isn't she?" he asked.

"Yes," I agreed. "Tell me more."

"Well, she was real nervous. She wasn't here too long, maybe half an hour. She did most of the talking, from what I could tell. Tom sat there listening. When they were done, I took Tom back to his cell. He didn't say anything, which was unusual because we've become good friends—he's painted some pictures for my kids and all. I opened the cell door and he went in, and then he turned around and slammed the door shut. He stood there staring at me, gripping the cell bars. 'Better cool down,' I told him, and he said, 'Fuck you, pig.' I was pissed, but I went back to the kitchen area and walked his girlfriend back to the office. She was shook up. I asked her what happened, and she said she told Tom she was breaking off their engagement and getting married to someone else. So I went back down to Tom's cell when she left, and Tom was throwing stuff around in his cell, crying, and then he smashed an old wood chair in his cell to pieces on the concrete floor, saying he was going to do the same to Dottie's boyfriend's head. I told him he had enough things to worry about and had better shape up. He did after a while, but he may still be feeling bad about getting dumped, you know what I mean?"

I thanked the deputy. He opened the door to the jail unit and led me inside to the kitchen area. The kitchen was messy with lunch dishes, a half-eaten loaf of white bread, a package of sliced baloney, and mayo and mustard bottles on the counter. A bowl with the remains of a cucumber-onion salad in a vinegar sauce sat on the table.

Tom's appearance shocked me. His hair had grown long, and his shirt and pants, the same clothes he had worn at the July hearing, were falling apart, holes forming at the elbows and knees. He looked defeated. His head was hanging low, eyes downcast. When he was seated and the deputy gone, he lifted his head and broke into a big grin.

"Surprise. Making it up for the peanut gallery," he said, moving his pursed lips in the deputy's direction.

"You had me fooled. I heard what happened and expected you to be down, but not that down. Sorry about Dottie. There'll be others."

"It hurts real bad, man. She understood me. I could tell her things I've never told anyone else. I needed her. She's 'thy sweet love' from the sonnet. Now I've got nothing."

"Maybe she'll change her mind. You never know," I said, my advice sounding dumb as soon as I said it.

"No, it was stupid of me to think it might still work out. What's the point in waiting around for me? I'm not getting out, am I?"

"I don't know. What did the doctors at the hospital say?"

"They didn't tell me anything. It's not like they ask you a bunch of questions, give you a few tests, and then say, 'Well, Mr. White Hawk, you tested crazy. You can go back now and tell the judge.'"

"What are you doing to pass the time?"

"Still painting some pictures. Painted one of me breaking the pole vault record in Minnesota."

He called back to the deputy, winking at me at the same time.

"Hey, I'd like to show Craig my pole vault painting. Would you run down to my cell and get it? I promise not to escape and ravish any young girls."

The deputy didn't bite, but he offered to escort Tom back to his cell if he really wanted to show me the painting. Tom went back with him and returned with the painting. A pole vaulter was at the peak of his jump, about to release and catapult over the bar. A few spectators were watching; one was taking a photograph of the vault. The horizon in the background was painted in layered pastels, lending a surreal glow to the scene.

"I knew I was going to break the record as I approached the pit. My body coiled real tight that time, and I released at just the right moment, rising higher and freer than I had ever been."

"You captured that moment in the painting."

He looked at me skeptically and then set the painting back against the wall.

"What else have you been doing?"

"They let Willie and me out in the exercise area together now. It helps to have someone to talk to other than Leonard and the other deputies. I get tired of talking about rocket science with them," Tom said, eyes mischievous. "I like Arnie, though. And Leonard. Willie and me are on good terms with them."

"What do you and Willie talk about?"

"Willie's real quiet. Mostly I ask him about that day. I can't remember much myself. When I was over in Yankton, the doctors asked me to write my life story—you know, thinking I'd write about what happened. I wrote about everything else in my life, boarding school and Shattuck, but not that. I suppose they thought I was being sly and didn't want to incriminate myself, but it wasn't like that."

"Still got headaches and stomach problems?"

"The headaches come and go. My stomach problems went away. I had my appendix out, just like Lee did, before I left for Yankton. Had it done right here in town at Dakota Hospital. Some of the nurses wouldn't care for me while I was there. Violated their principles, I guess, me being principally an Indian and a killer."

"You could use a haircut. And some clothes."

"Deb said she'd help with the clothes. The church has a rummage room in its basement. She's going to cut my hair too."

"She come often?"

"A few times since I've been back. I can talk to her. Not like I used to talk to Dottie, but it helps."

"Has Phil been back to see you? I saw him at the last hearing. He didn't look so good. Worried about you, I guess."

"Phil's always fussing about my partying or temper or study habits or girlfriends. I never lived up to his high hopes for me, the part about being a good boy, God fearing, clean cut, obedient, all that stuff. I can put on the act. I did it for him for years. I still do. I know he loves me in his own way and thinks of me as his son, but I always make a mess of it, and I sure have this time."

"You met him at boarding school?"

"Yeah, he was working at the Hare Home on the Rosebud. Phil came up with this idea that I should go to Shattuck. Seemed like a good idea to me. I was tired of reservation life, the drunks wandering on the roads, the hopelessness everywhere. People eating out of tin cans, when they ate at all. Mostly they drank. Phil filled out the application materials. Made the arrangements for a trip to see the place over Easter vacation my freshman year. We stayed at the Hotel Faribault, my first time in a hotel. We had a room with a queen bed. It was late when we arrived, but Phil insisted on unpacking everything, prancing around in his undies, neatly stacking our clothes in the drawers of the hotel room's dresser as if we were going to stay there a week. The next morning we went over to the school, and I met everyone and then had some time to kill, so I put on my track shoes and worked out for the coaches, and the next thing I knew, I had a scholarship. Phil got a counselor job there too, not at Shattuck but at St. James, a boys' school down the road a mile or so. These were all Episcopalian places, you know. Phil had some pull with them. His dad is an Episcopalian priest."

"By the way, I saw Lee this morning. At the Monogram News."

"What did Mr. Invisible say?"

"The psychiatrist reports will be important."

We were both silent for a few moments.

"Doesn't sound good. I feel like I'm on audition. Gotta show everybody how fucking crazy I am if I'm going to live," Tom said.

"Lee expected the defense psychiatrists would see you soon," I said.

"If and when," he said, eyes narrowing. "I wait on everybody for everything in here. I can't even take a piss without waiting on a deputy to escort me down the hall to the toilet, while I'm practically holding my crotch or butt to keep it in. I have time, plenty of it, to put the pieces together, to be shamed by it and depressed like I've never been."

Tom got up without signaling the deputy first. He opened the refrigerator in the kitchen, found a pitcher of Kool-Aid, and poured us both a glass. His prominent arm veins pushed out from under his tattoos, ballooning the figures. He shrugged when I looked surprised that he had helped himself to the Kool-Aid. "They trust us in here. Arnie lets us make our own meals when he's out of town."

"And here's the most fucked-up part," Tom continued when he sat back down. "I don't know why I did it, any of it, but that old lady enjoyed it. She smiled at me when I took my pants off and moved to the center of the bed to make it easier for me to get on top of her. I don't know why I did it. I got off, sure, but I'm not the only one with shame here."

I sat silent, trying to think what to say.

"You don't have to say anything," he said after a few minutes, sensing my hesitation. "Keep it to yourself, okay? I haven't even told Lee what happened that day. He hasn't asked, either—my own attorney hasn't asked. Can you believe it? You know what? I'm going down. After everybody gets a piece of me, the piece they love or hate, I'll go down and be gone, and nobody will care. The Indian boy's gone, let's forget about him. It's too painful. If you must, remember him on the field, on that last vault, soaring over the bar, when he was what we wanted him to be."

"It's not going to happen that way," I said without believing it.

"Get out of here," he said to me, rising up, looking around the corner for the deputy. "Visiting hours are over. It's time for my dreams. My only way out of here."

The business about Tom lying to me made a lot more sense after that.

11

The weather was hot over Labor Day. On Timber Road, heat waves were rising from the brittle field, and the corn was drying at a record pace, ready for picking weeks ahead of time. The roadside ditches were browning up. Cottonwood trees, planted for shade and shelter during the Depression, were dropping their yellow, triangle-shaped leaves. I didn't know Caitlin was back in town until she called the Friday leading into the holiday weekend, asking me to spend Saturday with her and Chris at High Line. Stop by late morning, she said. I woke the next day filled with longing for her but wary, worried the day would bring disappointment.

I knocked on their door and let myself in. Caitlin hugged me, the first time she had showed any affection for me in front of Chris. They were not ready. Their breakfast dishes were still out. A strong morning sun filtered through their kitchen window. Their belongings—clothes, books, dishes, kitchen utensils, framed posters, new stereo—stood everywhere in piles and in cardboard boxes. They were drinking Bloody Marys. I ran down to IGA for food while they packed for the day.

The river was much lower. The sandbars were wider and longer, slinking up and down the river. I easily threw a rock across the shrunken main channel, its width narrowed by the upriver dams holding the water back.

"The Corps isn't releasing the water yet," I said, repeating what I had read in a Bellman editorial in the last edition of the *Plain Talk*. He had taken on the Corps of Engineers, criticizing it for managing the river flows to the benefit of downstream states at the expense of states like South Dakota farther upstream.

"But they will be releasing water soon. The barge traffic in the lower states needs deep water in the fall. When they do, these sandbars will be underwater."

No one was interested in my civics lesson. We set down in our lawn chairs and opened the beer cooler. The sun beat down on us, trapped in the low riverbed without a breeze. High in the sky, a large bird circled, searching for prey trapped in the shallow ponds created by the shifting sandbars. Chris thought it was an eagle, a good omen. But as the bird drifted closer, hovering directly above us, its hooked red head and wide wingspan were that of the lowly turkey vulture.

"Craig, have you seen your Indian friend recently?" asked Caitlin.

"A few days ago. He's back from the hospital. The doctors finished their examination and sent him back to jail."

"Isn't he supposed to have more than one? Doesn't the defense get their own examination?"

"Yeah. I talked to his lawyer, McMillan. He expects his psychiatrists will see Tom soon."

"When's the next court hearing?"

"The trial starts in November, according to McMillan. In another town if a change in venue is granted."

"How's this guy Tom doing?" Chris asked.

"He's facing a murder and a rape charge. He did it. The judge told him he could get the death penalty at the last hearing. Insanity is his only defense. He has few friends, parents are both dead. Only a guardian, Phil. It's a bleak picture."

"A guardian?"

"Someone he's known for a long time. Caitlin met him at the last hearing."

"I met him, that's all. He's a strange bird. I'd plead insanity, too, if he were my guardian."

Caitlin paused, thinking about what she had just said. "That's too harsh. Phil was preoccupied with Tom's situation. He didn't have any time for me, and why would he?"

"What does Tom talk about when you visit him?" Chris asked.

"He's moody. But when he's in the right mood, he opens up. He seems genuinely puzzled by his behavior, by what happened that day in the Yeado home."

"What the fuck? That's pretty weird," said Chris.

"Anyone else visiting him in jail?" Caitlin asked.

"The Episcopal priest and his wife. I think she visits quite often."

"Are you talking about Deb Hubert?" Chris asked, surprised.

"Yes. Do you know her?"

"Yeah, I do. But that was before she married so well," Chris said, exchanging a look with Caitlin that triggered laughter at some inside joke they wouldn't share with me.

The start of school woke the town, the streets suddenly filling with cars, the sidewalks with students and faculty moving purposefully. The Greek houses were the first to be invaded. The actives came early to prepare their houses for rush week. The dormitories filled up a week later with hundreds of freshmen, the majority of them first in their family to attend college, patient and forgiving of the long lines and the university's incompetence. Older students arrived in cars stuffed with their possessions and made their way to off-campus apartments, free from parental and university supervision and anxious to be bad in some conventional way. Every store and bar and gasoline station was busy. The campus was crowded with fresh coeds eager to play a part in the experience they had heard so much about.

Paul showed up after the Labor Day holiday, his car packed with clothes and food and a blond console TV his parents gave him after redecorating their family room. I helped him carry everything up the flight of stairs to the apartment, piling the clothes on his bed. He looked around in his room for a moment, silently inspecting the place. I panicked for a moment, thinking he'd see the *Playboy*s were out of order, but he didn't notice. By the next morning he was unpacked, the kitchen and refrigerator stocked, the TV picking up all three channels. We sat on the couch in cutoffs and sweatshirts watching a soap opera, *As the World Turns*.

"I'm going over to the house this afternoon. You coming along?" Paul asked, as if I cared.

"I'm busy. I'm going over to the *Volante* offices."

"Come on. They'll ask where you are. What should I tell them?"

"I don't care what you tell them. Tell them Courtland deactivated me this summer, so I pledged Delt."

"Was Courtland here this summer?"

"I saw him a few times."

"Let me guess: on special duty, monitoring the White Hawk case?"

"Yeah. I don't know why he doesn't let it go. It's become a crusade for him."

"Have you seen Caitlin? Was she here this summer?"

"Yeah, but she doesn't have anything to do with my not wanting to go to the house."

"Of course not," he said, skeptical. "You've fallen in love with a hippie. Wait a minute. Turn to the side. Your hair is longer too. You're growing your hair, aren't you? Wait till the brothers hear about this."

"That hurts, coming from you of all people, Paul. It was your idea to move out of the house. I believe your words were the Greek life is 'too limiting.'"

"I believe I said 'too confining.' I wanted out of the house but not out of the fraternity."

"Give them a big Phi Alpha for me."

My first *Volante* editor, Tim, a vet with shoulder-length hair and the first pair of wire-rim glasses on campus, had graduated the previous spring. Tim was skeptical of institutional authority after his Vietnam tour but had not sunk into the cynical despair and drug habits of the vets who returned in later years, battered and humiliated by an ungrateful country that had turned against the war. Blair Carlon, a haughty, humorless political science major, replaced Tim as editor.

There was some money and influence in Blair's background. His father was a friend of Al Neuharth, the two of them returning to college after World War II to become news writers on the *Volante* and very big men on campus. After graduation they worked for newspapers in New York and Florida. Blair's father had gotten him the editor job, despite the fact that Tim had recommended several other, more qualified candidates to the selection board. Tim's ambition had been a more balanced paper covering a wider range of issues, but Blair returned the paper to its traditional role as a mouthpiece for the Greek system. The stories he assigned either had a Greek angle to them or dealt with campus and governing board politics, the training ground for the young politicians living on fraternity row. The *Volante* columns under Blair were filled with Greek gossip (**Campus Seen**: "The happy state of wedded bliss has claimed many campus couples this summer") or grooming tips (**For and About Women**: "Every so often, every girl needs to take a good look at herself for an honest, critical analysis to determine whether she has an up-to-date look").

Blair had no interest in the White Hawk case, to say nothing of Tom, and that was probably true of every student at the university. They didn't want to be reminded. I tried hard to impress Blair, hoping to get the campus politics beat. The first two stories he assigned were dull—not a single person asked me about them after they were printed—but I finally did get one sure to attract readers. In a recent editorial in the *Plain Talk*, Bellman had scolded the new university president, E. Q. Moulting, for allegedly using taxpayer money to buy liquor, readmitting a man and wife convicted of marijuana possession, encouraging hippies to enroll at the university, and putting his wife on the payroll. Because I knew Bellman, Blair asked me to find out more about the *Plain Talk*'s sources and then interview the president himself.

Bellman pretended to be surprised when I walked into his office. He was reading one of the national weeklies, where he found editorials for reprinting in the *Plain Talk*.

"Why, I didn't expect to see you for another couple of months. Nothing happening on the White Hawk case?"

"The *Volante* is following up on your column about the libertine behavior of our university president."

"I wouldn't take this so lightly, Peters. I think the regents made a mistake hiring this guy. He thinks he's slumming it out here. We're not now and never will be his beloved Ohio State.

Have you noticed he can't suppress a half sneer when he is forced to praise his employer, the University of South Dakota, at public functions?"

"I have an appointment to interview him tomorrow. How did you get the information in your column?"

"A letter from a local person has questioned several actions he's taken at the university. A second person, inside the university, came to see me. Someone I trust," he said, slightly offended. "I'll leave it at that."

I liked E. Q. and his lusty wife; her tight sweaters and Kentucky accent seemed a grade or two above his rank. E. Q. wasn't a pipe-smoking, reserved academic. He swept his thinning hair straight back, showing too much scalp; had bad teeth; and wore thick glasses that blurred and enlarged his eyes. His breath smelled like cigar smoke. But he was funny and clever and scorned the idea that the university was a substitute parent. The students loved his irreverence.

E. Q. came out from behind his desk, gesturing for me to take a seat at his conference table. He sat at the end of the table. His office struck me as rather drab and unimposing for a college president's. The wall along one side of the conference table was filled with his framed Ohio State degrees and pictures of him with distinguished-looking people at ceremonial functions. He was always prominently placed in the pictures, next to the important people.

"What can I do for you, Blair?"

"I'm Craig Peters. Blair asked me to conduct the interview."

"Craig. Well, better yet," he said, lighting a cigar. "I remember now. You were working on the paper when we arrived last year. You wrote one of the stories on my investiture. Added the right amount of irony describing my masters, the regents, prancing around in their absurd academic robes and hats. Am I right?"

"You are."

"I suppose this interview is about that scurrilous column in the *Plain Talk* all but accusing me of being a Bolshevik fellow traveler."

"That's right, President Moulting."

"Okay, let me take these points one at a time. The liquor business. I understand why ordinary citizens are concerned about tax money being used to buy liquor. This issue comes up all the time when we're entertaining, promoting the interests of the university. No taxpayer funds—I repeat, no taxpayer funds—have ever paid for alcohol, nor will they ever be used for that purpose. We have other sources. Often I pay for it out of my own pocket," he said, with no trace of sanctimony.

E. Q. leaned back in his chair and put his feet up on the conference table. He began to smile.

"Between you and me, I know where this is coming from. The former president's wife. President Weeks and his wife were here for twenty years, and not a drop of the stuff was consumed the entire time. She's a charter member of the WCTU you know, the humorless blue hairs. My guess is she's the one whispering in the ear of that gullible fool at the *Plain Talk*."

Moulting trimmed his cigar ash off in an orange, modernist glass ashtray on the table.

"Next, the hippie question. Am I recruiting hippies to this pristine place, this sanctuary of learning? To that charge, I plead utter confusion. I am not even sure what a 'hippie' is. Do you know? Does having long hair mean one is a hippie? In that case, you may even qualify, given the length of your locks. Regardless, having long hair doesn't make you a bad influence, does it?"

E. Q. stared at me for a moment and then smiled again.

"As for the two students found guilty of possessing marijuana, they indeed have been readmitted, but on probation. We all deserve a second chance, don't you agree?"

"I do."

"The last charge, that my wife is on the payroll, is ludicrous. I know her beautification committee has raised some ire for the crime of suggesting we close some of the ugly, unnecessary service roads on campus and plant grass and flowers, but really. I'll call in the payroll clerk right now, and she will verify, the only Moulting on the payroll is me."

"Not necessary, President Moulting."

"This a farce, worthy of a Feiffer cartoon in your newspaper."

The *Volante* ran a Jules Feiffer cartoon every week. Hypocrisy was his favorite target.

When we finished, Moulting walked me out of his office and down the hallway of the administration building to the west entrance, elaborating on the injustice of it all.

I wrote the story from Moulting's point of view, portraying the charges as likely false and his detractors as narrow-minded vigilantes. Once I finished it, I went to see Blair in his editor's office. He was a Delt, which gave him reason enough to be suspicious of me, but there was more, probably the fact that I was an SAE in name only, that fed his patronizing attitude. Not having religion was worse than having the wrong religion.

"What is it? Still not happy with your assignments?"

"I liked this one. They don't get any better. But the others. There's only so much you can say about soda and candy vending contracts and the museum moving its collection to the old library."

"Several attractive A-Phi coeds commented on those stories at our exchange last Saturday. Wanted to know who wrote them."

"Be serious for once. White Hawk's trial begins in November. What do you say to a story each week while the trial runs?"

"Nobody on campus cares about that story but you. It scares people. He's a cold-blooded killer, an Indian. And he's guilty. Do I really have to tell you this?" he said, still patronizing but sympathetic for once.

I tried to make the argument that the newspaper owed the students this news, that it had something to tell the students about the world they lived in. His expression hardened.

"This is between the two of us, Peters, but the selection board advised me not to run any White Hawk stories in the paper. White Hawk is no longer a student here. It's no longer a student matter. Besides," he said, "you're too close to the story. You're friends with this Indian."

"I'm done here, then. I'll write the White Hawk stories for the *Plain Talk*."

"Be my guest. But you may not be working there for long either. I heard Bellman is selling the paper."

Quitting the *Volante* felt good. Quitting always does when you cook your own books, convinced you've taken a moral stand. I left with my notebooks and supplies under my arm among the students crowding the halls during the break between classes, their self-absorption annoying me. I tossed everything in the back of the Plymouth and drove over to Bellman's office. He was in. He denied the selling rumor with more righteousness than needed if he was telling me the truth. He assured me I would be covering Tom's trial when it started in November, and Willie's too, scheduled to begin in December.

A week later the *Volante* ran the Moulting story. Blair rewrote it, taking Moulting's responses out of context and making him look like a scheming and paranoid careerist. Less than a year later, E. Q. would resign and return to Columbus.

I lost interest in school after leaving the paper. I was registered in four upper-division courses but rarely attended them. I was in retreat from everything that wasn't Tom, his court case, or Caitlin. I became a pest at the jail, stopping by nearly every day, bringing Tom stamps and candy and books and helping him pass the time. The sheriff let me eat lunch a few times with Willie and Tom. On one occasion, after we had silently eaten our peanut butter sandwiches, potato chips, and Fudgsicles, I asked Tom to tell us about a big football game he was in, the one where Shattuck won the conference championship. He had played so fiercely he lost ten pounds during the game, with cadets cheering "Hawk, Hawk, Hawk" from the sidelines. I wanted him to relive the glory, but he told the story as if it were a lifetime ago, as if it were someone else on the field that day, a bird of prey no longer hunting.

I had to sign in each time I visited the jail. The log was in the sheriff's office on the secretary's desk. Tom's visitors were the same few: McMillan, the Shattuck friend who had dropped off the psychology textbook last summer, and the Huberts, usually just Deb. One afternoon I bumped into her as I was leaving. She was carrying a large cloth bag with a loaf of bread and an apple crisp for the boys. She wore a peasant dress with thin straps on her brown shoulders. In an ungentlemanly moment, I asked where Father James was. She blushed slightly and said he was away at a church conference.

"I'm sorry, it's none of my business," I said.

"That's quite all right," she said. Her arms, holding the basket in front of her, were full and soft, with a redhead's translucent white skin. She had a sexual undertone in every gesture, neither flirty nor contrived but natural, fully understood.

"I think Tom may be giving up," I said, hoping to prolong the conversation, when she started to leave.

She turned back with a worried look. "He's down. He can't see any way out of it. His headaches are bad. He gets dizzy and vomits sometimes. Bad stomach too."

"I thought the appendix operation took care of the stomach problems."

"Different symptoms. He's so alone. He needs so much help."

"If there's anything I can do, please let me know."

"I will," she said, and walked down the hall toward the door leading to the cell blocks.

Tom had not said anything to me about his headaches and stomach problems. Apparently he was saving that piece of himself for Deb.

12

Sheriff Wilson called me on a Saturday night, the second week of November.

"Tom has asked to see you. He's feeling pretty down. Can't see any way out of his predicament. Lee and the Huberts are here too."

Caitlin was over that evening. She wanted to come along but changed her mind as we started walking to the jail. I dropped her off at her apartment. The leaves had already fallen from the trees, and a harvest moon shone through the bare, twisted limbs, luminous white on the sidewalks. Some of the stores still had Halloween decorations in the windows. *Woman Times Seven*, starring Shirley MacLaine, was playing at the Co-Ed movie theater. The warm air felt good when I opened the side entrance door to the courthouse. The sheriff was in his office, sitting in his chair at his desk. Lee McMillan sat across from him. They waved me in when they saw me.

"You know Lee, right?" Arnie asked me.

"Of course. What's up?"

"Tom's trial starts on Monday," said McMillan. "He wants to change his plea to guilty."

"No insanity in the plea?" I asked.

"Nope."

"When did this happen?"

"Hard to say," McMillan said, shrugging. "In the last week or two. He wants it over with; he doesn't want any more attention, any more shame."

"What about the psychiatrists? What did they say?"

"Nothing we can use in his defense. A Sioux Falls doctor said Tom is seriously ill, mentally ill, but he knew right from wrong at the time of the murder. If our own doctor won't support the insanity plea, well…" McMillan said, his voice trailing off.

"Can I see him?" I asked.

"The Huberts are with him now, but they should be finished soon. They've been with him for more than an hour," the sheriff said. "I know he wants to see you."

"If he pleads guilty, he could get the chair, right?" I asked.

The sheriff gestured his neutrality, both hands raised.

McMillan sighed, looked away, and said nothing for a few moments. "I told you about my visit with the judge. He wouldn't commit. If Tom pleads, it's in his hands."

"There's nothing else you can do? Your defense strategy relies on a doctor's opinion?"

"His plea was not guilty by reason of insanity. If a psychiatrist isn't going to back him up on the stand, he's got nothing. With no supportable insanity defense, we're done."

"What you're saying is *you're* done. You have no idea how to defend Tom, do you? This is your first homicide defense, there's no money in it, and you want it over. Going through the motions so you won't be disciplined by the bar."

"You self-righteous son of a bitch. We didn't ask you here for a lecture on how to defend this case, as if you have any fucking idea. Tom is facing the death penalty with virtually no credible defense. That's not my fault, it's his. Understand?" McMillan said, lighting a cigarette, his right hand shaking a bit, the lighter flame wobbling.

"I understand, Mick. I understand you've given up without much of a fight," I said.

The sheriff got out of his chair, grabbed my arm, and led me out of the office and down the hallway toward the jail. He stopped outside the main door.

"I like you, Craig, but you pushed too hard in there. Mick's doing his best."

"That's bullshit, and you know it."

"Maybe you haven't figured this out yet, but you're not the only one pulling for Tom. Each of us has a job, and right now you're not doing yours. Wait out here while I see how much longer the Huberts will be."

The sheriff returned almost immediately, the Huberts trailing behind him.

"How is he?" I asked.

"He wants to plead guilty. Something's changed in him. He seems to have given up," said Father James. Deb looked as if she had been crying. She was holding her husband's hand.

"Did he say why he's changed his mind?"

"You know how he is. He doesn't explain; he doesn't have second thoughts. I pray he'll seek some guidance from the Lord, but he's not interested in prayer right now."

"Has he talked to Phil Zolbach?"

"Yes, on the phone. He didn't share what they discussed."

Tom was in the bathroom when the sheriff sat me down at the table in the jailhouse kitchen. The clock on the wall read 12:35 a.m. I expected Tom to be down, resigned, tired, but his mood was almost perky. He asked if I wanted a sandwich. He was going to make one for himself. He made two peanut butter sandwiches. There was some milk in the refrigerator.

"How's school going?" he asked when we were both sitting at the table, eating the sandwiches.

"I'm flunking out. My midterm average was D-plus."

"Sounds familiar. You caught my disease. You better stay away from me."

"Too late now."

"Did I tell you about the letters Phil sent me when I was flunking out, thinking about leaving college?"

"No."

"Three-, four-page letters full of advice on how to bear down, stay disciplined, and it will work out. He wouldn't hear of me dropping out. When I told him I thought maybe I should see a doctor about my depression, he told me I didn't know what I was talking about. 'You don't really need to see a psychiatrist, now, do you?' he said. 'I guess not,' was all I could say."

"Have you talked to him about changing your plea?"

"Talked to him this afternoon. He surprised me. Said it was my decision. I thought he'd at least try to talk me out of it. He's probably given up on me too. I haven't made it easy for him, you know."

"Did you read the doctor's report?"

"Yeah, Lee gave it to me. Here's the short version: The patient was having headaches that felt like someone had driven a hot poker through the side of his head. The patient was drinking until a few minutes before he entered the home. The patient killed the jeweler, raped his wife, and claims not to remember his actions. The patient is lying about not remembering what happened. The patient knew right from wrong at the time he committed the crime. End of report."

Tom paused, as if a door had slammed shut, and then sat in silence.

"I'm going to get the chair. I know that now."

"Don't change your plea. You're only increasing the odds."

"I get the chair either way. Why go through the motions? The dirty shame of it all, the dishonor. Those two helpless people and the warrior, ha ha ha. Tomahawk, my Shattuck nickname. Tomahawk not so fierce after all. Try living with that hour after hour, day after day. With only Willie, the original silent tongue, as a cellmate."

We laughed hard at that.

"Why did you ask to see me tonight?" I asked.

"Phil, the Huberts, the others, they want to save their little Tommy. They want Tommy the orphan back. The lonely and rejected Tommy, the Tommy of their imagination. That's all we talked about tonight, the Tommy everybody thought they knew. I can't pretend anymore. Maybe Courtland was right, the miserable bastard. Even the people who hate you are right about some things, aren't they?"

"Sometimes."

"Here's what I want everyone to know. I didn't know who I was those weeks leading up to the murder. I was in a dream, high, floating. I don't know why I did it—these dime-store psychiatrists don't know why I did it—nor do I remember everything about how I did it. But I did it."

"You don't have to do this, Tom."

"Yes, I do. You know why? Because there's not going to be any forgiveness, and I'm not asking for it. Ask Tommy the orphan or Tommy the track star to beg forgiveness. This Tommy won't, nor does he expect anyone to forgive him. I want this over, done with. I want everyone to know it will end soon."

Tom covered his head with both hands. He got up without saying goodbye a few minutes later and walked back in the direction of his cell. His shirttail hung out of the back of his pants, covering his flat butt. I signaled the deputy, who was playing solitaire, to let me out. I couldn't face my empty apartment after that. I went to Caitlin's, woke her up, and we smoked a joint. When I was inside her, I came almost immediately and then held her close, real tight, having seen what it's like to have nothing left to lose.

Monday morning Caitlin and I drove over to Armour, where Judge Brady had moved the trial, a town north and west of Vermillion. Tractor-pulled corn pickers were busy harvesting brittle cornstalks. Cloudy skies obscured a faded sun, previewing the gray days of winter. The Douglas County courthouse was the largest building in town, visible from the east as I braked the car's speed once inside the city limits. All the parking spots were taken in front of the courthouse. We parked down a block and, as we got out of the car, heard the far call of geese. We looked up to see them high overhead, in a V formation pointed south.

Inside the courtroom, every seat was taken. People stood along the walls on either side and at the back. We took our seats in the section reserved for the press. Other than the judge, the court officers were all in place. The court reporter was still practicing his speed, the prosecution and defense in position at their respective tables. Phil Zolbach was there. I didn't see the Huberts in the courtroom. No reason for them to be here now. They knew the outcome.

Everyone rose on cue when Judge Brady entered. He carried himself like a young man, no trace of stiffness, erect, confident. He sat down in his chair. On his right hung a portrait of General Pershing, the general notorious for fighting World War I with the previous century's tactics, leading to unnecessary American casualties. He and the judge bore a serious resemblance to each other, right down to the carefully trimmed mustache and the unsympathetic eyes. On the judge's left hung a framed copy of the Declaration of Independence.

Lee McMillan stood as soon as the judge appeared to be ready. He asked for a conference in the judge's chambers. Brady's mustache twitched. He didn't seem to know Tom was about to change his plea. He announced a recess—reluctantly, he told McMillan—and then led the defense and prosecution teams to his chambers. They came marching back out in about twenty minutes, Volesky leading the way, a disappointed expression on his face after discovering the game wasn't going to be played—the other side had forfeited.

When everyone was seated, the judge turned and looked directly at Tom. The judge asked him to stand. On his feet, he stood at attention, a Shattuck cadet pose he'd assumed many times, this time without epaulets on his shoulders and a service cap shading his eyes.

"It is in my uncontrolled discretion to impose either a death sentence or a life imprisonment sentence, and I want to be distinctly and clearly understood that, in the event that you enter a plea of guilty, I am not now and have not committed myself as to the penalty which is to be imposed. Do you understand that?" the judge asked.

The courtroom was dead quiet. The radiators at the back of the room started to clang, hot water warming the flues. Tom spoke very softly. In the first row, we could barely make out what he was saying.

"Yes, I do."

The judge asked Tom whether anyone had influenced his decision.

"The only influence is myself," Tom said.

"And this is your own conclusion, of what you feel you should do and want to do. Is that it?" the judge asked.

"Well, Your Honor, feeling and wanting to do are two different things," Tom said.

The distinction surprised the judge. He pressed Tom for an explanation.

"Are you making a clean breast of it with this guilty plea, hoping I will show some leniency? Is that what's going through your mind?"

"No, it's not," Tom said.

There would be no plea for mercy or forgiveness, only the suicidal plea of guilt.

The judge didn't like it. He shook his head, and then, realizing he was showing his reaction to the courtroom, asked Volesky to read the charges agreed to in the conference. Volesky bolted up and read them, emphasizing the phrase "murder with malice aforethought." Premeditated murder was back in the charges, with, I presumed, no objection from McMillan.

"How do you plead, Mr. White Hawk?" the judge asked.

Tom didn't move and didn't respond for several moments. He swallowed hard.

"Guilty, Your Honor. Guilty."

On our way out of the packed courtroom, Caitlin in front of me, I felt a hard poke in my back. I turned around. Courtland. He was looking off in another direction, as if someone else had stuck their finger in my back. I kept walking. He poked me again, harder, but I didn't look back this time.

Caitlin and I didn't talk much on the way home. The sun was already setting, fading light at our backs as we drove eastward past skeletal shadows in fields where the corn stover would be gleaned by cattle during the long winter. A party of pheasant hunters was exiting an unharvested field at one of the four-way stops. Their carrying straps were filled with birds. It looked as if they had filled out their limit.

13

I dropped Caitlin off at her apartment and went home to write my *Plain Talk* story. There wasn't much to say. The trial had lasted less than an hour. The guilty plea ended the debate, if there ever was one. Bellman would still want his 350 words, though, so I threw in some description of the courtroom and the disappointment of the audience at the curtain coming down so quickly. They had been expecting drama, a recounting of what had happened that day in the Yeado home. The rumors had run from absurd to ritualistic. Body parts were found chopped and floating in blood in a frying pan on the stove. Some were eaten. The jeweler was castrated, his testicles stuffed in his mouth. He was beaten with the frying pan long after he was dead. The Hollman twins inspired the rape by sunbathing in tiny bikinis next door for Tom to see that warm afternoon in March. But they had been cheated of all that, and I had been, too, in the sense I had nothing to write about. Still short of the necessary word count, I called Fred Barton for his reaction to Tom's guilty plea.

"I didn't think the boy had the guts to admit it. He surprised me. But it doesn't change a thing. He turned me, a good Catholic, into a nonbeliever. No God would allow this to happen. Jim lost his life, and I lost my faith because of what that boy did," he said and hung up the phone.

Bellman cut that quote out of the story before printing it.

At the trial on Monday, following Tom's plea, Judge Brady had scheduled an aggravation and mitigation hearing to be held in Vermillion later in the week. Caitlin couldn't make it. She had a class.

The temperature had fallen. Everyone was wearing their winter clothes. The courtroom was full, many of them familiar faces: the Huberts, Zolbach, Barton. I didn't see Courtland. He had the outcome he wanted.

Tom looked tired and distracted from where I was sitting, impatient with something McMillan was telling him. He looked as if he was done trying to impress anyone with what a good Indian boy he was.

McMillan approached the bench as soon as Judge Brady called for order. His client, he told the judge, loud enough for everyone to hear, had requested that the hearing be closed. The judge gave McMillan a quizzical glare, as if he ought to know better and should have advised his client accordingly. The judge said that the law was clear. Aggravation and mitigation hearings are open to the public.

As soon as the judge adjourned the trial on Monday, Volesky had angrily stuffed his papers and files into his briefcase and strode out of the courtroom, pushing people aside, his large lower lip protruding in a pout. He had been ready for a fight that day, but Tom's plea change left him in his corner, the match called before he could throw a punch. On this day his sarcasm was running high as he questioned witnesses on the stand. He grimaced, his face twisted, as he showed pictures of the dead man to the state investigator, who confirmed the victim's identity. He shifted to silent horror and disbelief as the assistant police chief identified the frying pan and broken handle as the instruments that had bludgeoned the dying jeweler to death. He practically fainted himself when he raised the butcher knife found by the cleaning lady in the Yeado house after the murder. And, his face contorted with pain while listening to the coroner's description of the jeweler's wounds, he suggested that the punishment should fit the crime.

Volesky's fifth and final witness was a psychiatrist. Dr. Maloney practiced in Council Bluffs. He had the air of an academic and dressed like one in baggy, light-brown corduroys and a cardigan sweater. Earlier, before the hearing started, Volesky had conferred with him in the rotunda area. Maloney smoked a pipe, looking faintly bored with whatever Volesky was telling him. Tom told me about the day Maloney examined him. The psychiatrist showed up unannounced, made a fuss over not being able to see Tom immediately—Tom and Willie were exercising—and then spent less than three hours with him. Tom spent most of his first hour with Maloney filling out forms and completing a standard set of psychological questions. Maloney did not look Tom in the eye the entire time he was with him. At the end of the interview, as Maloney was preparing to leave, he told Tom he should plead guilty. "It will go better for you if you do, son," was his parting advice.

Maloney sat back in the witness stand once he was sworn in, relaxed, as if he were settling into his office chair. After several questions verifying his credentials and experience, Volesky asked the doctor to describe Tom's mental condition.

"Mr. White Hawk is not psychotic. He is and was completely aware of what was going on. He definitely knows the difference between right and wrong. His personality makeup is technically described as a passive aggressive personality," he said.

Tom sat at the defense table, showing no emotion but clearly interested in the testimony.

Volesky was pleased with the response. His case for the death penalty rested on the M'Naghten rule, the question of whether Tom knew right from wrong at the time of the murder.

"Could Mr. White Hawk's disorder be effectively cured or adjusted, making him conform to ordinary norms?" Volesky asked his witness.

"It has been pretty well accepted that personality patterns have a rather poor prognosis in treatment," Dr. Mahoney said.

Lee McMillan called one witness, another psychiatrist. Dr. Richard Levander was a tall man with a robust, efficient Scandinavian persona. He was on the faculty of the medical school and practiced psychiatry on the side. I'd seen him drive up to the courthouse in a green-blue Triumph Spitfire and half expected him to jump out with a pilot scarf wrapped around his neck. Tom had shown me Levander's conclusion, underlined in the report: "Our clinical evaluation of this individual leaves much to be desired, and actually, our feeling is that we have here a sociopath who we are unable to give much defense for."

On the stand, McMillan questioned Levander about Tom's diagnosis in more detail and then followed up with a question seeking to clarify the clinical terms.

"Would you state that, in your medical opinion, he is mentally ill?"

"There are two schools of thought on this, at the present time, in terms of these personality disorders. He is a sociopath. One group puts sociopaths in a criminal classification of insanity, and the rest feel they are distorted and warped and yet are competent and responsible for their actions."

"And which theory do you agree with?"

Levander tugged at his goatee for a moment and then answered, "I am riding the rail at this time."

That, from Tom's psychiatrist.

"Did you ask Mr. White Hawk what went on during the murder scene?"

"This is what I would like to know, but I don't think we ever will know. Mr. White Hawk does not give us a consistent story. His recollection is a vague reproduction of what happened, something like you would expect to get from an individual who had been quite intoxicated the night before and as a result can't quite remember what he was doing."

It was an opening McMillan should have been looking for—the mixture of alcohol and psychosis that pushed Tom over the ledge, in effect reviving the insanity plea—but McMillan was going through the motions now. He dismissed his witness and then requested a presentence investigation, which Judge Brady agreed to order.

I glanced up at Tom. He was angry, whether with McMillan, the psychiatrist, or the judge, it was hard to tell. He turned away from McMillan, who was talking to him, and stood up from the defense table. Surprise tinged with a flash of fear fluttered through the audience, like a sudden breeze whipping cottonwood leaves. He walked directly to the deputy sheriff standing guard and held out both hands, signaling his desire to be cuffed and returned to his jail cell.

Outside the courtroom, Phil Zolbach was waiting for me near a window. He was wearing a plaid western shirt and jeans. In his arms he held a parka with a hood and a pair of canvas chore gloves. It looked as if he wasn't sleeping well. His left eye had a tic.

"What are we going to do?" he asked. "Tom's given up. We're going to lose him. He left the judge's chambers on Monday without a plea deal. McMillan knew that was a mistake. He wrote me a letter last month saying Tom would be stupid to plead without a deal, and now he's let Tom do exactly that."

"I want to see that letter. If he said that, McMillan's in trouble."

"It's home in my office. I'll send it to you. For all the good it will do now. It's in Brady's hands, and he's not sympathetic."

"How do you know?"

"I waited for him outside the courthouse in the parking lot after the trial on Monday. He didn't see me at first, lighting a cigarette, humming a tune on the way to his car, until I got out of mine and greeted him. He stepped back, as if I might hurt him, even though he's nearly a foot taller than me."

"What did you talk about?"

"I told him I'd worked with young boys all my life and that Tom was one of the best, a God-fearing, quiet boy who may have had athletic success and some advantages many Indian boys are never given but was orphaned and had lived with rejection and loneliness all his life. The judge was unmoved. He seemed offended, at what I wasn't quite sure. I asked if he would please not sentence Tom to death. His crime was awful, but Christ taught us forgiveness was the most difficult but the most god-like of virtues. And then he said something I didn't expect."

"What was that?"

"He brought up Mrs. Yeado. How that poor woman was living with the terror of that night, the loss of her husband and home. And then he excused himself and got into his car. I watched as he drove out of the parking lot, stopping momentarily before he entered the street, and then disappeared into the distance, like Tom's future."

I didn't understand Zolbach. He was not easy to love or even like. I felt as if any display of sympathy on my part made me odd too, as if it would rub off on me. A man loving a boy was frightening and repulsive to me, more so because Zolbach was not sexually attractive. He was losing his hair, and he walked funny, and his breath was bad. But how could I fault his heart and what he had done for Tom, even though it had grown out of something I didn't understand?

"What happens now? What can we do?"

"I don't know. Wait and pray. Pray the judge is a Christian."

"Since when has that made a difference?"

"In case you hadn't heard, this isn't a philosophy class. Someone's life is at stake."

Zolbach and I walked out of the courthouse and over to his car in the parking lot. As he was about to get in his car, he stopped and gazed plaintively into the distance, not looking me in the eye.

"You know Tom. Was that Tom the psychiatrists described in the courtroom today? It's not the Tom I know. It's some textbook profile they read and memorized in school, modified to fit the circumstances. They should be ashamed of themselves. So long. I'm not coming back for the sentencing. I can't bear it. Here's my number at St. James. Call me when it's announced."

The sky was overcast, the wind creating little whirlwinds of dead leaves on the asphalt parking lot. Lights burned in the county offices inside the courthouse. The talk in Vermillion was about the university's football game against South Dakota State on Saturday. The White Hawk story was old news. No one cared.

14

I finished my story on the aggravation and mitigation hearing in record time, liberated from classes and research papers and exams.

At the *Plain Talk* offices, the cute girl with the bandanna was the only one working. The scarf was gone now, her hair longer and frizzy, like one of the hippies Moulting was accused of harboring on campus. She was friendly but not as interested in me as before. A framed snapshot of a guy stood on the corner of her desk.

"Hey, there."

"Hi. No one here but me today."

"Where's the boss man?"

"In some meeting in Sioux Falls. Secret business."

Bellman printed my latest story verbatim, the first time. He had probably lost interest, like everyone else.

A few weeks later, as I returned to my apartment after coffee with Caitlin, the phone was ringing.

"Peters, this is Lee McMillan."

"Mr. McMillan. To what do I owe the pleasure?"

"Have you seen Tom recently?"

"No."

"He's got it into his head that he should testify at Willie's trial. I can't talk him out of it."

"Why would he do that? What's he got to gain?"

"Nothing. He's pleaded guilty. Nothing he says in court will change that. But he seems compelled to do it. A bad decision. I've about had it with him."

"Why are you calling me?"

"He'll talk to you and maybe even listen. Willie's lawyer, Ramon, will make Tom out as the killer and Willie as someone who was only tagging along. Ramon's good. Brady's the judge on this case too. It won't help if Brady hears about Tom's role in the grisly murder and rape while he's sitting in the courtroom. Remember, Judge Brady decides whether Tom lives or dies."

"Is Volesky behind this?"

"I don't think so. Tom volunteered, and Chuck is happy to let Tom hang himself, but it's Tom's idea all the way."

"I'll do what I can."

It snowed heavily that night. The next morning I stood on my apartment's porch in a parka, stocking cap, and gloves, ready to shovel out my car. The sky was clear, and the wind had died down—the after-storm calm. The snow had drifted onto the porch, covering the chairs Caitlin and I had sat in, listening to the sounds of summer, so long ago now. The street was un-plowed; a brilliant white drift piled on top of my car. No one was out yet on the street, but I could hear shovels scraping against sidewalk concrete and the city snowplows in the distance. My street still wasn't plowed by the time I had dug my car out, so I trudged through the snow to the courthouse. Along Main Street, the business owners were shoveling the sidewalks in front of their stores while the city trucks dumped snow in the middle of Main Street, creating a huge windrow that divided the street.

The sheriff and his deputy were drinking coffee in their office, standing at the front counter in overalls and hunting boots. Snow was melting off their boots, forming puddles on the floor. They were the only people in the courthouse, along with Tom and Willie down the hall in jail. They smiled at the sight of me bundled up, stomping snow from my boots, with sweat running down the side of my face after trudging through the deep snowdrifts.

"Is Tom in this morning?" I asked.

They both laughed, the sheriff's eyes brightening. Leonard was a good cop, too, one with a sense of humor.

"As a matter of fact, he is," the sheriff said. "He's in his office right now. Follow me."

Tom sat down at the table in the kitchen. I expected the jail area to be cold on a day when the snow was piled high and the temperature only in the twenties, but the jail was warm and stuffy, the courthouse oil furnace on high flame. Tom had a white T-shirt on. When I'd visited him before, there was always the attitude and then the gradual warm-up. Today he seemed determined to stay hidden behind indifference.

"Hey, big snow out there today. What's so urgent?"

"Nothing much else to do. The town's completely shut down. Dead."

"Dead, huh? You'll get no sympathy here. Try staying in this hotel."

"I'll take a rain check. How's Willie?"

"Who knows? Nothing fazes him. I beat him in checkers again this morning. You'd think he'd win a game or two after the first hundred, or quit playing, but he plays on, telegraphing his moves, never getting mad. It doesn't matter to him. He would never have made chief."

"How about you?"

"No. I'm a warrior, not a negotiator. More like Crazy Horse, always moving. Fearless."

"Is that why you've decided to testify at Willie's trial? Because you're fearless?"

Tom's face dissolved into a determined glare, his eyes showing disappointment in me.

"You've been talking to Lee."

"He called me. He's worried. He thinks Willie's lawyer will make it worse for you. Brady's the judge. He'll be sitting there, listening to the lawyer grilling you about the murder, about raping Yeado's wife. All this before he sentences you."

Tom had turned his head to the side, staring at the wall while I spoke.

"I thought it would be over when I pleaded guilty. But it's not," he said.

"Talking about it in court is not going to help. Willie's lawyer will only make it worse."

"It hangs over me every day, every moment. But I'm not like the man in the sonnet. He had a lover to console him. Dottie is gone; I have no one. Phil's busy with his life at St. James. I'm alone, but that will change if people understand."

"Tom, you can't explain it in a way people will understand. Even the Indian people are confused. There was no sense to it."

Tom rose up from his chair and waved to Leonard that he was done.

"I'm sorry, Tom," I said, "but McMillan is right about this one. It's a mistake."

"I am the mistake," Tom said firmly, his voice no more than a whisper. "And I am the only one who can fix it."

Willie's murder trial was held in the Yankton County Courthouse, in the same town where the state hospital was located. The courthouse was a poorly designed building constructed at the turn of the century with cheap river wood, thanks to some corrupt county commissioners. The building was structurally unsound. Bellman made a joke about how I should wear a hard hat at the trial. His interest in the White Hawk affair had risen again with the prospect of both Willie and Tom on the stand, expecting the testimony to confirm his image of two cold-blooded killers who deserved nothing less than the chair. He gave me explicit instructions to spare none of the grisly details, should they come out in the testimony.

Willie's father, Joe, sat up front with his wife, several relatives, and their friends. Two Benedictine nuns from the Sacred Heart Convent in Yankton sat behind Willie's family. Ramon Roubideaux was with Willie at the defense table. Roubideaux enjoyed the attention. A gregarious man, he draped one arm casually over the back of Willie's chair while chatting with Joe and the others. No performance jitters. Chuck Volesky glowered, all coiled energy, a tornado on the prairie. The jury looked like they were ready for a movie to start. I expected to see someone eating popcorn. Tom was not in the courtroom yet. He was being held somewhere in the courthouse, waiting for his call.

On the first day, Volesky laid out the prosecution case, describing Willie as an equal partner in the crime, as another Indian thinking the law didn't apply to him. Volesky didn't call Tom to the stand.

The second day was more interesting. We rose for Judge Brady at the start of the proceeding. When the judge was finished with the preliminaries, Roubideaux wasted no time, calling his client to the stand. Everyone knew what Willie's lawyer was up to. With his questions, he drew a picture of a quiet boy who followed the rules at the boarding schools on the Rosebud Reservation and in Flandreau, where he'd attended an Indian high school. Willie was also a member of the Young Christian Society, whose purpose was to discourage young Indians from marrying early. Willie was portrayed as lonely at the university until he met Thomas White Hawk, who, Willie testified, "appeared to be more like an Italian or some other nationality other than American Indian, and he seemed to have a lot of friends." I suppose Willie was referring to Tom's SAE pledge class, some of whom lived in Julian and were probably in Tom's dorm room at times. And then Roubideaux asked a question his defense argument would hinge on. He asked Willie if Tom had any outstanding characteristics. For instance, was he stubborn?

"Yes. I think I would label his character, in that respect, obstinate. I tried many times to persuade him into doing the right thing, and I had difficulty doing that," Willie said.

Willie's attorney had prepped him well. I was quite sure Willie had never used fancy expressions like "in that respect" or "obstinate" before. Roubideaux asked several more questions. Willie claimed not to know they were on their way to the Yeado home that morning and that once he realized what Tom had in mind, he tried to talk him out of it. The only reason he followed Tom inside was to keep him out of trouble. Willie said Tom stuffed a number of things in Willie's pocket before he left that morning, one of them being Mrs. Yeado's diamond ring. He didn't realize he had the ring in his possession until he was back in his Julian Hall room.

Roubideaux and Volesky finished with Willie near the end of the afternoon. The judge adjourned the proceedings.

Everyone left the drafty, cold courtroom quickly, chilled by the cold air seeping through the windows all afternoon.

Tom made his appearance the next day. McMillan was there, too, sitting in the audience a few rows behind the press. He looked slightly miffed—present but not happy about it. The courtroom hushed when Sheriff Wilson and Leonard escorted Tom in. Tom looked confused, his eyes blinking in the bright room, unfamiliar with the courtroom layout. The judge pounded the gavel a time or two, more to draw the attention away from Tom than to quiet the room. Both attorneys approached the bench when the judge said he was ready to proceed. They spoke too quietly for anyone to hear, the shorter, amiable Roubideaux standing a head lower than the ever-scowling Volesky. Whatever the issue, Roubideaux apparently lost the argument, for he shrugged his shoulders in a you-win-some-you-lose-some manner and returned to the defense table.

The argument was apparently over whether Lee McMillan would be allowed to sit at the counsel table while Tom was on the stand. The judge announced that Mr. White Hawk's court-appointed attorney would be allowed to do so. Tom was then sworn in and took his place on the stand.

Volesky questioned Tom about the events leading up to and during the murder. His questions were designed to show Willie was an accomplice rather than the scared-kid-tagging-along image Roubideaux had conjured with his questions. Under Volesky's questioning, Tom said Willie knew the purpose of breaking into the house. And Tom acknowledged that he and Willie split up the cash in Yeado's billfold, but he was firm about not giving Willie the diamond ring. Tom also testified that he would not have broken into the Yeado home that day if Willie hadn't willingly followed him into the house.

"So, you're Thomas White Hawk," Roubideaux asked with exaggerated scorn when he began his cross-examination.

"Yes, I am," Tom said.

"Well, Mr. Yellow Hawk, I believe that you have entered a plea of guilty to the premeditated murder of James Yeado. Is that correct?"

"Somehow we switched names here," the judge said. "We now have a Yellow Hawk on the stand."

"Oh, my mistake. Pardon me," Roubideaux said with exaggerated regret. "It's White Hawk, isn't it," he said, turning to Tom.

"I'm not yellow," Tom said.

"Of course you're not," Roubideaux said.

"That'll be enough, counsel," the judge said.

Ramon Roubideaux was a smart man and a sly attorney, asking questions with no basis in fact, loaded with innuendo, requiring Tom to deny them while establishing doubt in the minds of the jury. Tom seemed to be sinking in shame with each response, panicking, drowning. When Roubideaux finally told the judge he was through with the witness, Tom took an extra moment to regain his composure and started to leave the stand. The judge motioned across the room for the sheriff and deputy to escort Tom out of the courtroom. Sheriff Wilson instinctively moved to drape his arm over Tom's shoulders, almost immediately regretting the spontaneous show of affection and withdrawing his arm quickly.

The next morning the judge gave the jury members their instructions. I spent the rest of the day playing cards with Roubideaux, the sheriff, his deputy, and an AP writer in a back room, waiting for the verdict. Roubideaux kept us laughing the entire time, cracking jokes and making fun of Volesky, who disdained to join us, preferring to wait in the empty courtroom with his briefcase full of work. Willie's father, Joe, played a few hands with us, too, chain-smoking the entire time. Finally, fourteen hours later, at 1:30 a.m., Friday morning, the jury returned. They brought Willie out for the verdict. He was sweating; Roubideaux was nonchalant, as usual. The nuns were there, too, gripping Bibles in their laps.

The murder verdict came in not guilty. Sheriff Wilson immediately arrested Willie on charges of burglary and grand larceny and returned him to the Clay County jail. A few months later, he would plead guilty to the grand larceny charge and would be sent to prison for eight years.

Bellman seemed happy enough with my story on Willie's trial. He should have been pleased—I'd spent the entire weekend on it, not having much else to do while Caitlin and everyone else were studying for finals. But there was something different about Bellman's mood, and I suspected it didn't have anything to do with the story. He was reading a report of some kind when I entered his office, unusual for him, in that he would typically be frantically editing the Thursday edition copy on a Wednesday morning. After he'd finished reading my story, I asked him again whether he was selling the paper.

Bellman looked at me as if it were none of my business, but then he had a second thought. He got up and closed the door to his office.

"The rumor happens to be true. I am selling the paper. This document," he said, pointing to the report he was reading, "is the buyer's due diligence. The basis on which they made their offer. It's a good offer."

"What does this mean for my job?" I asked.

"From what I gather, the new owners are not going to cover local news. Mostly wire service stuff and local announcements and advertising. The White Hawk story is not something they'll want to run in their paper. I should have told you before this."

I didn't realize how much the pitiful job at a semiweekly newspaper with community announcements on the front page meant to me. I left the *Plain Talk* offices that morning feeling lower than ever, over the pointless job and over Tom and what I could or couldn't do for him now. What anybody could or couldn't do for him now.

15

We sat alone in the Armour courtroom for several minutes before a courtroom employee turned the lights on. She didn't see us at first, calmly turning a bank of light switches on and then shrieking softly when she saw us sitting in the third row. We apologized for letting ourselves in, explaining that the doors were unlocked and we thought it would be okay since the clerk of court's office was closed. Caitlin had driven over with me after we had spent the night together at her place. The temperature was in the forties, and the snow was melting and running in tiny streams along the curbsides and into the latticed grates covering the storm sewers outside the courthouse.

We made fun of the Pershing portrait on the wall behind the judge's bench while we waited for the hearing to start, imagining that old, stiff Brady was spying on the courtroom behind the portrait, peering through two holes in the eyes of the observant general. A few minutes later, an AP news writer rushed in, expecting to see a crowd and showing his surprise when he saw that so few people were at the sentencing hearing. He took a place in the front row. Tom and McMillan came in next, followed by Sheriff Wilson and Leonard. Volesky was the last to arrive, acknowledging only McMillan as he took his place at the state's table.

Judge Brady entered the courtroom, businesslike as always, showing no indication he had been burdened with a life-or-death decision. Sitting at the bench, he took his time arranging the papers in front of him and then gazed up at the courtroom, turning to Tom as he began.

Brady explained that Tom had pleaded guilty to premeditated murder and the time for his sentencing had arrived. He paused, his face showing a flicker of uncertainty—or was it empathy?—before his face hardened with conviction again. He asked Tom whether he was insane at the time he had committed the murder—a legal protocol in murder cases but nonetheless an absurd question. Of course this lonely and tormented boy was insane the day he committed murder and rape. But Tom wanted it over. He responded without emotion, saying he was not insane when he committed the murder. He looked back at Caitlin and me after he answered, curious to see how we would react. It was a lie. Tom knew it. The judge knew it. Volesky and McMillan knew it. The whole fucking state knew it.

The judge asked Tom to stand.

"Mr. White Hawk, is there anything you wish to say before the sentence is read?"

"Yes, Your Honor, I would like to say a few words."

Tom hesitated, as if he were still unsure what he wanted to say after all this time, day after day in that jail cell alone with his thoughts, preparing his statement, unable to sustain any coherence.

"I shot Mr. Yeado the night he died. It was accidental. I did not intend to kill him before, during, or after. Our plan was to take him down to the jewelry store. I knew he had quite a bit of cash in his safe. I raped Mrs. Yeado. I did not intend to kill nor did I rape with any pleasure. I have disgraced my relatives and accept my punishment for these acts. That is all, Your Honor."

Tom caught Brady off guard by finishing so quickly. Brady told him to remain standing. The judge reached for a manila envelope on his desk. He opened it, and out slid a single sheet of paper. He held the paper in front of him for a moment and then read for everyone to hear.

"It is the sentence and judgment of this court that, by reason of your conviction of the crime of murder of James Yeado, you, Thomas James White Hawk, suffer death by electrocution, and may God have mercy upon your soul."

As soon as Brady finished, he rose from the bench and walked around to the defense table. He pulled out a pack of cigarettes from inside his black judicial robe and offered McMillan one. McMillan turned it down. Brady was talking quickly, nervously, saying he would provide Tom and McMillan a copy of the letter he sent to the governor explaining his reasons for the death penalty. Tom and McMillan sat silently, Tom looking away, McMillan staring directly at the judge as he talked. I doubt they heard anything the phony bastard said.

The next morning the *Argus Leader* ran a story on the hearing, a single column alongside a much longer story on the construction of a second Barrel Drive-In restaurant in Sioux Falls. If there had been a story in the *Plain Talk,* it would have read about the same. There wasn't much more to say.

White Hawk Sentenced to Death

ARMOUR, S.D. (AP)—Thomas White Hawk, 19, has been sentenced to die in the electric chair for the March 1967 slaying of Vermillion jeweler James Yeado.

Sentence was handed down in Douglas County Courthouse on Monday afternoon by Judge James R. Brady.

Only half a dozen people were in the courtroom when the sentence was pronounced, including Clay County State's Attorney Charles Volesky and White Hawk's court-appointed attorney, Lee McMillan, both of Vermillion.

There have been no death sentences carried out in South Dakota since George Sitts died in the chair at the South Dakota Penitentiary 20 years ago for the shooting of two western South Dakota police officers.

AND JUSTICE FOR ALL

1

Second semester began in late January, soon after Tom was sentenced to die. Before classes started, I went over to the political science department and met with Dr. Farber, the chairman. Doc reminded me of the Munchkin mayor in *The Wizard of Oz*, elevated in his office chair, with two miniature feet resting on a step, thumbs hooked into the side pockets of his sweatervest and stubby fingers dangling like link sausages. Doc selected his favorite political science majors and awarded them with advice, scholarships, and trips to broaden their limited experience. No favors would be dispensed that day. The purpose of my meeting was to decide whether I should be allowed to stay in school.

"You have really outdone yourself this semester," Doc said, my grade report in his hand. "How did you manage a D in Comparative Governments, when all the other grades are Fs? Excellent work, my boy!"

"Somebody up there is watching out for me, I guess."

He liked irony. He liked irreverence in his favorites, but I was pushing it.

"What's happened? You've quit everything. Classes. The *Volante*. Ye gods, man, you're throwing it all away."

He was still smiling, but without mirth.

"I got caught up in the Tom White Hawk business. I wrote several stories about the murder and the trial. He shouldn't have to die. The state is going to electrocute a man who has little recollection of his crime."

"It's a tragedy, but it's not your tragedy. There's nothing you can do about it now. But if you're not ready to accept that reality, perhaps college isn't the place for you at this point in your life. Take some time off. Find a job. You can always come back."

I had not yet shown Doc my full-blown righteousness, my anger at how morally indifferent everyone else was.

"Tom didn't get justice, he got revenge. Is that what we teach in political science courses? Let's examine this case. The defendant is an Indian. Oh, and you say a guilty Indian? He must die, then."

Farber looked at me for a moment, taken aback but not upset, and then he sighed. His secretary was typing in the outer office, the IBM Selectric ball whirling back and forth as she tapped the keys. I could hear Farber's next appointment arriving and introducing himself.

Farber sat watching me, not unkindly, forming his diagnosis, and then he slid off his chair—quite deftly, as fat people often can—and walked me to the door.

"Well, my boy, it's settled then. You'll take some time off to find yourself. Come back ready to hit the books," he said, offering a handshake. His hand felt tiny and soft in mine, like a child's. I'd expected Farber to put me on probation, suspend my scholarship for a semester, pat me on the back, and tell me it would all work out. Maybe even encourage me to go back to the SAE house. I felt I had been tricked into something, but I wasn't quite sure what. What the hell would I do now?

I walked back to the apartment, fighting a southwest wind and a subzero temperature that penetrated my windbreaker and jeans, a bead of snot running down my nose. The Dutch elm and sugar maple trees in the campus quad, stripped of their leaves, swayed back and forth with the shifting wind, whistling a raspy, frigid overture in a winter symphony. My cheeks were stinging with the cold, my eyes watering when I got back. I jumped into bed and under the covers to warm up.

The doorbell rang about an hour later, startling me because no one ever used the ringer downstairs at the porch entrance; usually people would walk up the stairs and knock on the door. I went to the window that looked out on the street and saw a '64 Ford pickup, the model with a snub-nosed front grill, parked out front. A vaulting pole and cardboard boxes filled with books and canvases were piled in the truck bed. It had to be Tom's possessions. His pole vault painting would be in one of the cardboard boxes.

I went down the stairs and opened the door. Phil Zolbach stood there in the cold in his shirtsleeves, shivering.

"Come in, Phil. Let's go upstairs, where it's warmer."

I offered him something to drink. He turned it down. We sat on the couch. The coffee table in front of the couch was piled high with textbooks Paul had purchased for the spring semester.

"I saw the boxes in the back of the pickup. Tom's possessions?" I asked.

"Yes, they are. I picked them up at the sheriff's office. They transferred Tom to the penitentiary in Sioux Falls yesterday. Sheriff Wilson was kind enough to box everything up for me. They were all sad to see Tom leave."

"You had better get a tarp to cover everything if you are driving back to Faribault."

"I'm on my way to the hardware store. One of the deputies gave me your address. I wanted to see you before I left town."

"Why is that?"

"I know you've grown close to Tom over these last few months. Now you know why he means so much to me and why I am so disappointed in him. I had high hopes for him. I sacrificed so much for him."

Zolbach studied the books on the table as he talked, and then he turned and looked at me, waiting for me to respond.

"No one asked you to do anything for Tom, including him," I said, trying to understand where he was going with this.

"Oh, yes, he did. When he first came to the Hare Home, he was a broken child. Withdrawn, suspicious, so lonely. He didn't, he couldn't, put it into words, but he needed and wanted me as only a child can need and want a loving adult in their life."

"Maybe so, but that's not what I heard from Tom."

"Tom will tell you whatever works for him at the moment. If it helps him get what he wants, he'll say anything. He'll lie to you with the most sincere, honest-seeming face you have ever seen and walk away without a shred of guilt."

"Isn't that what you do to survive in his world?"

"Only in Tom's version. I tried so hard to instill the importance of buckling down, of staying concentrated on his studies, of waiting to experiment with alcohol and girls until he was through with college and medical school. But he couldn't escape his upbringing."

"You mean his being an Indian?"

"Of course not. Why do you think I left a good job at Honeywell and went to work at the Hare Home? The Indian people have been given a raw deal. Tom would have been in medical school or law school by now if not for the poverty and lack of opportunity in his life. Being an Indian had nothing to do with it. But now he'll never escape."

"What is it you wanted to ask me, Phil?"

"I have a question. A very difficult one, but I must ask it."

"What is it?"

"Does Tom blame me for this—for this terrible trial he's facing?"

"Are you thinking about the rifle? The fact that you gave it to him a few days before the murder?"

We both knew he wasn't thinking about the rifle, but I didn't know where to start.

"I've been over that a thousand times in my mind. He would have found another weapon. He was in some kind of state. Having a .22 rifle didn't trigger his psychosis. Whatever was going on in his mind did," he said.

The memory of Tom's crime transformed Zolbach's face into a sad, drooping mask.

"Tom's never blamed anybody but himself. He's still trying to understand why he did it," I said.

I knew Zolbach wanted to know what Tom might have told me about those camping trips and hotel stays and the spare bedroom in the Zolbach home in Saint Paul, but I didn't have the words nor the courage to bring it up. I chose to console him, to leave that image of a naïve or compliant or denying Tom in his mind. Was it right to leave it that way? I didn't know then and still don't.

"I have been tortured about this for months," said Zolbach.

"Do you remember the Shakespeare sonnet Tom sent you in a letter last summer? Sonnet twenty-nine? He recited it for me one day while I was visiting him in jail."

Zolbach started to sob, controlling it only after great effort.

"Now you know why I love that boy so much. And now he's going to die," he said, starting to sob again.

Zolbach left a few minutes later. I walked him out to his pickup and took a last look at the painting of Tom soaring to heights he'd never reach again. I gave Zolbach directions to the hardware store downtown, where they were sure to have tarps, and ran back upstairs, two at a time, to escape the cold. The telephone was ringing when I opened the door. A writer from the *Minneapolis Tribune* wanted to talk to me about Tom's case.

2

The *Tribune* writer calling was Gerald Vincent. I knew nothing about him. I had never seen his byline in the *Tribune*. Vincent had read the AP story on Tom's sentencing and then read my *Plain Talk* stories. He wanted to know more about Tom and his case. Would I help him? We agreed to meet for lunch the next day at the Chimes Café.

After Vincent's call, I went over to Caitlin's apartment to share the news with her. I should have called first. No one answered my knock at the door. When I turned to go back down the stairs, the lower entrance door opened, frigid air rushing in with Chris, who was returning from grocery shopping. I helped carry her grocery sacks up the stairs and into the apartment. She was wearing a high-pointed red stocking cap with a white reindeer design. Her straw-blond hair poked out from underneath the cap.

"I haven't seen you in a while," she said, setting the grocery sacks on the kitchen countertop.

"Not been around much."

"You mean like class? Caitlin told me you've blown off everything."

"Not everything. School. And maybe a few other things."

"You aren't a dropout. It's not in you. Once a frat boy, always a frat boy," she said. Was that contempt or irony I heard in her voice? Either way, she had landed a punch.

"I need something more real than school," I said.

"I get it. Existence before essence. Very Sartre."

I shrugged, on the ropes.

"Seeing as how you're no longer Mr. Straight, shall we get high?" she asked.

Chris found a leftover roach in an ashtray. After a few hits, we sat in the living room and listened to *The Sounds of Silence*. The late afternoon winter sun, low on the horizon, shone weakly through the kitchen window, the pot smoke floating in the dull light. Getting high in the afternoon felt uniquely liberating, *rebellious* in the exaggerated way the word was used in those days. An hour later I realized what bullshit that was and wished I weren't high anymore. When Chris started to clean the kitchen, it was my signal to leave, even though Caitlin hadn't shown up yet. I left a note on her bed and went back to my apartment.

The next morning Caitlin called and asked that I pick her up on the way to the Chimes. I had not seen her since the sentencing. We walked down Main Street silently, bundled up in our parkas, the snow crunching under our boots. The restaurant's front windows were steamed up. Inside, the humid air and cooking smells felt homey and safe. The place was crowded. The tables were all taken, but we found a side booth where a waitress was clearing dishes. Seeing the waitress reminded me that Dottie once worked here. I doubted she did anymore, but I asked the waitress.

"No one by that name works here," she said after pausing for a moment, shaking her head and handing us the laminated menus.

"The lunch special today is hot beef sandwich," she said, and left with her tray full of dirty dishes.

I sat facing the front so that I could signal Vincent when he arrived. Caitlin sat across from me. She looked lovely in a navy turtleneck, jeans, and stocking cap, the same one Chris had worn yesterday.

"I thought that was Chris's cap?"

"It is. We wear each other's clothes all the time. I'm surprised the rich frat boy hasn't noticed before this," she said.

"I wish you'd give up on the idea I come from privilege."

"Your father's a lawyer, right? You have a fancy car, right? And he wrote a check for your tuition and books, right? He sends you money, right? That's how you've been getting by all these months, right? Where I come from, Dad gets paid peanuts for teaching, climbs ladders, and paints all summer when he's not selling Perfecta and Daily Double tickets at the dog tracks. He grumbled and swore, 'Jesus Christ, this is a lot of money,' when it came time to write a check for my freshman college books, making me feel like the family wouldn't be eating for the rest of the week thanks to me. And by the way, it was the last check I got from him."

"Let's talk about this later. And by the way, I'm not that many rungs above you on the ladder. I caddied at the country club many summers to pay my SAE dues."

"Ha ha ha."

Vincent hadn't told me what to look for, but I recognized him as soon as he walked in, comfortable in a strange place, eyes searching the tables without appearing to be actually looking for someone. Average height, thin. He dressed with an urban flair that set him apart in this backwater.

Caitlin moved over to my side of the booth to make room for Vincent opposite us. We introduced ourselves.

"A packed house. Good sign in a lunch place," he said, reaching for the menu. "What do you recommend?"

After ordering, Vincent started in like a reporter, asking me a number of questions about how I came to know Tom and what my continuing interest in the case was. When he seemed satisfied with my answers, he told us why he had come to Vermillion.

"I'm working for the *Tribune*, as I told you on the phone, as a columnist, not as a news writer. The paper wanted more personal testimony on issues of poverty and race in Minneapolis. I'd been raising hell at community meetings on these issues for some time. They asked me if I wanted a bigger stage. I took them up on it. But it's time I moved on to the next thing. Tom's story might be it. Looks to me like he got railroaded," he said.

"What do you have in mind?" Caitlin asked.

"First we get him a decent lawyer. Pleading guilty without a plea bargain is outrageous. I have some ACLU connections. Then we write up his story, the background, the influences in his life, the factors that led to his sickness. We publicize that story to an audience more sympathetic than a hanging judge in Indian country," he said.

"What do you need from us?"

"You know the story, at least the major elements. And you know the people involved. You can help me with access. Help me with the research. People around here may not always want to talk to a commie ACLU type who's also an Indian."

That surprised me. Vincent didn't look or act like an Indian. Not his dress, his manner, or his skin color. He saw the doubt in my expression.

"You know what your reaction to finding out I am an Indian tells me?" he asked.

"What?" I said, my back up. Caitlin looked at me as if I had lost my mind.

"That you're an unconscious racist. That you have certain preconceptions or stereotypes in your mind about what Indians look and act like. I guess I didn't fit that image. Perhaps I should have worn my moccasins today."

That was Vincent, uncompromising even when he needed something from you.

"Look," he continued, "your reaction is a common bias. How would you know any better until it's pointed out to you?"

"I suppose I should thank you," I said, trying but not quite managing a smile.

"So here's what I'd like to do next. I want to meet Tom, but he doesn't know me. I need a reference, someone who will put him at ease. Will you introduce me? Come with me tomorrow to the penitentiary, and we'll meet him. You're welcome to come along, Caitlin."

I agreed to do it. To my surprise, Caitlin did too. On the way back to her apartment, she apologized for the lecture on whose life was more difficult.

"I was being a bitch," she said. "But then, you know that by now."

3

Visitors were only allowed on Tuesdays and Thursdays at the penitentiary, so we waited another day before driving up to Sioux Falls. The road rose steeply to the top of a bluff, where the penitentiary overlooks the city. We could see the looming pink quartzite walls of the building, granting no quarter, an outdated fortress of iron and stone. The outside air was rancid, the meat-processing stench from the nearby Morell plant fouling the air. We walked through the main entrance and had finished filling out the visitation forms when Phil Zolbach came through the security station. He came right over when he saw us.

"This is a pleasant surprise. Tom will be so happy to see you. He's having a rough time, you know. He's in isolation, a single light bulb in his cell. Really. I'm serious. Nothing to read. The Clay County jail wasn't a picnic, but this place is a dungeon. I'm going to write the warden a letter," he said.

"I thought you were back in Faribault, Phil?" I asked.

"I was, but I had to see Tom again, especially after our discussion the other day. Tom needs me more than ever."

"Excuse my manners," I said, wanting to change the subject. "Do you remember Caitlin? You've met before. At one of the hearings. And this is Gerald Vincent. He's a writer. Works for the *Minneapolis Tribune*. He wants to help with Tom's case."

Zolbach took two short, quick steps toward Vincent and then extended his hand, shaking Vincent's rather formally.

"I've read some of your columns in the paper, Mr. Vincent. I'm from the area. My parents live in Saint Paul. Are you thinking about writing about Tom?"

"That's a distinct possibility, but I need to know more about Tom and what happened before I commit to it," Vincent said dryly.

"Let me know what I can do to help. Craig has my address and telephone number. I must be on my way now. The boys at St. James will be wondering what happened to me."

"Do you work there?" Vincent asked.

"Yes, I am an adviser and Episcopal layman at the school."

"That must keep you busy."

"It certainly does. The boys are a handful. I really must go. I told them I would be back this afternoon," Zolbach said, zipping up his parka. He pulled his gloves and hat from a side pocket and left the building.

The visitors' room was not far from the security station, down a hallway past the warden's office. We were seated on one side of a long table, where we waited for Tom. Tall, narrow windows were secured with iron mesh on one side of the room. Snow drifts filled the prison yard, with whirlwinds of fresh snow softly blowing up against the windows. Two guards brought Tom into the room, where several prisoners and their visitors were gathered around tables. His hands were handcuffed, and he was wearing an orange jumpsuit. One of the guards unlocked his handcuffs. Tom looked up at us but did not say anything. They had cut his hair, purging the Indian like the boarding school practice of his youth. Humiliating as the jumpsuit and hair were, he was still striking and dignified in a way few white men would be in the same circumstances.

"Tom," I said, "this is Gerald Vincent. He's a writer. He's here to help you."

Tom kept staring straight ahead, not acknowledging Vincent, glaring at me as if I had done something wrong.

"You didn't tell me they don't have room service in this joint," he said. "If I had known that, I wouldn't have left the Clay County jail. Sheriff Wilson knows how to treat a prisoner," he said, still straight faced until Caitlin was the first to get the joke, laughing gently.

Then Tom turned to her.

"You must be Caitlin. Craig's told me about you. I saw you at some of the hearings," he said.

"Yes, how are you, Tom? We're so sorry it's come to this. We'll do anything we can for you."

"You can come as often as you like," he said quietly, difficult to hear in the room full of conversations.

Vincent leaned forward in his chair, not to be put off, intense.

"Tom, you don't know me and don't know what I can do for you. I understand that. People in Minneapolis are outraged by what's happened to you. Your lawyer simply didn't know what he was doing. He presented no credible defense, when there were several strategies available to him. There was no plea deal, something completely unheard of. The judge overreacted. He gave you a harsher sentence than the law required given the circumstances. I am on the board of the Minneapolis ACLU. We can get you a better lawyer. There is a way to get a new trial in this state. Or maybe a reduction in the sentence."

"Why would you do all this?" Tom asked.

"We can learn from your experience. White and Indian. I want to write your story. You have not been treated fairly or humanely," Vincent said.

Tom smiled faintly. "My story? My story is I sit alone all day and all night in that cell. Wondering why I did what I did. If I don't understand it, how can you make anyone else understand it, much less forgive it?"

"I can't promise that. But I will promise you this. I will do everything in my power to change that thinking. Many people are willing to take this fight on."

"Why would you do this? You don't even know me."

"Look, I know very little about you, Tom, but my guess is that people have been helping you all your life, always expecting something in return. I'm no different. I want something in exchange, for sure, but I'll be straight with you. You'll always know what's in it for you and for me."

"In case you hadn't noticed, I don't have a whole lot to give. Nor a whole lot to lose, either," Tom said, holding the thought for a moment. "Unless orange is your color, and in that case I'd give you the jumpsuit off my back."

Caitlin and I laughed. Vincent's face stayed frozen, dead serious.

"Tom, if you want, I'll talk to Phil Zolbach," Vincent offered, although his tone of voice made it clear he was not in the habit of asking permission for anything he did.

"That won't be necessary. What do you need from me, Mr. Vincent?"

"I have some questions. We'd better get started," Vincent said, pulling a yellow legal pad from his briefcase.

Vincent spent the rest of the hour asking Tom questions about his life. He wanted to know more about his parents, his brothers and sisters. Did his parents work? Did they drink? What was it like growing up in boarding schools? How did he meet Phil Zolbach? Why did Zolbach leave a good job at Honeywell in Saint Paul to work on the reservation? Had McMillan researched the Shattuck shot put incident? Why did Tom change his plea? Why hadn't McMillan negotiated a plea deal? Why did he testify for the state at Willie's trial?

Our time was up long before Vincent was finished with his questions. He told Tom he would be back next week. He knew an ACLU lawyer in Minneapolis and hoped to persuade him to take Tom's case. He promised to bring this lawyer along with him the next time.

Tom stood up when the guards approached, rolling his eyes at the sight of his keepers, and then turned serious. "Thank you for coming."

We watched the guards lead him out through the door that led to the cellblocks. We sat without saying anything for several minutes while Vincent continued his notetaking, pushing hard on his pen as he wrote furiously. When he was finished, we left the visitors' room and made our way through the security station and out the front entrance. The wind had picked up some, blowing snow across the sidewalk. The sun reflected off the snow, bright and glaring as we walked across the parking lot to Vincent's car.

"He's not what I expected," Vincent said when we were on the interstate, southbound toward Vermillion, driving as fast as I had ever seen anyone on that route. "He's not like most who have grown up on a reservation. I didn't realize he had spent so much time in boarding schools. Does he talk about that experience?"

"At times. Depends on his mood."

"It's what most people hold against him," Caitlin said, leaning up from the back seat. I didn't think she was following our conversation, assuming she was reading her book. I remember the title, *The Confessions of Nat Turner*, because Vincent made a point of complimenting her when he saw the title.

"What is it they hold against him?" Vincent asked.

"The fancy schools. The athletic talent. The promise. And then he went out and murdered an old man and raped his wife. How ungrateful, they say. Why? Nobody understands that."

"That's the right question, Caitlin," Vincent said. "Somewhere in his psyche, in his experience, lies the answer. We have to find it before they fry him."

Vincent talked as fast as he drove the rest of the way, the snow piled high on either side of the road making it seem as if we were speeding down a tunnel. He asked for our help researching Tom's background. Caitlin said she was taking a full load of classes and working at the *Volante* but would help when she could. Vincent tried not to show his pleasure at Caitlin's response. I said I had nothing but time. When do we start? He said he would call me when he returned next week with the lawyer.

I asked Vincent to drop us off at Caitlin's apartment. Inside, we started arguing before our jackets were off.

"Why did you get out here?"

"I thought it would be okay. I'm over here quite often."

"It's not where we both live. You were signaling to him I'm yours. That you have a claim on me."

"That's ridiculous. I thought it would be easier this way."

"It would be easier if you went home."

And so I went home to my apartment. Paul was studying, his class notes and an art history textbook carefully laid out on his desk. Paul wasn't an iron butt in the mold of a Zinner or a Harvey, competing for the highest grade in every class. Paul blew many of them off—the general education stuff—but the ones where his interests and future lay, he worked obsessively hard on, absorbed in the subject. I envied his sure-handed grasp. He knew what he wanted.

"Are you up for a drink?" I asked him as he ran his fingers through his spiky, coarse hair, standing up and stretching.

"Hard day at the office?"

"I'd call it miserable. The last part, anyway."

"Sure, give me a minute to get dressed. Where are we going? The Char?"

"Unless you have a better idea."

Paul sat across from me in a booth, sipping beer while I drank boilermakers.

"You're pathetic," he said.

"Among other things."

The room spun like a merry-go-round until I finally fell asleep that night. I awoke in the morning knowing less about myself than the night before.

4

Gerald Vincent made good on his promises. The *Minneapolis Tribune* ran a story the next week on the ACLU's reaction to Tom's death sentence. ACLU officials said that a guilty plea generally results in judicial leniency, not the application of the harshest sentence available to the judge. "I must say that I have never in my experience heard of a case where the death penalty was invoked after a guilty plea," said an assistant legal director. The story went on to say the ACLU would take up Tom's case in a nationwide effort to abolish the death penalty. There were pictures of Tom and Willie in the story, mug shots, and a large one of the ACLU officers gathered on one side of a long table at a press conference discussing the case. Gerald Vincent sat at the center of the table, speaking into a microphone. In a follow-up story two days later, Lee McMillan acknowledged the offer from the ACLU to take over the case and said he was strongly inclined to accept it. Caitlin and I had a good laugh about that one.

A few days later, Vincent called and asked me to join him and the ACLU lawyer who had agreed to take Tom's case for lunch at the Chimes Café. Gary Hamill was a quiet man who waited you out, not playing his hand as quickly as Vincent. He had a kindly, professorial air about him, a gentle irony in his eyes. He sat back in the booth, smoking a pipe, listening to Vincent explain his research methods. Vincent would travel to the Rosebud and interview relatives, boarding school staff, and anyone else willing to talk about Tom White Hawk. "I'm the Indian," he reminded me. He asked me to travel to Faribault, Minnesota, where Tom had attended Shattuck Military Academy, to see what I could find. "Talk to everyone. The headmaster, faculty, coaches, other cadets, the janitors. Take notes on everything. No detail is unimportant," he said. "I'll decide later what to keep and what to leave out."

They asked me to stay and have lunch with them. I ordered a California burger, fries, and a Coke. Hamill took his time reading the menu and then ordered the hot beef sandwich, a slice of roast beef and bread covered with gravy and mashed potatoes. Vincent didn't look at the menu. He asked for more coffee, toast, and some peanut butter on the side.

Hamill asked what I knew about Lee McMillan and Chuck Volesky, where they went to law school, what kind of law they practiced, that sort of thing. Hamill said he was not familiar with South Dakota criminal law but thought a new trial was possible given what Vincent had told him about the case. But he wanted to meet Tom before he would take him on as a client. We decided to drive up to Sioux Falls and visit Tom in prison that afternoon.

Tom was happy to see us, breaking into a smile as soon as he spotted us across the room. Two guards flanked him, a special privilege for death row inmates. He sat down and then got up again to shake Hamill's hand when the lawyer extended his. I had not seen Tom shake someone's hand since the SAE smoker, so long ago. He held his hand out shyly, almost embarrassed by the gesture, and lightly shook the lawyer's hand.

Hamill did most of the talking that afternoon, asking Tom a number of questions about the murder and his defense. My mind wandered while listening to the familiar material. It was mostly working-class women and clergy visiting middle-aged, white inmates. Poor company even if Tom had had the consolation of their friendship, which he didn't. Death row inmates were confined to their cells and released for an hour each day for exercise. Tom had no one to talk to, to distract his thoughts from the impending date on the calendar, the suffocating surge of fear drowning him.

A guard signaled Tom that his visit would end in five minutes. Tom asked Vincent and Hamill to leave then so that he could discuss something privately with me. Hamill got up immediately, but Vincent sat for a moment longer. He looked hurt and then gathered his papers and notes from the table, stuffed them with a little more force than necessary into his briefcase, and left.

When Vincent was out of the room, Tom asked if I had seen the Huberts. "Are they still in Vermillion?"

"I saw Father Hubert a few days ago. He's helping organize a campaign to repeal the death penalty in South Dakota. A legislator from Watertown is going to sponsor the legislation."

"Was Deb with Father Hubert?"

"Yes. They were in the IGA, grocery shopping. She was going to make some kind of vegetarian dish that night. Their cart had all sorts of strange-looking plants in it."

"I miss Deb. I could talk to her."

"Is that all you wanted to do with her?" I asked, thinking it a joke.

Tom's expression didn't change.

"I want you to do me a favor."

"Name it."

"Ask Deb to come see me. It's important."

I told Vincent and Hamill about Tom's request on the ride back to Vermillion. I should have kept it confidential, but I was eager to impress them, and what better way than to show them that Tom had shared some intimate detail with me? Vincent didn't say anything at first, staring intently at the road ahead, smoking, all three of us silent. When he caught my attention from the rearview mirror, I saw in his eyes that he had an angle, a theory he had developed in those few moments of reflection.

"I don't know this person. Who is she?"

"She's the wife of the Episcopal priest in town, Father Hubert. They were frequent visitors when Tom was in the county jail. She baked cookies and bars for him. Brought him extra clothes, even cut his hair."

"Did she visit him alone, without her husband?"

"A number of times."

"Attractive?"

"Yeah," I said. "Not sorority pretty, but earthy, natural."

"Tom's lived in two worlds most of his life. He's probably attracted to this woman, stirring more doubt in him, more confusion. If I were you, I wouldn't say anything to her about Tom's request."

Hamill agreed to take Tom's case before they dropped me off at my apartment. As for me, Vincent agreed to pay my expenses and a daily salary if I would drive over to Shattuck and conduct some interviews. I dilly-dallied for a few days but finally got on the road on a late February afternoon. I ran into a ground blizzard outside Mankato. The snow skidded sideways across the asphalt highway, my car headlights pointing ahead through the streaming white blur. The storm lost its strength an hour later, and soon enough I arrived in Faribault, Minnesota, where the prep school was located. Shattuck sat on a rise north of

Faribault above the Straight River, its frozen surface reflecting the moonlight.

Tom didn't tell me what a grand place Shattuck was. It had a tall, wide concrete arch at the entrance. A drill field was surrounded by elegant faculty and administrator residences, shuttered windows, wide brick chimneys, and screened porches. At the far end of campus were several large Gothic Revival buildings constructed in pale-white limestone, their towers and peaks etching a spiked line against the blue winter sky. I parked my car in front of Shumway Hall, the tallest and most imposing of the buildings, where Vincent had told me Burgess Ames, the headmaster, would be expecting me.

The headmaster's office was on the first floor, at the end of a long hallway. Pictures of cadets who had graduated and gone on to successful careers, mostly in business and the military, hung on the walls. I didn't recognize any of them, but the headmaster's secretary, an older woman who was wearing two sweaters and gloves to keep warm in the drafty building, had known most of them when they were students at Shattuck. She shared their biographies with me while I waited for my appointment to begin.

"But," she said, "the school's most famous alumnus doesn't have his picture in the hallway."

"Who's that?" I asked, expecting it to be some Episcopal clergyman or perhaps a famous politician like Eugene McCarthy, an alumnus of a similar school, St. John's Prep, north of Minneapolis.

"Marlon Brando."

"You're kidding me."

"He was a legacy. His father went to school here too."

"Did you know Brando?"

"I sure did. It was my first year here, 1942. A very pretty boy, like a girl. But after he left Shattuck, he broke his nose and it changed his looks," she said, sounding relieved.

"I was working in this office," she went on. "He had several appointments with the headmaster. He got into trouble for mouthing off to a visiting officer. The faculty ended up voting to expel him. He acted in some theater productions on campus. But he was an angry young man, scowling a lot."

"Like Tom White Hawk?"

"Oh my, no. Tom was very quiet. And the other boys looked up to him. He was so polite—not like Brando, who acted as if the world owed him, you know what I mean?" she said, pausing as she appeared to be thinking about Tom. "Is that why you're here? Is it about Tom?"

"Yes. I am helping research Tom's background for an article on him. To help Tom."

"We were all shocked to hear about the murder. Tom was so gentle. He was here a few times to see Headmaster Ames. He would sit in the same chair you are in now, staring quietly at the floor, never conversing with me like the other boys would. Even Brando would talk, though with him, always snotty."

"Always in character," I said.

"There was one thing that was strange, though. About Tom, I mean."

"What was that?"

"The tattoos on his arms. They were so out of place on Tom, and so ugly. He came back for his senior year with them. He and another Shattuck student had spent the summer in California."

"Tom told me what happened. He and his friend drank a quart of vodka in less than an hour one night. They went to a tattoo parlor in the Tenderloin, in San Francisco. He woke up with his arms stinging and swollen with tattoos. He didn't even remember picking out the designs."

"He wasn't embarrassed about them. But I always thought they were out of character—to use your description—until I heard about the murder."

The telephone rang on the secretary's desk. The headmaster was ready for me.

Burgess Ames walked around his desk and shook my hand without looking me in the eye. He was a tall, long-legged man with an aristocratic air, formal in his manners. He had gone to Yale and Oxford and then returned to the US for a job as assistant dean at a private school in Connecticut before coming to Shattuck.

"Please, sit down, Mr. Peters," he said, gesturing to a conference table and chairs near a window that looked out over the drill field. A few boys were horsing around on the field, which had been cleared of snow. They tossed a football back and forth, their breath turning to steam in the cold air.

The headmaster sat across from me at the table. The room smelled of cherry-blend pipe tobacco.

"The reporter from the *Tribune* called. He asked for our help. We're happy to do what we can. This is a private school. We all knew Tom," he said, his eyes blinking, looking at me one moment and then turning away.

"Did you know Tom very well?"

"It's my job to get to know all the students. He was a superior athlete and won many awards. I had many opportunities to observe him, to interact with him."

"Was there anything about him or his behavior that would have predicted what happened?"

"That's difficult to say. Tom was very hard to get to know. He would seldom open up, though you knew there was a lot going on inside his head. There were a few times on the playing field when he'd make a mistake—drop a ball or miss a basket—and he would storm off the field, angry at himself. At other times, he'd explode at a fellow cadet. I had to speak to him once or twice about his behavior when he was a floor proctor his senior year. He took the hazing stuff a little too personally, as if he were releasing his own frustration rather than disciplining the underclassmen."

"What else?"

"He was never insubordinate, never talked back or disobeyed those in authority. He was a favorite of the faculty. They awarded him the Harvard Trophy, the best-liked student. He swept all the major awards at graduation."

"Was Phil Zolbach around often?"

"Of course. He was the only adult in Tom's life, to my knowledge. Phil works down the road at St. James. Many of our boys are St. James graduates. Phil would attend the athletic events, cheering Tom on, when he wasn't tied up at St. James. And holidays, of course. He'd be there waiting for Tom as soon as the last class dismissed, parked outside of Dobbin Dormitory, where Tom lived. Most of the time Phil took Tom to his home in Saint Paul, where Phil's parents lived. Sort of like two boys home on holiday, though Tom would occasionally come back early, before the holiday ended. We'd have to open up Dobbin for him. He was a lonely kid, but he never wanted your pity. He wanted to be left alone."

"That sounds like Tom."

"Do you know him?"

I explained how I knew Tom. Ames was curious about the trial, so I told him about the whole sorry mess.

"No one contacted us about Tom before or during the trial. Not a single phone call or letter. He had a serious accident while here. He was struck in the head by a shot put. He didn't lose consciousness, but he had sixteen stitches and suffered migraine headaches. I can only imagine how bad they must be now."

"There are days he can't get out of bed."

"He was in and out of the infirmary after the shot put incident, for headaches and a lot of other athletic injuries. Our coaches had never seen anyone play with such abandon. He was in the infirmary every week with this or that injury. Dr. Rumpf, our physician, isn't here today. But I had copies made of Tom's visits to the infirmary. You can see for yourself what a time he was having."

"May I take them with me?" I asked.

"Of course. We made them for you."

"Did he ever get in trouble?" I asked.

"Sure was a young man, and young men will push back in environments like this. He was disciplined for stealing a couple of times, once for breaking into the infirmary for phenobarbital to relieve his headache pain. There was a drinking violation. He went to the dean's review board for that. Adolescent hijinks."

"Tom told me he had a girlfriend here. She went to St. Mary's."

"He did?" Ames asked. "I wasn't aware of that."

He appeared to be thinking about it, and then his expression changed.

"Oh, yes, now I remember. There was an incident. Tom was caught out after hours with a girl. Phil intervened with her parents, and it ended quickly after that."

"Do you remember her name?"

"I don't. Is there anything else, Mr. Peters?"

"I'd like to visit with a few of the students in his dormitory. Did you say Dobbin Dormitory?"

"Yes, I'll walk you out and show you which one it is."

Outside the headmaster's building, Ames pointed to Dobbin.

"Dobbin will be full of boys this time of day. I am sure they'll have plenty of Tom White Hawk stories for you. They called him Tomahawk, you know, a perfect image of Tom," he said, contemplating what must have been a memory of Tom earning the nickname.

Ames's expression turned puzzled.

"I can't imagine how it's come to this, Mr. Peters. Is vengeance so powerful a motive your state would put a nineteen-year-old boy to death for what was clearly an insane act? When we heard Tom pleaded guilty and nevertheless received a death sentence, we were shocked. I wrote the governor."

"Did you hear back?"

"Still waiting."

Dobbin Dormitory smelled like sweat and analgesic balm, with boys running around in high spirits, dressing for dinner. The first two I asked had not met Tom, but Andre Luc remembered him and was willing to talk, pulling up a chair for me beside his bed.

"Yeah, I remember Tomahawk. How could I forget him? He was a proctor my freshman year. He was an animal, a big, intimidating asshole who terrorized everyone on the floor. You never knew where he was coming from, you know what I mean? He'd be your best friend one day, and the next you'd be dropping your drawers and he'd be paddling your butt until you practically fainted. He walloped me one day in the chest so hard I fell backward and knocked my head against the bedpost, hard. It hurt for weeks."

Another cadet stopped while we were talking, pulled in by Andre's testimony.

"Andre, if you hadn't razzed Tom about his guardian, he wouldn't have been on your case so bad. I mean, Tom went ballistic," said the other cadet, whose name was Christian, a brawny blond with freckles and big teeth, one of them missing. Christian said he had played football with Tom, the two playing defensive tackle on the team that won a conference title.

"What did you say?" I asked Andre.

"I said his guardian was a homo, only stranger."

Christian whistled. "Man, did that set Tom off. You had it coming, Andre."

Andre shrugged. "Maybe so, but that guy always took it to extremes, you know what I mean?"

"He was nobody to fuck with, that's for sure."

The sun, a reddish globe in the cold sky, was setting behind the trees on the Shattuck campus when Andre walked me out to my car.

"I painted a pretty ugly picture," he said. "I should be more forgiving. Tom had a rough life, orphan and all. It's hard to feel pity, though, for someone who never returned it," he said as I got into my car. "Well, time for chapel and then dinner." He jogged back to the dormitory.

I drove around the drill field once more before leaving Shattuck, trying to imagine Tom in his uniform, marching on the field, taking his turn at leading the exercises. Covered in snow, the track and football fields farther down the road were as quiet as graveyards, Tomahawk's fearless play on them buried and forgotten.

The stars shone brightly in the moonless sky as I drove back home. Nearing Sioux Falls, I found an FM radio station broadcasting the news. The announcer, with little apparent interest in his voice, said the South Dakota legislature had defeated a bill to repeal the death penalty that afternoon. The bill, the announcer said indifferently, was an effort to save the life of a young Indian man who had killed a jeweler in Vermillion last year.

5

I typed up my interview notes the next day and sent them to Vincent's Minneapolis address. I waited anxiously for his response, as if I had sent a piece to *Playboy* or *Esquire*. Vincent called a couple of weeks later and thanked me for the work, but he didn't seem that interested in Tom's Shattuck experience. I had the impression that whatever haunted Tom, in Vincent's opinion, had entered Tom's soul long before Shattuck. But he thanked me for the effort and promised he'd send a check in the mail. In the meantime, he was on his way to the Rosebud Reservation.

I didn't hear from Vincent again until he showed up during spring break one day, returning from his Rosebud trip, on his way back to Minneapolis. It was a freakishly warm day, reminiscent of that Easter a year ago. Caitlin was in the apartment with me. We had settled into a kind of truce by then. I held back on my soaring desire, stronger without the distraction of school or a job, and she in turn came over when the spirit moved her to talk about books and politics and other subjects that held no interest for Harlan, who was back in the picture again.

"The conditions are difficult where Tom grew up in Mission," Vincent said, "but the people are open and kind and love to laugh and tease one another." He sat next to Caitlin on the couch, and I went to the kitchen to make coffee for everyone. "These once-great warriors and their families are living in poverty, many surviving on commodities alone. Sweet, generous people whose only crime was to be here, in this country, first. I thought the urban Indian had it rough," he said.

"Where did you go? Who did you talk to?" I asked, carrying the coffeepot and three cups into the living room. I placed the cups, two of them stamped with a gold SAE crest, on our shabby coffee table, its veneer peeling off the stained top. Vincent reached for a cup—one with a crest—poured himself some coffee, and lit a cigarette.

"I started at the Hare Home, where Tom lived for a few years. It's a boarding home but also a working farm for young Indian boys in Mission. John and Emily Artichoker run the place for the Episcopal Church. I thought this Zolbach character was Tom's legal guardian, but according to the Artichokers, they are. And here's another piece of interesting news. The Episcopal bishop, Conrad Gesner, forced the Artichokers to take Zolbach on as a maintenance man. Zolbach's father apparently has some pull with the bishop. Zolbach stepped in and assumed responsibility for Tom's care, and of course the Artichokers were happy to let him, with all the boys they have and so little money to go around. The bishop and the local priest were always on their backs about expenses. They said Zolbach did everything for Tom. One can only imagine what that included. From there I went south to the town of Rosebud, where Tom went to boarding school after his mother and father died, before he was transferred to the Hare Home. Rosebud's nestled into some rugged, rolling hills, beautiful vistas right out of a Hollywood western. Not a bad place to grow up, but the boarding school is a bleak place, just a set of barracks and classrooms where the conversion activities took place."

"The conversion activities?" Caitlin asked.

"Removing all trace of the Indian. Converting them to whiteness and Christianity," Vincent said sardonically. "As Indians, they're no good, to themselves or others."

"What did you find out about Tom's family?" I asked.

"The people at the Rosebud school were very helpful. They remembered Tom and his parents. Tom's father was a real brute. He beat Tom's mother mercilessly and then would force her to have sex practically in front of all the in the hut they lived in. Really sick stuff. He was unemployed most of the time. The mother never worked."

"When I first got to know Tom, he lied to me about his parents. Told me his father was an electrician and his mother a nurse," I said.

"Tom's good at creating a story of his own making. He fought the shame drummed into him with his own myths."

"Did you find his home, where the family lived?" I asked.

"The boarding school people told me where I could find Charles White Hawk, Tom's uncle. He has a ranch, a successful one. Charles is a big, powerful man. He showed me a picture of himself and Tom's father when they were still in high school. They could be twins, they're so similar. Charles drove me over to the cabin where Tom was born. It's two big rooms, a sodbuster kind of hut with leaky walls and no plumbing. No electricity. A wood stove for heat. When Tom's father was killed in a car accident, the kids were all sent to foster homes. Nobody lives in the cabin now."

"What are you going to do next?" Caitlin asked.

"I'm going to the penitentiary tomorrow and talk to Tom. I've got more questions for him. Then it's back to Minneapolis to write this up. I've got to get it done and published. The clock's ticking."

Vincent stayed a while longer and then left for Sioux Falls. I waited for him to ask for my help, or pay me for the Shattuck trip, but he said nothing about either subject.

I didn't hear from Vincent again until the middle of April, when he sent a copy of his manuscript, asking me to review it. I was disappointed not to have played a bigger role in the production of his article, a well-written and far more penetrating work than my amateurish *Volante* and *Plain Talk* pieces, which seemed juvenile and shallow by comparison. Reading it helped me understand how Tom, the obedient student and star athlete with attractive mixed-race features, became the white man's idea of the perfect Indian. A white Indian. Tom suffered from those unrealistic expectations, developing what Vincent called cultural schizophrenia.

Vincent's article was published by a press in Minnesota and distributed to a list of people he and Gary Hamill and the Episcopal bishop of South Dakota put together. Vincent paid for the publication and mailing costs out of his own savings, which were about gone. He would have to go back to work soon in Minneapolis.

Vincent was always looking for the underlying prejudice in every gesture or statement people made around here, claiming people actually used the word "Injun" and that he was once denied a hotel room in Vermillion because the proprietors discovered he worked for that commie organization, the ACLU. Having the ugly truth rubbed in your face each time he uncovered it was annoying, but he put it all on the line for Tom, when nobody else would.

Vincent thought the Episcopalians had something to atone for in all this. The Hare Home and Shattuck were church boarding schools, institutions run by Episcopalians, where daily chapel and service to the faith were required. Why did Tom, so soon after being untethered from their oversight, kill a defenseless jeweler and rape his elderly wife? Why hadn't they detected that darkness in Tom and done something about it? Vincent asked the Episcopal Church those questions when he approached the local bishop asking for help. The church must have agreed. The bishop wrote an editorial for a national Episcopalian newspaper, highlighting the inexperienced defense, the absence of a plea bargain, and the unusually harsh sentence. He requested financial support for Tom's new defense counsel and his fight for a new trial. The money poured in. In a few months, enough money had been raised to pay Hamill.

Not long after Vincent's article was published, in late May, Caitlin told me she and Harlan were moving to Texas. Harlan had found a job working as a chef in an Austin restaurant. She told me a few days before they were to leave, had wanted to tell me for weeks, but the time was never right. I didn't know how to fight the Harlan thing. I felt rotten, an ache deep in my gut, struggling with the doubt. What was it about Harlan that was so much more attractive than me? Why was she willing to leave school and virtually everything she valued to be with someone she found so much fault with, especially his zany ideas, modest ambition, and drug-soaked friends?

The last night Caitlin was in town, she invited me over for the evening, our last hurrah before she would leave the next day. Harlan was at his home in Iowa saying goodbye to his parents. Chris had already left for a summer job in Wyoming, where she was interning at a speech therapy clinic in Cheyenne.

I walked up the stairs to Caitlin's apartment that evening with a bottle of Mateus and a couple of Paul's LPs, the Beatles'

Sgt. Pepper's Lonely Hearts Club Band and Van Morrison's *Blowin' Your Mind!* I didn't know much about music, but Paul did, and he told me that these two LPs would cement my reputation with Caitlin as a sophisticate, maybe even persuade her to change her mind about leaving. I knew that wasn't going to happen, but I was determined to make it a memorable night.

Caitlin opened the door when I knocked and brushed past me and down the stairs. She was always more beautiful in casual, everyday glimpses like this one, and none more so than that evening. She was wearing jeans, sandals, and a pale green T-shirt that tightened across her breasts. She had just washed her hair and was wearing Loves Fresh Lemon for the first time in a long while.

"I'm out of chili powder," she said. "I'm going to run down to IGA to pick up some. Make yourself at home."

She didn't invite me along. A wave of disappointment rippled through me. I wanted to be seen with her one last time.

I put the Beatles album on and helped myself to a beer in the refrigerator. Several IGA cardboard boxes were stacked on the couch, full of her possessions. A suitcase and makeup bag sat on the kitchen table. Posters and craft art were still hanging on the walls. It looked like Chris's stuff.

I didn't like the first two songs on the Beatles album. They were too cheery for my mood. I was putting the Van Morrison album on the turntable when Caitlin returned from the store.

"Nice choice," she said when she saw the album cover.

I reached for the grocery bag, brushing against her arm and her waist. "Spring is finally here, huh?"

"The lilacs are blooming," she said. "Did you see the huge one next door? We have one like that in our backyard in Sioux City. Lilacs are Mom's favorite."

"Are you making chili?"

"Yep."

"I don't know why you are leaving. You haven't graduated yet. You're not even sure you love him."

"This can be hard, or it can be easy tonight. You decide. I prefer easy, don't you?"

"Either way is painful. I'll try easy."

After chili and grilled cheese sandwiches, we decided to take a walk, wandering through campus and then down Plum Street, where the sorority houses, dark and vacant now that the semester was over, lined the street. The girls had discarded what they no longer wanted or needed in overloaded dumpsters and garbage cans, an odd scene, where everything was usually so manicured and tidy. I never thought to ask Caitlin before this, but the sorority houses triggered the question.

"Did you go through sorority rush when you were a freshman?"

She thought for a moment and then looked at me as if she were about to make a confession.

"Yes, I did. I pledged Chi Omega. Stayed with it the first semester, went through orientation and activated. I made a few friends. One of them was Skyler. You met her last fall."

"I remember her. She was the one who looked the part of a sorority girl but swore like a longshoreman. How long did the two of you stay with it?"

"Skyler and I were roommates in a campus dormitory, Richardson Hall. After the first semester, we moved into the Chi-O house. We were skeptical of the bullshit, but it was cheaper than living in the dorm. And then second semester rush started. After the new girls came through rush, the actives all gathered in the television room downstairs to discuss the new candidates. There were about twenty-five of them. The rush chair had a projector, and she flashed each girl's picture up on the wall and everybody offered their comments. You should have heard those bitches. 'She bites her fingernails.' 'She's a slut.' 'She's got thick thighs and is pigeon-toed.' 'Did you see her outfit?' And on and on. The next day Skyler and I moved out and back into the dorm."

"I had no idea."

"It's not important. I had no business pledging in the first place. My mistake, not theirs."

Back in her apartment, we drank the Mateus and listened to more music. I had not touched her all evening, but the wine made me braver. Sitting together on the couch, I leaned over to kiss her. She withdrew, reluctantly, I thought, and then got up and cleaned up the kitchen. I got up to help. Her hair fell forward, covering her face, as she leaned forward above the sink, washing the dishes. When we were finished, she went into her bedroom, disappearing for a few minutes. She seemed more relaxed when she came back, as if she had decided on something.

"Let's go to bed," she said coolly.

Last summer, during the days we spent together in my apartment, our lovemaking had been spontaneous, heedless of anyone or anything when the passion arose. Caitlin would cry softly after her orgasm, lying under me, collapsed in pleasure. When school started in the fall, after a break of several weeks, we were awkward in bed again, as if we had fallen out of practice. The passion became ironic, the mutual laugh substituting for the mutual orgasm. That night, more of the same. We undressed on either side of the bed, Caitlin jumping under the covers with her panties on, me embarrassed that I wasn't as hard as I wanted to be. After several tries, the final a last-ditch effort to rescue my self-respect, we gave up and started laughing at the absurdity of it. I knew my recent performance wasn't why she was leaving with Harlan, but I also knew that it made it easier for her to do so.

The next morning I woke to the sounds of the Sinclair station next door opening up for business. Someone pulled up the station's garage doors, letting the fresh air into the mechanics' bays. One of the mechanics must have been changing a tire, loosening lug nuts with a power wrench, the whirring, rat-a-tat-tat echoing against the walls of the station. Caitlin was lying on her stomach, facing away from me. Her long, straight hair spread out across her back. I kissed her on the cheek, but she didn't turn over, offering her hand instead and then squeezing mine as hard as she could. I dressed and left, knowing Harlan would be arriving soon.

My Caitlin affair was a zigzag romance. The emotions spiked frequently—attraction one day, friendship the next. We never quite figured it out. We tried hard at the loving and the sex, which seemed more abundant then. I never saw Caitlin again, but it seems as though she were here only yesterday, lying next to me in bed, the lemony fragrance in her hair, those seductive lips asking to be kissed and to share a laugh when it was over.

6

I went back to school in the fall and registered for twenty-two hours, an overload. There wasn't any point in taking all those hours, but I had something to prove. If Tom had to face the prospect of the electric chair in five months, I sure as hell could take a few more classes. Paul was living in the apartment, but our schedules were such that we seldom saw each other. He was still active in the SAE house and was engaged to be married.

Vincent called right after Labor Day. His article had generated a surge of interest in Tom's case. Donations to Tom's defense fund were increasing. A letter-writing campaign requesting that the governor commute Tom's death sentence to life in prison had erupted spontaneously, though Vincent was skeptical the letters would have much effect.

"Weepy letters won't persuade this or any future governor in this Injun-hating state," he said. "Our focus must remain on the hearing for a new trial."

"Has it been scheduled?" I asked.

"That's why I called. It's scheduled to begin in late September. We're driving to Sioux Falls tomorrow to meet with Tom to prepare testimony and review the psychiatric report."

"You have a psychiatric report?"

"Gary contacted the Menninger Clinic in Kansas. Dr. Joseph Satten was here three weeks ago and examined Tom. He's the same psychiatrist who examined Hickock and Smith, the

Clutter family killers. We have his report. Gary thinks it will persuade a judge that a new trial is warranted."

"That's good news, Jerry."

"It is. Come on up to the prison tomorrow. We haven't seen you in a while."

I arrived early and waited for Vincent and Hamill in the reception area, where the visitors passed through the security station. The warden was there, talking with two visitors, a man and a woman. The top half of the man's head was white and bald, the lower half tanned and leathery. She wore a sundress. A scarf covered her hair. They were clearly uncomfortable. I listened to their conversation, pretending to read a magazine. Their son was serving time for manslaughter.

Warden Herman Salem introduced himself to me when the couple left to see their son. The warden was a retired army colonel, a Korean War commander, strangely unjaded by his military experience and still harboring a faith in human nature.

His expression showed surprise when I told him I was there to see Tom White Hawk.

"So you are here to see Thomas. I have grown quite fond of him."

"How's he doing?"

"He grows more distant, separating from us a little more as the day grows closer. But he's holding up. He's been through a lot. He's accustomed to being alone with his fear."

Vincent and Hamill arrived. The warden turned to them and introduced himself. We talked for a few minutes. The warden knew a hearing date on Tom's request for a new trial had been set. He was quite interested in the hearing and Hamill's analysis of Tom's chances. Hamill surprised me when he offered to send the warden a copy of his brief. The warden might not be the enemy, but he worked for him. Hamill later told me his legal strategy was already a matter of public record. He'd provided his brief to the hearing judge. Chuck Volesky would have read it several times by now.

There was a problem this morning, however.

"Gentlemen," the warden said, "we recently implemented a new policy. No more than two visitors at a time. One of you will have to wait out here in the reception area while the other two visit with Tom. Whoever sits out now can see him after the other two have finished. You have one hour."

I told them to go ahead but to leave me a few minutes toward the end of the hour. Vincent and Hamill started on their way, but Hamill turned back, reached into his briefcase, and handed me a stapled typewritten report.

"Here's the Satten report Jerry told you about. It's confidential. I don't want to see any of it in a news story, if you know what I mean. But I want you to read it. I want to know how much of it squares with your understanding of Tom," Hamill said, handing it to me. "We'll leave some time for you to see Tom," he assured me as he left to catch up with Vincent.

I took the report from Hamill and found a chair and table in a far corner of the reception room, where I could read without interruption. Before I started reading, though, the warden came over, wanting to talk more, curious about my role in Tom's life. I went on too long, flattered by his attention and charmed by his amiable manner. Half an hour later, I began reading the report.

CASE SUMMARY

Patient's Name: Thomas White Hawk
Age: 20
Referred by: Gary Hamill, Attorney
Physician: Dr. Joseph Satten, M.D.
Date Exam Began: August 15, 1968
Date Exam Completed: August 16, 1968

BACKGROUND DATA

The subject was born April 30, 1948, on the Rosebud Indian Reservation of South Dakota. His parents, Dorothy McLean and Calvin Edward White Hawk, were Sioux Indians from the reservation. The subject reports himself as the oldest of six, but the United States probation officer has noted that there were two older children born out of wedlock.

The subject's father was unstable, drank heavily, and frequently beat the mother. He worked irregularly as a farm laborer and often could not support his family; the subject both feared and hated him. The subject felt much closer to his mother and, though protective of her, described her as a "kleptomaniac" and somewhat loose in her morals. He both loved and hated her.

The subject was normal and healthy at birth and presented no unusual problems during his childhood. When the subject was about two years old, his father enlisted in the United States Army and served in Korea, while the family continued to live with a brother of the mother in an Episcopal Guild House near the reservation. When the father returned about two years later, they rented a small house on a cattle farm near Mosher, South Dakota, and the father worked irregularly as a ranch hand.

The family's social and economic difficulties led to a number of moves, and there were times the children lived with other relatives when their own parents could not care for them. As a child, the subject spent much time playing by himself and helping with his younger siblings, toward whom he felt quite protective. Due to continued difficulties in the family, the subject and the younger children were sent to the Rosebud Boarding School in Mission, South Dakota, when he was eight years old, and he continued on and off at the federal school for Indian children for the next five years.

When the subject was about ten, the White Hawk family group was relocated to Chicago, Illinois, by the Bureau of Indian Affairs so the father could obtain steady employment. The move was unsuccessful, and the family returned to the Rosebud Reservation the following spring and for a time lived with Charles White Hawk, a brother of the father and a fairly successful Indian rancher.

The subject recalls many times that the father beat the mother without provocation, and often these beatings were related to sexual activity afterward. One particular episode of violence between his parents stands out in his memory and frequently recurs to him in nightmares. Once, the family was driving back from a drive-in, and an argument between the parents started in the car. The father dragged the mother out of the car and beat her with a board he found in the ditch.

Another episode of violence involved the father's rage reaction when some meat disappeared from the refrigerator and the father jumped to the conclusion that a neighbor's dog—a beautiful collie named Laddie, who was a frequent visitor of the home—had in some way opened the icebox and taken the meat. The father got his rifle, demanded that the subject find a flashlight, and the two of them went searching through the house for the dog. The father started shooting at the dog when he saw him, at the same time berating the subject for not holding the flashlight properly, and then he beat the dog to death with the butt of the rifle. Later that evening, the dog's owner, a girl of eighteen or twenty, came over, sobbing and crying, and slept there in the house beside the dead dog. The patient has a confused recollection of being in bed with her that night, becoming frightened when she asked him to play with her genitals, and starting to cry when she would not let him withdraw his hand from her vagina.

A short time later, when the subject was about eleven, his mother died suddenly of what was thought to be a stroke. The subject was given contradictory stories about the cause of her death—one that she died in childbirth and another that she had a brain hemorrhage—but he has always suspected the father beat her to death. The defense attorney's report of the hospital record gives a history of her being beaten prior to admission but lists the cause of death as "viral encephalitis." The subject was very upset following the death of his mother and for months would cry himself to sleep at night. He was angry with his younger brother and sister because they didn't seem to care about the death of the mother, but now he feels they didn't really realize what was happening. He recalls withdrawing from people and not letting anybody "get" to him since that time, but the intense loneliness that he felt after his mother's death lasted about two years.

The family continued living with the father's brother, but the father continued his frequent alcoholic binges and neglected the family. The children were returned to the Rosebud Boarding School, where they spent most of their time. In the winter of that year, the father was fatally injured in an automobile accident. Although the subject felt somewhat sad and depressed following his father's death, the feeling was quite different from that following the death of his mother. He didn't cry much after his father's death; rather, he experienced some sense of relief, recalling the times that he'd wanted to kill his father. While still lonely for his mother, the subject had a sense of well-being, of being "free" of his father and being on his own.

Local welfare workers arranged adoptive placements for the younger children in the family, but it was felt that the subject could manage on his own by going to boarding school. He was later placed in the Bishop Hare Mission Home, operated by the Episcopal church in Mission, South Dakota. A counselor at the home, Mr. Philip Zolbach, assumed responsibility for the planning and supervision of the subject, and a close relationship developed between the subject and Mr. Zolbach.

On a number of occasions, Mr. Zolbach wished to adopt the subject, but subject would not agree. Although he never said anything about it, in the back of his mind the subject had hoped that his uncle, with whom the family had lived intermittently, would adopt him. He was too proud to ask to be adopted by his uncle, but he did not want to do anything that would prevent such an adoption and therefore would not agree to being adopted by anyone else.

The subject and Mr. Zolbach spent a great deal
of time together while subject was at the Hare
Mission Home, fishing, camping, and traveling
back and forth to Rapid City and St. Paul, where
they would spend holiday weekends at the home
of Zolbach's parents. The subject enjoyed getting
out of the home for a few days but dreaded the
overnight accommodations, which always ended
up with Zolbach near him in the tent or in the
same motel room or bedroom. Zolbach would
wait for the subject to fall asleep, or pretend to
fall asleep, and then masturbate under the covers while they lay in the same bed. When the
subject was younger, in his first years at Hare,
Zolbach would often accompany him to the
bathroom, where he would watch the subject
urinate and give him hygiene lessons on how to
care for his uncircumcised penis. However, the
subject maintained that Zolbach never touched
him sexually.

With the help of Mr. Zolbach, arrangements
were made for the subject to enter Shattuck
Military Academy, where he completed tenth,
eleventh, and twelfth grades. The subject very
much wanted to go to Shattuck, not only because
it was a good private military school but also
because he wanted to get away from reservation
life, from his painful past, and make something
new and different of himself. He had hopes and
aspirations of being a doctor but wasn't sure that
he was good enough to be able to accomplish

that goal. The subject liked Shattuck very much and was an outstanding athlete there, but he tended to keep to himself and did not "put out" in his relationships to others. In the spring of 1964, while on the athletic field, he was hit on the head with a shot put and required sutures to repair the laceration.

Six months after that injury, when he returned to school the following fall, he began to have severe migraine headaches with disturbances in his vision, and he frequently reported to the physician, Dr. C. W. Rumpf, who prescribed medication to ease the pain and the tension. Also to ease the tension, the subject found himself playing football very hard, and occasionally he was knocked out on the field. Although his grades remained passing, he found it increasingly difficult to keep up his level of work. He had a C average during his sophomore year, a C– during his junior year, and a D average during his senior year, but he graduated successfully in June of 1966.

The medication given to the subject by Dr. Rumpf, which contained phenobarbital, seemed to help a little, and on one occasion, the subject broke into the infirmary in order to get an extra supply of pills, which he continued to take whenever he could. Although they seemed to give him a sense of well-being, they also seemed to induce peculiar, dreamy states, which bothered him and made him decide from time to time not to take any pills. During the time that he was at Shattuck, he worried much about his headaches and the possibility of losing his sight, and he had many nightmares and dreams from which he would awaken crying.

Also going on during his senior year was a relationship with a girlfriend at St. Mary's, a nearby school. Although they liked each other very much, she had to cut down her contacts with him in order to keep her grades up and remain in school. Intellectually, he agreed with the decision, but emotionally he felt rejected. The subject later discovered that Mr. Zolbach had intervened with officials at St. Mary's, leading to the girlfriend's sudden interest in academics.

HISTORY OF PRESENT ILLNESS

Although, in retrospect, it is clear that emotional difficulties began to show themselves while the subject was at Shattuck, the level of the difficulties seemed to intensify following his graduation. Although Mr. Zolbach had encouraged the subject to become a doctor and to start his premedical work at the university in September, the subject wasn't "really set" on being a doctor. He wanted to join the marines first and get that out of the way. Taking Zolbach's advice, he started in at the university but felt some conflict about the course of action.

Soon after his enrollment, he met Dottie McBride, an Indian girl about a year older than him, whom he had known in grade school. They began to go out with each other, and soon he felt extremely close to her, almost "dependent." She seemed to "understand" his moods, and he felt he could "trust" her in a way that he could trust nobody since the death of his mother. The subject also joined a fraternity that fall, Sigma Alpha Epsilon, and he enjoyed the prestige factor. The pressures of pledge life and being "different" began to build up, even though he was accustomed to the harassment after suffering abuse at the hands of upperclassmen at Shattuck.

Sometime toward the end of October and the beginning of November, the subject felt himself getting tense, and in an attempt to cope with the tension, he started drinking and taking phenobarbital again. During this time he and Dottie began having an affair and started to talk about marriage. The affair left him in a state of acute conflict; he enjoyed the sexual relationship but was angry with Dottie for being "weak" and giving in to his demands for sexual activity. He began to fantasize that, if they were married, she might become unfaithful to him.

Shortly before Thanksgiving, the subject and Dottie had a quarrel, the cause of which is not clear. In any event, he accepted an invitation to spend the Thanksgiving weekend in Minneapolis with the family of a classmate, but at the same time, he promised to spend at least part of the holiday with Dottie in Vermillion. He felt tense and restless and didn't sleep very much in the few days prior to the Thanksgiving weekend.

When he and his classmate arrived in Minneapolis, they spent the evening together and then went to the movies. Although the subject was extremely tired, he wasn't sleepy when they returned, and for some reason that he cannot understand, he told the family that he wanted to go to his guardian's place near Wayzata. He was dropped off near there, but he didn't really want to go in, and he started walking down the street. He was wearing summer clothes, and it started to get cold, whereupon he walked into the garage of a house, sat in one of the cars, and tried to get warm. He recalled that he was aware of what was happening around him but that he was moving automatically and not really thinking. He was aware of having promised Dottie that he would get back before the end of vacation and spend part of it with her, so he switched the wires on the car and started it. As he drove down the street, he kept hoping a policeman would stop him, a thought which puzzled him.

When he was apprehended in Vermillion after a minor accident, he felt relieved. He told the authorities part of what had happened and was relieved to have confessed to the crime but felt he could not describe all of his thinking lest people think he was "crazy." The probation officer in his presentence report notes that the crime was out of character for the subject and that, in spite of the subject's cooperativeness, he was really at a loss to explain why the subject had committed the offense. (It is irresponsible that these signs of mental disturbance were not recognized then, prior to the commission of the more serious crime.)

Early in December, something happened at the fraternity that ended the subject's membership. The subject and a fraternity brother were involved in a bloody fistfight after this person called subject a "prairie nigger." The retelling of the fight caused the subject to get angry again, his fists clenched.

In the meantime, the subject and Dottie decided to become engaged, although it was not to become official until Christmas, when he would give her an engagement ring. A short time later, for some unknown reason, the subject and Dottie got into a fight, and he struck her, following which she broke off the engagement. She later accepted his apologies, however, and reinstated the engagement within about a week. The subject gave her the ring for Christmas as planned, and the holidays were pleasant.

Early in January, the subject and Dottie again had difficulty with regard to their affair, and for reasons he cannot clearly define, he began to feel some pressure from Dottie that they get married soon rather than wait the two years they had originally planned. He did not resolve the conflict with her and increasingly felt a sense of being trapped because he felt that he was not "smart enough," both to get married and to continue with his work at school. On top of that, he felt that if they were to have a child soon after the marriage, he would not be able to go on with his studies. Also during this time, he pleaded guilty to the car theft charge, and after a presentence evaluation, he was placed on probation. His sense of tension and irritability continued, and his college work suffered. He drank even more and resumed taking phenobarbital.

Sometime in March of 1967, approximately two weeks before the crime, the subject called Mr. Zolbach and told him he thought he needed to see a psychiatrist. Mr. Zolbach dismissed the idea, and subject did nothing about it. The subject's sense of conflict and confusion continued, and about ten days before the crime, he began to have the idea that he must have some money in order to get married.

On Wednesday before the crime, Mr. Zolbach came to visit the subject and in response to subject's request, left a rifle with him. The subject had said that he wanted the rifle for hunting, which was partly true, but he was also thinking that he would use the rifle in a robbery scheme of some sort. He felt, in some way that he cannot clearly define, that he would get the money he needed from the Yeado Jeweler store, where he had bought the engagement ring and he was known. The fact did not deter him; quite the contrary, in a strange way it seemed to pull him there. The following day he told Willie Stands about some of his ideas and asked if Willie wanted to join him. The subject did so because he felt he needed someone along to "build up his courage." Willie felt he also needed some money and agreed to join in the robbery.

Vincent and Hamill returned as I happened to look up from my reading. The report told me a lot about Tom that I didn't know and that there was a lot I had thought to be true that wasn't.

Vincent was in a hurry, as usual, walking quickly, reaching for a cigarette and heading for the door.

"Sorry, I have to have the report back. It's my only copy," Hamill said, reaching for it.

"And, as you can see, Jerry has to get back to Minneapolis and has not a minute to spare," he said, eyes rolling slightly, "but I'll call you soon to talk about the report before the hearing."

"Thanks for letting me read it. I didn't finish it. Only got through the background stuff."

"I'll send you a copy."

"How's Tom?" I asked.

"I think he's ready for the hearing. He knows it's not going to be easy. He's going to be asked questions as if it were an actual trial. Questions about the murder and the rape."

Tom was sitting at a table in the visitation room, waiting for me, wearing the same orange jumpsuit. When he saw me, the look in his eyes warmed, but his expression stayed glum.

Tom was still in isolation, separated from the general population. His guards, and the warden, were his only day-to-day contact with human beings.

"We don't have much time, Tom," I said. "Is there anything I can do for you? Anything you need?"

"Are you serious?" he asked.

"Shit. I'm sorry."

"Did you read my story?"

"What story?" I asked, somehow finding the presence of mind to stall him with the question. Had Vincent and Hamill showed him the Satten report?

"Jerry's article. My story."

"Oh, yeah, Jerry had me edit it before publication. Did you like it?"

"Wouldn't change a word," he said. "But it's not going to save me. The people who want me dead don't read that sort of thing. Gary's right. It comes down to a new trial. If I don't get one, I'm riding that big chair down the hall. The chair is in this building, did you know that? And do you know who has to pull the switch? The warden. By law he has to do it. Herm, he's tougher than he seems, but I know he's worried sick about that. Praying to his God that I get a new trial."

"We all are, Tom. There are a lot of people pulling for you."

"Tell them I want to live. I didn't a few months ago, but I do now," he said, his chest heaving, as if the specter of his death took his breath away.

"You will get a new trial," I said.

"It's fall," he said. "I should be playing football, not rotting in here. Why aren't I on a field somewhere, stuffing a running back? I was fast, broke through the line easily, saw the fear in the running back's eyes, knowing he was going to get hit, hard. They cheered from the stands when I got a tackle. 'Hawk, Hawk, Hawk,' they'd chant."

Tom got up and signaled the guard he was ready.

"Come back again when we have more time," he said. "But be prepared for a background check. They screen my visitors," he said, smiling. "Only the privileged make it through."

I drove back to Vermillion, cheering to myself, "Hawk, Hawk, Hawk," for the boy I had read about in the report, the boy whose young life knew triumph and fear in great but unequal measure. Now this boy, Hawk, would soon die in an electric chair.

7

The hearing requesting a new trial for Tom White Hawk was held in the federal courthouse in Sioux Falls. The presiding judge of the state circuit wanted a neutral site. The thought of Tom eluding the death sentence had reignited the anger of the hotheads, Vincent's "Injun killers."

There was a lot of talk, Tug told me authoritatively one morning at the Monogram News. "If that Indian boy gets off, justice will have to come another way. A lot of people in town won't be happy until he's dead," he said, his hand trembling as he dropped the change in my open hand. He looked at me through his tired eyes, red rimmed and watery, holding my gaze longer than needed, as if I didn't understand his message the first time.

The hearing lasted three days. I skipped the first day—too many classes—and drove up to Sioux Falls for the second, a Thursday. The federal courthouse was downtown, on south Philips Avenue. I knew the area well. When I was growing up, my mother often took me shopping downtown, where all the retail stores were clustered. The only movie theater in town, the State Theater, was on Philips too, an art deco classic where I'd watched Saturday matinees featuring Rocketman, the man in the atomic-powered suit and sleek, steel helmet who flew through the sky and destroyed evildoers, triggering dreams of flight in his cheering adolescent male audience. The street began to change in the late 1960s when the Western Mall was built, triggering an exodus to the outskirts of town, where developers built parking lots large enough to accommodate the shoppers rushing in from small towns around Sioux Falls. When I turned onto Philips on my way to the hearing, the street was almost empty.

I put a dime in the *Argus* newsstand on the front steps of the courthouse, opened the hatch, and grabbed the paper on top of the pile. Lee McMillan and Sheriff Wilson, on the stand the first day, were quoted in a front-page story. The same story ran a picture of Tom entering the courthouse through a side door. He had gained some weight, making him look healthy and well fed, and he was wearing a dark suit Hamill had purchased for the hearing. He was handcuffed. The camera had caught him in a wolflike smile. I was sure that was not his mood or intent, but the damage was done. No need to even read the story.

The courtroom was much larger than the Clay or Douglas County courtrooms, a magnificent room with intricate images carved into the oak paneling on the walls. The judge's bench towered over the spectators and counsel tables. Tom had been here once before, when a sympathetic federal judge, Fred Nichol, gave him probation for stealing a car and a pep talk on life's challenges before sending him back to the university.

The doors to the courtroom were closed when I arrived. Several people were waiting outside in the hallway: Vincent; Zolbach; the press; Tom's uncle, Charles White Hawk; Charles's wife; and a young woman conducting interviews for the university's oral history center. I went over to Vincent, who was with Charles and his wife.

"Charles, this is Craig Peters. He knows Tom. Craig helped me research Tom's story," Vincent said.

Charles stood with his head bowed. He glanced up at me when Vincent made the introduction and then looked away again. His hair was cut short, thick and graying. He wore a western shirt—a yellow, faded one with snap buttons—and blue jeans, with an oversized silver buckle on his belt. His frame was muscular and athletic, clearly a White Hawk. Charles would sit in the front row throughout the day, arms crossed, staring intently at the judge, lawyers, and witnesses.

"Jerry, I have something to discuss before the hearing. Can we talk for a minute?" I asked, pointing to the benches down the hall from the courtroom entrance.

When were seated on the bench, I asked Vincent to tell me more about the defense strategy.

"I thought I sent Gary's brief to you. My apologies. He argued five points in it," Vincent said. "Some are stronger—in my opinion—than others. Let me see if I can remember all of them. The first had something to do with criminal law process. Too esoteric. The second argues that the sheriff's interrogation after Tom's arrest was unconstitutional. The third, and most obvious, of course, was that his counsel, Lee McMillan, seriously fucked up the case. I think the fourth was that the death penalty is unconstitutional—not a great argument, since we're killing an Indian, here. They don't quite count in this state. And the last one is that Tom was sick, mentally ill, at the time of the murder. That one has the most promise."

When everyone was seated, the hearing judge, Judge Winter, opened the proceeding. Hamill rose immediately and asked the judge whether Mr. White Hawk's handcuffs could be removed. Hamill had already asked the penitentiary guards, who did not object. Judge Winter winced with the question, seeming to signal sympathy for the defendant, but he denied the request. Tom would hold both arms and hands clasped together under the table throughout the hearing.

Hamill called Dr. Satten to the stand. Sitting next to Tom at the defense table, Satten walked quickly to the clerk's chair, where he was administered the oath. Satten was a diminutive man with big, black glasses, long sideburns that flared out, and a weak chin. He wore his pants too high and spoke a million miles an hour in a Brooklyn accent. The room fell very quiet as Hamill approached the witness. At the previous hearings, Tom's gaze had been downcast, usually fixed on some object, but today he was looking directly at the witness as one might on the first day of class, curious to hear what Satten would say after all those hours answering his painful questions.

Hamill began by establishing his witness's credibility. Satten held a medical degree from New York University and was on the staff at the Menninger Clinic in Topeka, Kansas. He'd served as an expert witness in a number of cases involving criminal insanity, including the Clutter murders. Responding to further questions, Satten explained the methods he'd used in Tom's examination, described Tom's background and early influences—the stuff I had read in his report—and concluded with his diagnosis, a personality disorder.

When Satten finished, Hamill turned the pages of his yellow legal pad, as if he had lost his place. Satten looked at him quizzically as he continued to search for it. Sitting next to me, Vincent sighed irritably.

"Oh, here it is," Hamill finally said, looking up at the judge. "Dr. Satten, now that you have described Mr. White Hawk's background and shared your diagnosis of his mental illness with us, I would like you to help us understand what his state of mind was on the day of the murder."

Satten leaned forward in the stand, pausing for a moment for effect. This was not his first rodeo.

"At the time leading up to the burglary, his state of mind—he was in emotional turmoil and was not really himself. My opinion is that this was not a deliberate homicide. The only question in my mind is whether he was already in an extremely disturbed state of mind when he entered the home or whether the accidental shooting of Mr. Yeado triggered the lapse into a more disturbed state of mind, during which his behavior was almost totally irrational for a good part of the day. The anger that had been present in him in relation to his father, and in relation to Mr. Zolbach, erupted in relation to Mr. Yeado, with a shooting that may have been either accidental or, as we psychiatrists would say, unconsciously determined," Satten said.

"Dr. Satten, you previously described Tom's relationship to his father, but you did not mention Mr. Zolbach. Yet you said that Mr. White Hawk's actions that day were also motivated by his relationship to Mr. Zolbach. Would you help us understand what you mean by that?" Hamill asked.

"Philip Zolbach was an adviser at the Hare Mission Home, and he took an interest in Tom which gradually developed into a very special interest," Satten said.

Vincent leaned over and whispered in my ear, "Special interest and a whole lot more."

"Tom, for a long time, felt feelings of gratitude and responsibility toward Mr. Zolbach, but as he grew older, he began to resent the rules, the demands on his time, and the sexual tension. He wanted more freedom, much as a young adolescent wishes from a parent, and the relationship with Mr. Zolbach gradually developed into an intense, what we psychiatrists call, a mixed relationship. Tom had mixed feelings of love, warmth on the one hand, and anger on the other hand. The intensity of this relationship increased, with Tom gradually feeling more and more trapped in a web of obligation. Those intense angry feelings increased following his start at the university and in the months and weeks leading up to the crime, finally erupting that fateful night in the Yeado home."

Judge Winter called a lunch recess at 11:30 a.m. The hearing would reconvene at 1:30 p.m. Zolbach was one of the first to leave, pushing through the courtroom's swinging doors in a hurry. He was dressed more formally than he usually was for these court hearings, wearing a sport coat, tie, and khakis. I pushed my way through the people making their way out, turning a couple of heads with my rude behavior, and caught up with Zolbach on the steps outside the building. We all knew where this was heading, most of all Zolbach, but I felt compelled to console him, if that was possible. I wouldn't have felt that way if he had not stopped to see me shortly after Tom's sentencing, but it had become more complicated, no matter how disgusting the details.

"Phil, stop, please," I shouted at him. "I want to say something."

He finally stopped at the bottom step and turned around. He wasn't as upset as I thought he was. He looked at me with a blank look, his eyes magnified behind his thick amber lenses.

"What is it? I'm late already."

"Phil, I want you to know there are many ways to look at this."

"Why would I conclude that? What are you talking about?"

"The testimony about who's to blame."

"Are you talking about the psychiatrist's testimony? Frankly, he wasn't describing the Tom I knew, nor our relationship. Tom's fabricating a story he thinks the doctor will fall for and get him out. Is that what you're so concerned about?"

I felt bewildered, stupid as hell for even bringing it up.

"Yeah. The psychiatric stuff. I wanted to make sure you were okay."

Zolbach shot me a puzzled look and then left. He was due back at St. James for a choral concert that afternoon, he said. He was conducting the choir.

Hamill finished with Satten well after three in the afternoon. Volesky was next. He had pretended to be bored during Hamill's questioning, exhaling heavily, checking his own notes—at one point reading the newspaper, until the judge threw him the stink eye and he put the newspaper away. He rose slowly, ran his hands through his flat-top a few times, and strode up to the witness box where Satten was sitting. After four-plus hours of Hamill's slog through the psychiatric details with Dr. Satten, everyone was looking forward to some courtroom drama.

"Dr. Satten," Volesky began, holding what appeared to be Satten's report high in one hand, "you state—on page thirteen of your report—'In this particular case, we have an Indian boy, the oldest in the home, living in a situation of more than average poverty and social instability with parents who were far from ideal.' Dr. Satten, how familiar are you with Indian reservations?"

"In a general way," Satten said.

"In other words, not at all. Isn't that right, Dr. Satten?"

"I have many colleagues, including the director of the institute I work for, Dr. Karl Menninger, who are quite familiar with reservations. I consult with them on a daily basis."

"I'll state my question another way. Have you ever been on an Indian reservation, here in South Dakota or anywhere else?"

"I have not."

For the next two hours, Volesky hammered away at Satten, questioning his expertise, his conclusions, his motives. He countered the struggles in Tom's early years with the life of privilege he had led at the Hare Home; at a summer camp he had attended for three summers in New Hampshire; at Shattuck, an exclusive military academy for wealthy Episcopalians. Volesky played his role, a natural one given his personality, of a Yeado friend and local citizen angry that the killer might yet escape his punishment because some celebrity psychiatrist had found a way to explain it all away. When he was done, Volesky returned to his chair, smugly triumphant, confident he had delivered an impressive performance.

The judge asked Dr. Satten to remain on the stand. The judge had some questions regarding the M'Naghten rule, a nineteenth-century English legal concept embedded in the criminal code of many states, including South Dakota. The M'Naghten rule was used to determine the criminal responsibility of persons claiming an insanity defense. The question the rule posed was deceptively simple: Did the person committing the act know right from wrong at the time of the crime?

"Do you have an opinion on whether Thomas White Hawk knew the difference between right and wrong, under the M'Naghten rule, at the time he committed this crime?" the judge asked.

"First of all, my concern is that this is a legal question, not a psychiatric opinion. I think psychiatrists get out of their territory when they address themselves to legal opinions. This is one of my criticisms of the previous psychiatric reports," Satten said.

"Both the prosecution and defense psychiatrists expressed an opinion," the judge stated.

"They did. I feel this is not proper. I feel that is the province of the court and the jury and that my job is to bring as much evidence as I can that's relevant to those issues. Once I start giving opinions about the M'Naghten rule, for example, I am no better judge than anybody else, because I'm not in my field of experience," Satten said.

"The M'Naghten rule is the rule of South Dakota; therefore it seems to be quite important to the court to come up with an answer to the problem of whether he knew right from wrong at the time he committed the act. Was he aware of a wrongness of the act at that time, and the quality of it?" the judge asked.

"I have stated my opinion, as requested," Satten said.

"Yes, you have. Thank you, Dr. Satten. You are excused. Well, the time is late. I think we'll begin with Mr. White Hawk tomorrow morning, unless counsel objects," the judge declared.

I looked to see Tom's expression. It did not change with the news he would have to wait another day before he would tell his story, or what he remembered of it. I wasn't sure if the guards would allow me to talk to Tom, but I gave it a try, opening the gate at the railing that separated the courtroom audience from the judge and lawyers, walking through it toward Tom and Hamill, who were both getting up, Tom a little awkwardly with the handcuffs on, Hamill stiff with age.

"Tom, I can't be here tomorrow. I wanted to be, but it's not possible," I said.

Tom shrugged and turned toward the guards, who nodded at him, signaling for him to come their way.

"It doesn't matter," he said, the respectable, dark-suited image Hamill had tried to create undermined by the handcuffs. "You can't be up there with me, can you?"

"No, I suppose not. I'll see you soon. I'll be up to visit."

He had already turned his back to me and was walking out with his guards.

I told Vincent on the way out I would not be at the hearing the next day. I said I would call him to find out how Tom did.

He advised me to read the newspaper. The *Argus* would no doubt cover it in all its gruesomeness.

Saturday morning I went downtown, surprised to see so many people on Main Street until I remembered it was the university's homecoming weekend. The homecoming parade was approaching downtown as I arrived, the crowd swelling in front of the Monogram News. I worked my way through the jovial throng, most of the students quite drunk already, and went into the store. Sure enough, the newspapers, piled high next to the cash register, carried a story on Tom's appearance at the hearing. I bought one and left the store, avoiding eye contact with some SAEs across the street who were cheering on the fraternity's float, which had several blitzed pledges on the flatbed, drunkenly swaying back and forth.

According to the story, Volesky made several attempts to draw the details of the murder scene out of Tom, but he stuck to his story, remembering only a patchwork of flashes and sensations. He depicted the rape more coherently, remembering that the noon siren echoed loudly on that quiet Good Friday, that Mrs. Yeado hadn't resisted him. After admitting he had stuffed one of Mrs. Yeado's nylons in her mouth before raping her, Tom broke down, sobbing for several minutes, according to the story, silencing the courtroom while he recovered. I didn't read on. That was enough. The Indians had lost again.

Judge Winter denied the petition for a new trial a few weeks later. Vincent sent me a copy of the decision. In it, the judge referenced Dr. Satten's diagnosis of Tom's mental health before and during the crime but deferred to the earlier psychiatric reports that said "the defendant was legally sane at the time of the commission of the act." The judge also implied that Satten's refusal to render an opinion under the M'Naghten rule weakened his testimony. In effect, the judge had distilled the question of guilt or innocence into the limited confines of M'Naghten.

There was no possibility of appeal at this late date. Thomas White Hawk had three and one-half months to live, unless the governor commuted his sentence.

8

Jerry Vincent thought the decision denying Tom a new trial had a silver lining. He predicted that the Injun haters' gloating would boomerang on them, creating sympathy for Tom where there was little before. Over the following months, Vincent was proven right. The Episcopalians were shamed by Vine Deloria Sr., who threw his clerical collar on the floor at a diocesan meeting discussing Tom's fate when they resisted helping Tom. Deloria said that's what he thought of a religion and church that would not help, that would condemn a young boy to die.

Soon after, the Episcopalian congregations began writing letters to the governor, pleading with him to commute Tom's sentence. Jim Hubert and a law school professor organized a campaign to abolish capital punishment. An abstract constitutional argument, they reasoned, stood a better chance to save the Rosebud orphan than an emotional plea for his life. A producer from NBC News called Jerry. NBC wanted to feature the White Hawk story on *First Tuesday*, a news feature program. The program would be based on Vincent's pamphlet. The producer and staff flew to Minneapolis and interviewed Vincent and Hamill and then drove out to the Rosebud to film the reservation and conduct more interviews. Sander Vanocur narrated the story in his gruff, can-you-believe-this-shit-really-happened tone, portraying Tom as a lonely, confused young man, uncertain of his identity, crushed by the white culture's expectations.

The reaction to Tom's plight was global and diverse, with support coming in from the Swedish Section of Amnesty International; the University of New Mexico Kiva Club; the staff at the Albert Schweitzer Hospital in Pucallpa, Peru; the Lakota Omniciye Club at Black Hills State College; the Rosebud Sioux Tribal Council; and hundreds more. It seemed a corner had been turned, and then Manny Marshall's letter hit the editorial pages of South Dakota's newspapers.

> Dear Editor:
>
> We have read in the newspapers about campaigns to do away with capital punishment and listened to television commentators tell us that the man who killed a 60-year-old jeweler while he was lying peacefully in bed now wants to live. He wants to live in the comfort of his cell, with his books and TV and free meals, a better life than what most of his people have on the reservation. Why is this man afraid to die? He was the sole judge of whether Jim Yeado was to live or die. He voluntarily shot and bludgeoned Jim Yeado. He raped Jim's wife while the jeweler lay bleeding to death in the next room. No, I don't think Thomas White Hawk's sentence should be changed to life imprisonment, and I am speaking for 90% of the people of South Dakota.
>
> Have the people who are working so desperately for Thomas White Hawk ever said, "If you give

us Thomas White Hawk's life, we will give him to you to put into prison until his death?" No, they are asking for life imprisonment, and life imprisonment means he has a chance of parole after a few years. If Thomas White Hawk were to ever go free, it would not be hard for him to get another .22 automatic rifle, another skillet, and another butcher knife.

If Thomas White Hawk's sentence could ever be commuted to life imprisonment for the most senseless and brutal murder and rape ever committed in the history of South Dakota, then I see no reason for legislators or any civic-minded organization to waste their time trying to get capital punishment abolished. In my judgment it will already have been abolished. No criminal will ever have to worry about capital punishment, whatever his crime might be.

Manny Marshall

Vermillion, S.D.

Manny's letter left all of us feeling Tom was as good as dead.

And then, another shift in the South Dakota wind. In January, after Frank Farrar, the new governor, was sworn in, Jerry received a phone call from Farrar's chief of staff. He wanted a copy of Jerry's White Hawk pamphlet. The staffer said the governor had received hundreds of letters regarding Tom's death sentence. Jerry assumed the letters were opposed to the execution, influenced by his pamphlet. Perhaps the governor was leaning in that direction. His interest in Jerry's article had to be a good sign. But there was no news forthcoming from the governor's office as the execution date grew nearer.

A week before the planned execution, I visited Tom. He had not heard from the governor and didn't expect to so late in the game. If the governor was going to commute his sentence, Tom concluded, he would have done so long ago rather than let him suffer through this agony. Tom seemed unshaken by his impending death, resolved to its inevitability and the extinction that followed. He did admit, though, that he listened—respectfully if not credibly—to the prison chaplain's message of Christian consolation, the afterlife hope.

Early on a Friday morning, three days before the scheduled execution on Monday, February 3, the warden approached Tom's cell, his eyes full of news, suppressing a smile.

"Thomas White Hawk, good morning. I have the distinct pleasure of informing you that Governor Farrar will be holding a press conference in Pierre at ten o'clock this morning, at which time he will announce that he has commuted your death sentence to life imprisonment."

Tom was shaving at the time, pulling a dull razor across his cheek in the dim light of his cell. He collapsed to his knees in relief.

The *Volante* ran a one-paragraph story on the governor's announcement, as did the *Plain Talk*. *The New York Times* published a three-column story, focusing on the Indian community's sense that Tom's death sentence was an act of racial revenge. Father Hubert called on the afternoon of the announcement, in case I hadn't already heard the news. He was beside himself with joy but said he and Deb agreed that a celebration of any kind would undermine the greater cause of abolishing the death penalty in South Dakota.

The SAEs hosted an exchange with the Thetas that night. Paul came home quite drunk, banging around in the kitchen looking for food. He came into my bedroom, sat on the end of the bed, and ate a piece of cold pizza while regaling me with his plans to start an advertising firm after graduation, plans that included me, he said, slurring his words. Bar talk, I thought. Paul never brought up the subject again.

Tom wrote a letter two months later, explaining how he felt when his execution was called off, how sweet the prospect of life in prison seemed at that moment. He asked me to come visit him soon. He had something he wanted to talk about.

The next week I drove the sixty miles to the penitentiary on a Tuesday afternoon. The sky was bright blue, promising spring, but the frozen fields were still in winter's dying grip, black clumps of dirt poking through the snow cover from a late March storm. I was thinking about Tom, about what his life would be like now. The governor had made it clear in his remarks before the commutation announcement that he would not consider a further reduction in Tom's sentence. He made a point of discouraging future governors from doing so too. Manny Marshall and others bitterly registered their disappointment in letters to the local newspapers, as if a life-in-prison sentence were time at a resort hotel in Puerto Vallarta. But there was a grain of truth in Marshall's complaint—as true now as then—that Tom had not only escaped extinction but also the sorrow and humiliation of his own people. For Marshall, it all came down to one basic fact. One had died, and so should the other.

Tom was late for my visit. He was breathing heavily, his T-shirt stained with half-circles of sweat under his arms. He wiped the sweat off his face with a red bandanna and looked at me, smiling.

"I'm out in the general population now. Just finished a basketball game. The skins were cellar-dwellers until I arrived. Now we're kicking ass," he said, and then pointed down at his expanding belly. "I need the exercise. Two hundred and twenty pounds. I vaulted at one seventy-five."

"Think you could still clear thirteen feet?"

"I do, most nights," he said, pausing, "in my dreams."

We talked for a few minutes about what it felt like to receive a last-minute reprieve. He was thankful for it, but each day he grew angrier at Farrar for waiting as long as he did. *The Indian kid must suffer a while longer.*

His Shattuck girlfriend continued to write, he said, and then he asked if I had seen Deb Hubert. She had still not visited him in prison.

"She and Father Hubert split up," I said. "I think she left town with someone closer to her age. Sheriff Wilson was thinking about charging Father with cradle-robbing until she left him."

Tom thought that was funny.

"Is Caitlin still around?" he asked.

"She left with her boyfriend. Look at us. Two lovesick teenagers," I said.

Tom grinned, appreciating the connection to a world that was slipping out of his grasp. We needed a red beer and a snooker table.

"She left for Texas. She and Harlan are working in a restaurant in Austin."

"I'll trade endings with you," he said and then got serious.

"I've been thinking about something that happened when I was growing up. My parents were still alive. We all, my mother and brothers and sisters, went to Rapid City one day. Dad had a job with a construction company in Rapid. He was on the job a week, and then he got fired, so we drove over to Rapid to pick him up and bring him home.

"Mom gave us all a bath before we left, in the same water, and it grew dirtier and colder with each kid. We tried to look the best we could in the clothes we wore every day. Mom called Uncle Charles, and he agreed to let Mom drive his car to pick up Dad and bring him home.

"When we got to Rapid, Mom decided she would treat us to lunch first, knowing Dad would never take us to a restaurant. We stopped at Tally's, downtown. It was my first time out of the rez and the first time I had eaten in a restaurant. I was maybe seven or eight years old.

"We sat in a booth with shiny red leather seats and one of those little jukeboxes on the table with the napkins and salt and pepper shakers. We weren't there a few minutes when another family, a white family, a mother and two kids about our ages, came in and sat in the booth across from us. The white kids were familiar with the restaurant, not awestruck like we were, and got to order for themselves, which they did without looking at the menu first. The youngest white kid, a girl, pointed at us like circus animals. But we were fascinated with them. They were so clean, clean like we'd never been, and dressed perfectly with new clothes, not the worn hand-me-downs we wore day in and day out.

"And then their orders came and they each had what they wanted. All we could afford was two hamburgers and an order of fries, for the whole table. I wanted to be them, that's how bad it gets. I was envious of them. I wanted to wake up in a warm house and a clean kitchen like those kids did and not have to worry about getting beat up or whether there would be enough to eat that day.

"We left Tally's and talked in hushed tones in the back seat of Uncle Charles's car, still in awe of what we had seen, and then picked up Dad. The mood changed immediately. He had his last check and cashed it on the way out of town, bought a case of beer. He had the first six down before we were out of town. By the time we were back on the rez, he was in a drunken rage. One of the kids let it slip that we had stopped for lunch at Tally's before picking him up, and he stopped and pulled Mom out the car and into the ditch, where he beat her with an old two-by-four in the trunk."

"Man, that is a sad story," I said.

"My stories always end sadly. You know that by now."

"Why are you thinking about that one now?"

"I have had a long time to think about things. About how I got here. It started with experiences like that, the shame and confusion over what I was. I understand that now—too late, but I understand it."

9

I graduated from the university in the spring of 1970, a year later than planned. The commencement ceremony was held on Inman Field, the university's football field, with the commencement stage set up in the west end zone. It was a warm spring day. The sky was clear of clouds, and the lawns overnight sprouted bright, undulating yellow beds of dandelions. My dad brought along his new Kodak Instamatic camera to take pictures. He enlisted another parent in the crowd to take our picture. I stood between Mom and Dad, taller than both, my long hair falling out the back of my mortarboard down to my shoulders, sunglasses on. Mom wore a dark-blue dress with a wide white buckle and had a pageboy haircut. Dad was in character, dressed as if he were on his way to the office: worsted wool gray suit, dark tie, and a black handkerchief in the coat pocket. To their credit, my parents had tolerated my erratic behavior, paid the additional tuition and living expenses with no patronizing lectures, and shown a genuine interest in Tom White Hawk's story. They contributed to the White Hawk defense fund; they were Episcopalians.

Moulting's successor, an Irish Catholic historian, handed out the diplomas. I crossed the stage to accept mine, the audience quiet until someone yelled, "Phi Alpha!" I was worried that might happen but surprised when I appreciated the cheer, even though whoever called it out wasn't serious. After the ceremony I told my parents I had a party to go to and they were free to return home. They were relieved. Dad was starting a new trial on Monday and needed the preparation time.

I found a job that summer working at the *Argus Leader*, covering business news. I romanticized the job in my eagerness to find work, in part misled by the editor who hired me. He implied I'd be writing *Wall Street Journal*–like analytical pieces, but those story assignments never materialized. My stories were nothing more than announcements for new businesses, expanding businesses, and bankrupt businesses, along with the occasional feature story, generally on a local family business. When I wasn't churning out these formula stories, I did whatever my editor asked me to do, mostly editing copy and answering the business desk phone.

And then my big break came. A story broke in the western part of the state, a murder involving an Indian man and a rancher with a familiar South Dakota political name. The rancher shot the Indian man during an argument, calling it self-defense. There were no witnesses. A coroner's jury cleared the rancher. The incident would have been forgotten if not for Norman Little Brave's widow, who pressured the Mellette County attorney to prosecute. One of the *Argus* editors decided to send a reporter to White River, where the trial would be held. I volunteered, offering my amateurish White Hawk stories as evidence of my expertise, and I got the assignment. It was the opportunity I had been waiting for, and it came gift-wrapped: the rancher's name was Baxter Berry, Courtland Berry's father.

10

I took the long route to White River, driving south through Vermillion and then west toward Pickstown, crossing the Missouri on the Fort Randall Dam. Deep ravines and draws crowded with scrub oak and cedar run along both sides of the Missouri. The turbines in the deep water below the dam churn furiously, turning the water into electricity. The landscape gradually changed as I drove west, fewer farm places—home, barn, equipment shed, and shelterbelt—and more rangeland. The rangeland was bordered with ragged fence, worn by cattle and wind. I reached Winner, about fifty miles from my destination, toward late evening. The town was a narrow strip on the distant western horizon, the only light in the sky. I checked into the Philips Hotel on Main Street.

Lee Goodwin, the proprietor, checked me in. Lee was a talkative and entertaining man with a rapid-fire, rat-a-tat banter and the body of a nose tackle. There was a restaurant and lounge at the back, with a Closed sign perched on a small stand at its entrance. Lee said he had closed the restaurant during World War II for lack of food staples and kitchen help and never reopened it. But he still kept a private stash in the bar, inviting me in for a drink when I told him I was a reporter here to cover the Berry trial.

Lee led me to the back and turned on the lights, cracking the old joke "How many Czechs does it take to change a light bulb?" The lounge was in pristine condition, a relic of dark-brown leather booths bordered with nail heads, cocktail tables, and a shiny bar that gleamed even in the dim light. Lee brought our drinks to the table, and we made small talk for a while. He confessed to being a politician, was in the South Dakota Senate, making Baxter Berry and Norman Little Brave his constituents.

"Are people talking much about the trial?" I asked.

"Right up there with what's on TV tonight."

"Do you know either one? Berry or Little Brave?"

"I know the Berry family quite well. Baxter's father, Tom, built a large ranch near Belvidere, some thirty thousand acres. A prince of a guy, and handsome as a movie star. He was governor in the late thirties, a difficult time in the state. His big mistake was the income tax. He signed a bill implementing one. Turned a lot of us into Republicans, including me."

"Did Baxter follow in his footsteps?"

"Baxter inherited the ranch when Tom died. He's spent most of his life living there, expanding the holdings, becoming a figure in cattle organizations. I think he leases a significant amount of rangeland from the Indians," Lee said, judgment sliding into his tone, a disappointment I couldn't pinpoint or define.

"He has a family, right?"

"One son and two daughters. Courtland is the son, and Diana and Peggy."

"Norman Little Brave?" I asked.

"I don't know him. He's a typical reservation Indian, from what I've heard."

"What do you make of it all?"

"Baxter's not easy to like or defend. This was some shameful business. No weapon on the Indian. Baxter didn't call the authorities for an hour or so after he shot him. And when the sheriff finally arrived, Baxter and two of his friends were out in the corral where the Indian was lying dead. They were just casually leaning up against a feed rack in the corral."

"Why didn't the sheriff arrest Baxter when he arrived?"

"You'll have to ask him that. I'm sure the lawyers will ask him at the trial."

"And the coroner's jury? Clearing him of the murder?"

"Again, ask the coroner. He didn't release the results of the inquest."

"How do you think this will end up?"

"Hard to say. As I said, there are no heroes in this situation. But it wouldn't be wise of me to go on the record, would it? Especially if it ended up in a newspaper story."

The next morning Lee, in a white starched shirt, brown tie, and cuff links, took me to a local café, where we ate breakfast. Several of the locals came up to our table to banter with Lee—"Mr. Republican," as he was known here in Winner. I left after breakfast and arrived in White River before noon, expecting the trial to last a few days, maybe a week.

Mellette County had built a new courthouse in 1965, a single-story, flat-roofed, plain-looking building that could easily be mistaken for a medical clinic or a small manufacturing plant. I took a seat in the courtroom near the front, where two other reporters were seated. The courtroom was filled in unequal measure, mostly white and some Indian, pitted on either side of the center aisle.

Courtland arrived late, in a western shirt and cowboy boots, his hair grown out slightly. The top half of his head, his forehead, was pale white, his face a dark tan. His two sisters and his mother were with him. Space had been reserved in the front row for the Berry family, closest thing to royalty in this county. Courtland was solicitous of his mother and sisters, making sure they were comfortably seated before he sat down. He turned back to the spectators then, casually inspecting the faces, and saw me in the press row. He got up and came over, surprising me with a welcoming smile.

"Peters, it's been a while. You stayed in journalism."

"I got the bug," I said.

"Court will adjourn before it gets too late this afternoon. Let's have a beer."

Baxter Berry's attorneys were two of the best criminal lawyers in the state, shrewd characters with a talent for spotting a weakness in a man or an argument. They both spoke in the colloquial language of the all-white jury, questioning relatives and friends of Norman Little Brave, trying to establish Norman as an unbalanced Indian who used peyote in his religious practices and harassed Berry over the years with his dogs and with stray rifle shots over Berry's head when Berry got too close to Norman's home. Who knows—it may have all been true or bullshit, but Norman wasn't there to explain himself.

The defense blamed the murder trial on "political do-gooderism" by people back east "who don't know anything about Indians." The tall, slightly stooped lawyer from Canton, Sam Masten, said Berry had been able to live with the Indians for sixty-three years, but he was "faced with a real threat." Berry's other lawyer said, "He only had one chance to defend himself, and that was with a gun. Otherwise, he'd have been another Yeado."

The lawyer let that sink in, pausing as if invoking a silent prayer. He returned to the defense table as the courtroom grew quieter.

The state's prosecutors questioned why Berry didn't run to his house when Little Brave arrived, rather than grabbing his pistol and holding his position at the corral gate. Berry pulled his pearl-handled .38 from the holster and waited for Little Brave to charge him, firing twice, watching Little Brave drop facedown into the March-cold mud and horse manure. The assistant attorney general from Pierre said Berry "showed the same remorse after shooting Little Brave as if he had shot an animal. The rancher didn't even look to see if Little Brave was still living." In conclusion, he told the jury, "the fact that Norman Little Brave was an Indian doesn't have a thing to do with this trial."

The judge adjourned the trial at four o'clock. The audience was dead quiet as they trailed out of the courtroom and gathered in small groups in front of the building. Courtland came over and said he was going to drive his mother and sisters back home but would come back and meet me at the Frontier Bar later.

Everyone in the Frontier knew Courtland. Polite greetings came from the tables filled with happy-hour patrons as he made his way toward my table. We shook hands. No fraternity grip.

"Craig, you look well. How are you?"

Courtland had never addressed me by my first name.

"I'm doing all right. How about you? Where are you living? You look like a rancher."

"That's because I am. I live here now."

A waitress arrived and took our orders, a tap beer for me, scotch and water for Courtland. Good Scotch too—Cutty Sark.

"I thought you wanted a career in the army. You were a lifer."

"I thought so too. I graduated and went through OCS and got a regular army appointment. Went to Vietnam and got in on the tail end of it. All I found there was futility, cynicism, broken lives. And drugs and alcohol just to get through each day. I put in two years—short of my commitment, but they let me resign my commission. The army was doing everything it could to shed junior officers as the war wound down. I knocked around a while and then came back here for good after Dad began to fall apart."

"I had no idea. Do you see any of the old SAE crowd?"

"Never. Those days are long gone. That's why today was so weird. Seeing you in the courtroom, and then our defense lawyer referring to Yeado and Tom White Hawk in his summation."

"What a coincidence. Are you sure he wasn't tipped off by an interested party?"

"I swear to God I didn't say anything to him. White Hawk grew up a few miles from here. People haven't forgotten."

Courtland set his Cutty down, the badass Courtland creeping back into his expression. "I've changed. Not as much as you might want, but I've changed some."

"Fair enough."

"The Yeado reference today. There's something I'd like to say about that time. I'm not proud of the way I handled myself. I see the whole situation a little differently now. Tom had a lot of pressure on him. He didn't have much to fall back on."

"That's big of you, Courtland. Why all the hate, though? Wasn't he like you in a lot of ways? West River guy. From the same neighborhood. Military background."

"You forgot about Shattuck. I applied to Shattuck a few years before Tom. I had good references and a prominent family, but they rejected my application. They never explained why, but it bothered me."

"Why didn't you just blackball him during rush? It would have saved you and him a lot of misery."

"What, and miss all the fun of pledge training? Humiliating him, riding him hard."

"You were an asshole."

"Like I said, I'm not proud of what I did."

Someone from across the room bought us a second round. Courtland went over to thank him and then returned to our table.

"It must be hard to watch this trial. Difficult for the family."

"We'll get through it, I suppose, but we've never been very close as a family. Dad was always distant. Depressed, I think."

"How do you suppose it will come out?"

"I hope you didn't travel all the way out here expecting a guilty verdict."

"I don't know what to expect. The prosecution made a powerful argument today."

"They did, but that's not how the jury looks at it. People out here, living close to the reservations, know the Indians got a raw deal. The problem is, we get tangled up in our daily lives and forget about context. That's for reporters and historians. I don't doubt Dad shot Little Brave when he could have handled it in a way that didn't end up with a dead Indian. But in that moment, the two of them, Little Brave coming at him, he had a right to defend himself. Should he have done more for Little Brave once he was on the ground? Of course. But that's not what Dad's being tried for."

The next morning at 11:00 a.m., the crowd filled the courtroom, everyone in the same seats. The judge gave the jury instructions, and they retired, emerging two and one-half hours later. Norman Little Brave's wife was sitting in the front, in the same upright position the entire time, dignified, showing little emotion. The jury foreman rose and read the verdict: not guilty.

11

I became the guy who wrote the Indian stories for the *Argus* in the 1970s. The editors, in a self-congratulatory gesture, replaced *Indian* with the term *Native American* in the paper's text, announcing it as if they were making amends for the broken promises of the 1868 treaty. The paper's coverage was still reactionary; that is, the stories were invariably about some protest or civil disobedience of one sort or another, usually led or inspired by a member of the American Indian Movement. It seemed that Natives only merited a story when they were threatening a white man's property rights or challenging his perception of frontier history.

The AIM leaders—Dennis Banks, Clyde and Vernon Bellecourt, Russell Means, Carter Camp—were an intimidating bunch, handsome warriors dressed in western shirts, wide-brimmed hats, and bone chokers, with feathers in their braided hair. The zeitgeist took a dramatic turn left, leaving Tom White Hawk, once the image of the "good Indian" in the eyes of white and Indian cultures, an anachronism. Whenever I asked an AIM leader about why they had not taken up Tom's cause, the response was usually sympathetic but skeptical that his plight had any political value—Tom was a head case, too fucking crazy and too old school to turn into a martyr. They didn't find Tom sympathetic enough, I guess, not the kind of injustice they could shout about in front of the television cameras.

The Alcatraz sit-in, the protest over Raymond Yellow Thunder's murder, the Trail of Broken Treaties march, and the Wounded Knee occupation all raised the national profile of AIM. In South Dakota the spark that inflamed passion and fear was a violent confrontation between AIM and law enforcement at the arraignment of Darald Schmitz. Schmitz had stabbed Wesley Bad Heart Bull in the chest outside Bill's Bar in Rapid City. AIM supporters drove through a snowstorm from Rapid to the Custer County courthouse, where the arraignment was to take place. When they arrived, they were met by local, county, and state law enforcement officers armed to the teeth. The county attorney told the AIM group no one would be admitted into the courtroom, despite the fact that there was room for everyone. He eventually changed his mind after some heated discussions and agreed to allow Ramon Roubideaux, Willie Stands's lawyer; Russell Means; Leonard Crow Dog; Dave Hill; and Dennis Banks into the courtroom. Sarah Bad Heart Bull, Wesley's mother, was refused entry. Fights ensued—tear gas thrown into the surging crowd, the nearby chamber of commerce offices burned down, the courthouse set afire, and a Texaco station's windows smashed in.

South Dakota freaked out.

Twenty-two people were arrested that day. Sarah Bad Heart Bull was tried for riot with arson and sentenced to five years. She ended up serving five months. Darald Schmitz was acquitted by an all-white jury and never served a day behind bars. Two years later, Dennis Banks was tried for riot and assault charges stemming from the same incident. Bill Janklow, who strangely enough began his career as a legal aid attorney on the Rosebud Reservation, prosecuted Banks.

Janklow was ambitious and colorful, a loudmouth Indian fighter. He ran for attorney general and won, capitalizing on the racial tension running high in the state. Janklow fortified the courthouse during the Banks trial as if the Indians were circling the fort. He acted out during the trial, petulant when he didn't get his way, gloating when he did, the highest law enforcement officer in the state behaving like a teenager. In the end, Banks was found guilty and ordered to report to prison in two weeks. Janklow was pissed, knowing Banks would flee, but the judge held fast. Banks fled, of course, but that turned out to be a gift for Janklow, who spent the next several years on an unsuccessful attempt to extradite Banks from California, solidifying his political stock and ego with every story the *Argus* carried on the subject.

Janklow knew he had a winning formula in demonizing AIM and a gift for expressing the fear and paranoia in white hearts. He may never have actually said it, but it worked in his favor when most voters thought he said "the only good Indian is a dead Indian." He played the AIM fear card with great skill, becoming governor in 1978 and in the process dealing Tom White Hawk another bad hand.

In late 1979 I was writing one of the many Janklow stories that appeared in the *Argus* over the years. I was disappointed, however, with the direction my editor wanted me to take the piece in and was back in my cubicle pouting. The newsroom receptionist made her way over, a pink telephone message in her hand.

"Hey, bawl-baby, you can write about it in your first book. Back to work now," she said, handing me the message. Jerry Vincent had called, asking me to call him back as soon as possible. I called, expecting bad news, but it wasn't. He and Gary Hamill were coming to town the next day. They had a meeting with Tom. They were working on an application to the parole board, hoping the board would hear Tom's request for a reduction in his life sentence. Would I meet them at the penitentiary the next morning? They had scheduled a two-hour visit with Tom.

Jerry Vincent had not aged a day, with his smooth, light-brown skin and black hair, dressed smartly in a tweed sport coat and black wool slacks. Gary was aging and looked anemic, with a few wisps of hair combed over his balding head. His mind was still razor sharp, though, and his humor keen. He teased Jerry about his new look, wondering why Indian men were always better dressed than their wealthier white brothers.

I asked them before we went back to see Tom why they thought the parole board would reduce his life sentence. The governor who had commuted Tom's sentence, Frank Farrar, had retreated from the sympathetic comments he made before commuting Tom's sentence. In a subsequent newspaper interview, Farrar had said, "For the crime that he committed, he should have died. There would have been an uprising if I hadn't commuted his sentence. I spared his life to save others."

"Farrar's not going to be any help, and we're sure not going to ask him for it. But he's been out of office for a long time now, and the people on the parole board were appointed by different governors," Hamill said.

"And you think the new governor will be any better? He's a new generation of Indian fighter," I said. "Ask AIM."

"Bill Janklow was a legal aid lawyer on the Rosebud before he became governor. He knows what conditions Tom grew up in," Hamill said. "And he's unpredictable. Doesn't like to be told how to think about an issue."

"AIM hasn't done a thing to help Tom. Janklow would love to shove that down their throats," Jerry said, grinning.

Security was much tighter at the penitentiary this time around. We marched through a metal detector, the machine's alarm triggered by Jerry's chrome-and-pearl-handled jackknife, and were frisked before we were allowed into the visitation room. A lone artificial Christmas tree with a white blanket wrapped around the base stood in one corner. The open area where visitors and prisoners sat around tables was divided into individual stations, with dividers for additional privacy. The prisoners now sat on one side of the station behind a plexiglass barrier.

Tom was waiting for us. He had grown enormously fat. His tattoos ballooned on huge forearms. Tomahawk must have weighed three hundred pounds. His hair was pulled back in a ponytail, falling down his back. As we were sitting down, he apologized for the smoke smell on his clothes. He was the new fire keeper for the Inipi, the prison's sweat lodge. He had built a fire that morning for a sweat scheduled later in the afternoon. He spoke softly, as he always did, his words hardly audible in the din of the visitation room, where the voices of prisoners and visitors echoed off the tile floor.

"It's good to see you, my friends," he said. "It's been too long."

"How have you been?" Jerry asked.

"Getting by. We have a library now, a good one. It has lots of books. The prison chaplain, Martin, brings me some too, mostly on Native religions. I'm up for a furlough. Going to visit Crow Dog's Paradise for a Sun Dance on the Rosebud. I haven't been home in a long while."

"Has anyone else been visiting?" Jerry asked. I knew he was curious about who was and who was not still interested in Tom and his fate.

"People on the inside. The chaplain, the teachers in the prison high school, Warden Salem. That's my social group," he said, smiling wryly.

We were quiet for a moment, and then he continued. "Arnie Wilson came to see me. He wanted to see how I was, whether I needed anything. I haven't seen Father Hubert."

"What about Phil Zolbach?" I blurted out. "What happened to him?"

"Phil came by in the first few years but then stopped coming. I guess I got too old and too fat," he said, pausing for our reaction. "The chaplain knows Phil. He told me he's working for the Boy Scouts in Minneapolis now. I wish him well. He thought he was doing the right thing."

"Have you seen Willie? Is he still here in prison?" Jerry asked.

"Once. Long time ago. He's out now. We didn't talk much. You know Willie. I blame him sometimes. He could have saved me if he had been stronger."

"We don't have much time, Tom. We'd better get started."

Hamill carefully outlined the arguments he recommended Tom use in his parole board application. Tom was engaged, asking several questions, employing legal terms I had never heard him use before. He said the other inmates consulted with him daily. He had become a jailhouse lawyer.

When it came time to leave, we all rose, not knowing quite how to say goodbye. Tom had a stack of papers, what looked like newsprint, in his hands. He turned to the guards and asked permission to give one to each of us. The guard nodded permission. Tom handed us a prison literary publication. Inside it were several poems and a short story about UFOs that he had written. We all promised to read his work and send our comments.

In the parking lot, I shook hands with my two friends. Gary knew what he was up against, expecting the board to be deeply skeptical, but he said he would do his best. He was retiring soon. This was his last piece of unfinished business.

I waved to them as they drove out, the cold air chilling me, fooled by the sun; it was all light and no warmth, reflecting off the pink-and-white quartzite walls of the prison. I was back in the newspaper offices a few minutes later but didn't get much work done. I read Tom's story and poems. They weren't very good, too self-consciously literary, a waste of talent. I cried then, wiped the tears, and went home for the day.

The board denied Tom's request, voting 5–0 against him. You didn't get on the board without a belief in the value of punishment. I thought Janklow had something to do with that vote, not wanting to have to deal with it if the board voted favorably, but I could be wrong about that.

ALL HIS RELATIVES

1

I received a message from Warden Salem that Tom wanted to see me the same week the parole board's decision was announced. I rescheduled some interviews and drove up to the prison that afternoon.

Tom was already in the visitors' room, playing a card game with a guard, when I arrived. He looked up without recognition in his eyes as I approached the table where he was sitting. His back was to a window, the natural light illuminating the space. The guard picked up the cards and left us. Tom was distracted; something was on his mind.

"Are you my friend?" he asked, his thin lips pinched shut.

"Of course," I said, surprised he'd ask such a question.

"It's in your power to free me. I want to walk with my relatives."

"Come on, be serious."

"I am very serious. Please, friend, it must be you."

"What is it I must do, then?"

"Read this," he said, handing me a spiral-bound notebook, its blue cover wrinkled with wear, the right-hand corners frayed and curling. He'd torn out many of the pages; the spine clogged with ragged strips. I leaned back in my chair and read his graceful, boarding school handwriting on the lined paper. It was his version of what had happened that warm morning in March.

When I finished, the man responsible for the horror in the story I had just read was so close I could touch him, hear his labored breath, smell the cigarette smoke on his clothes. I stood up and glanced at him. He had turned sideways, looking out the window onto the snow-covered prison yard at the pale December sun retreating in the western sky.

Turning to leave, I looked back at him. He thrust the notebook at me. "Take it," he said. "It's over now."

Writing his story had freed Tom. The truth, or what he thought was the truth, had ended his journey. I could see the transformation, the guilt and shame falling like scales off his eyes, as the Bible says. I left the visitation room, ignoring the guard's friendly nod, and walked out of the building without returning my visitor's badge to the security office. Release arrived that day for Tom, confusion and doubt for me. A zero-sum game.

2

I was troubled for months about what Tom wrote in that note-book, obsessing about the Yeados, the victims I had ignored in my zeal to expose the larger tragedy. I couldn't get the image out of my head of their bodies in the beds, one lying shot and bleeding to death, the other bound and gagged, while the boys debated what to do next, lounging in the living room downstairs. Would I have so ignored the Yeados' suffering if it had been my parents or relatives or friends? Would I have dismissed their agony in service of my ambition to be seen as a confidant of the killer? What of the Yeado children, who sent their father's body to Oregon to be buried, after he had lived in Vermillion for thirty years, raising a family, attending Mass each day, repairing keepsakes for the church ladies, and selling diamond rings to brides? What of Mrs. Yeado, who followed her dead husband to Oregon, selling everything before she left—the jewelry store, the inventory, her entire household and furniture, even her precious table china—in an auction that summer on her front lawn? Why had I ignored her humiliation and shame? Why were they the ones standing in the path of Tom's madness? Why had I chosen the deranged over the gentle?

I stayed on at the *Argus,* working the same statewide beat, but the real action was back on the business desk. South Dakota removed all restrictions on interest rates, attracting banking giant Citibank, which opened a credit card processing center in

Sioux Falls. The Citibank development spurred the retail and real estate markets, and soon enough Sioux Falls was a spiffy, sparkling commercial land of Oz. Trophy wives drove SUVs to Dayton's in the mall, where they bought Wolfgang Puck dishware and Saint Laurent bed linens. The rush for the perfect family, the big beige house, the jumbo mortgage, Pottery Barn interiors, three-car garages, Cozumel vacations, and multiple shiny credit cards was the point of it all. I played the game as well, the narcotic of possessions dulling the passage of time.

And then a familiar voice, Warden Salem, at the other end of a call late one afternoon in May 1997 while I was at work. The warden had been retired for several years but was still close to the penitentiary staff. They'd called him the previous evening shortly after Tom White Hawk had fallen to the floor of his cell, clutching his chest, dying a few hours later. The warden remembered that Tom and I were close.

"That man spent thirty years in prison," the warden said. "There wasn't a single undignified moment in all those years. Sure, he kept to himself, and he turned a little nutty in the end, sending that three-hundred-page treatise on the death penalty to the governor. You remember that. Seems to me you wrote a story about it in the paper. Janklow called me soon after and told me to throw away the key. Well, anyway, Tom hadn't been that sick boy who murdered a jeweler for a long time, but a judge and governor thought they knew otherwise. A waste. A shameful waste."

I thanked the warden for calling. I asked him how he was getting on in retirement and listened to a few of his memories of Tom in prison. He had a gift for narrative, building a story around a memory or a telling detail, stopping occasionally to release the emotion that gushes to the surface in old age, without embarrassment. I let him go on for as long as his memories lasted, ignoring an impending story deadline. The warden's Tom White Hawk was neither a symbol nor a psychotic; he was a boy and then a man who slept in a cell each night for thirty years, overpaying for an act he didn't intend or understand.

The next day, two more calls. The first was Gary Hamill, a weak, shaky voice on the other end of the line. Gary had fully retired. When he saw Tom's obituary in the *Minneapolis Tribune*, he tried to contact Jerry, who had moved to California and was on the faculty at UC Berkeley. So far he hadn't had any luck finding him.

"Even if I do," Gary said, "he's in California. I doubt he'll make it back for the funeral. That leaves you and me. Are you going?"

"Of course," I said.

"Happy to hear that. This old battleship needs your help. I can't drive the entire distance to the reservation. I'll drive as far as Sioux Falls and then hitch a ride with you. The funeral is at three o'clock on Saturday. What time should we leave?"

I couldn't say no to Gary. I gave him directions to my apartment.

The prison chaplain called and told me that Tom hadn't left a formal will or last testament, but he found a letter addressed "To Whom It May Concern" in Tom's footlocker, asking that he be buried on the Rosebud and that I be one of the pallbearers. Something opened up in me with that news. I saw the Indian boy again, standing alone in a room full of SAEs, near the fireplace, ignored in the rush to pledge those who most resembled themselves. The SAEs had ended up doing the right thing, though. They didn't know what was germinating in that beautiful boy standing alone, profoundly lost in the heart of white man's country.

I asked for a few days off after the funeral. I had some unfinished business. Having Gary along would make it easier. He always saw both sides of an issue: the temperament of a judge though a trial lawyer himself.

3

Saturday morning I was standing on the sidewalk outside our apartment when Gary pulled into a parking space. He arrived in a new car, an oyster-gray Volvo station wagon. I expected him to slowly pry himself out of the car, bent and stiff from the drive, but he slid out, easily stepped over the curb, and strode toward me, his hand thrust out to shake mine. He anticipated my surprise.

"Retirement's been good for me. I'm eating better, exercising, sleeping late," he said. "But the golf game is still pathetic."

"I didn't know you played golf."

"I don't."

"After the phone call, I didn't know what to expect. You sounded feeble."

"You don't say," the old coyote said, smiling. "A bad day, perhaps. We all have them. I'll need some strong coffee before we hit the road."

We left soon after. It was a glorious May morning, with the birds chirping their mating calls and the smell of freshly turned earth rising from the fields west of Sioux Falls sweetening the air.

The drive to the reservation would take about four hours. I drove well over the speed limit once we crossed the big bridge at Chamberlain. The prairie grasses were still brown, not the vivid green their city cousins were already sporting, juiced on a steady diet of fertilizer and regular watering. A few miles west of the Missouri bluffs, the prairie flattened, heaving like a sheet in the wind, becoming mile after mile of monotony until the turn off I-90 toward Highway 83 south, toward Mission and the town of Rosebud.

As we left the I-90 interchange, Gary woke from a nap he had been taking since Chamberlain.

"Had you seen much of Tom over the years?" he asked.

"Not as much. I tried to make it once or twice a year, usually around the holidays, although Tom never seemed to be much affected by them. He didn't have a store of happy holiday memories to depress him. The last time I saw him was around Christmas. He was applying for a furlough so that he could participate in another Sun Dance at Crow Dog's Paradise. He wanted to dance this time, and maybe do the piercing."

"I didn't know the prison granted furloughs. I'm happy to hear that. I'm sure it gave him something to look forward to. How was he holding up? I always feel guilty when I lose touch with clients I care about."

"There were visits when he was distant. He could be rude and offensive without saying a word. But most of the time he would open up and talk about his current interest, whatever that might be. He was curious but would grow bored with something once he had mastered it or had read everything there was to know about it. You know about the book-length piece he wrote on the death penalty, of course. I have a copy. It's full of quirky scholarship and paranoia, but an incredible feat of scholarship given the limited resources of the prison library. But that phase didn't last long. He was heavy into Indian and Eastern religions the last time I saw him."

"Did he ever show any remorse?"

"He did, but not in the way we're accustomed. I spent a long time second-guessing what I had done—you know, taking his side and ignoring the grief on the other side. The Yeados were the victims, but I looked the other way. So did Jerry. Maybe you did too."

"Standing for the rights of a murderer doesn't mean you lack empathy for his victims, if that's what you are talking about."

"Yeah, I'm talking about that, but also about a path of destruction out of proportion to what Tom had suffered in his life. I don't dismiss his background, but how many lives had to be destroyed because his was so fucked up?"

It took us an hour or so, but we finally found the cemetery, on a steep rise just below where the Ponderosa tree line began. Crow Dog's Paradise was a short distance down the road, where Tom would have danced that summer.

I thought we might be late, but I should have known better. We were the first to arrive.

When everyone had gathered at the grave site, an elder said a few words, welcoming Tom back to his relations. In Lakota belief, a person roams the earth forever unless they have a ceremony. We lowered Tom in his prison-issued casket into the hole that had been dug for him. The ropes slipped on one side halfway down, returning Tom to Mother Earth in a quick slide and triggering laughter and a gentle teasing of the pallbearer with the slippery hands.

The sound of the casket thudding on the ground gave death's final shape to Tom's life, a brilliant flame extinguished early, with maddening sadness at the close. The mourners watched the pallbearers shovel dirt over him, silencing forever Tom's soft voice. I was sweating in the warm May sun by the time we were finished.

Gary had taken off his suitcoat and was sitting in a folding chair a few feet from the burial site, all bold red suspenders against a white dress shirt and dark-blue tie. The mourners sensed something kindred in Gary, asking how he knew Tom, thanking him when they discovered what he had done to help him.

We stayed a few hours after the funeral, ate a meal with the mourners, and then got back in my car. Once we were back on the road, Gary asked that we drive to Pierre first and spend some time at the state archives. He wanted to read the letters sent to Governor Farrar, the letters regarding Tom's death sentence. I knew what he was up to.

"We can do that, but you'll have to agree to one more stop," I said.

"Where's that?"

"Vermillion."

"Sure," he said, surprised by the proposal. "Why Vermillion?"

"Another witness, counselor, this time for the people."

Gary was silent while I drove east on I-90, a ribbon of concrete running unobstructed into the horizon ahead of us. The prairie wind was surging from the west at our back, the stronger gusts making it seem as if the car were hydroplaning on a wet surface.

Gary wanted to smoke his pipe.

"Crack the window open," I said.

"What did Tom think of you?" he asked as he stuffed the tobacco strands into the bowl of his pipe.

"What do you mean?"

"He knew many people during the stops in his life. Family, boarding school, Shattuck, jail, prison. You knew many of them. Where did you stand in that cast of characters?"

"There was a time when I thought Tom and I were psychically dependent. He was many things I wanted to be. And I was, or thought I was, something he wanted to be. I loved him like a brother, strangely enough, after the crime. And now that he's dead, I feel that love again. Hard to look at the casket and not feel it today. But I came to understand a while ago that the people in Tom's life—the people who cared for him at the Hare Home, his friends at Shattuck, the clergy, Zolbach, Willie, the Huberts, Jerry, you, me—were all protection he bought with his beauty and grace, his sensitivity, his great promise."

"Protection from what?" Gary asked.

"I don't know. You read the psychiatrist's report. I don't think he had it quite figured out either."

We arrived late in the evening and checked into a Days Inn in Pierre. The state archives, we discovered, are closed on Sunday, and so we spent most of the rainy and weirdly cold next day in our respective rooms. I had brought work with me and concentrated on it, occasionally leaving my room for the still-warm chocolate chip cookies the Days Inn management set out in the dining area. There were no restaurants open on Sunday in Pierre when the legislature wasn't in session. We ate dinner at a Burger King.

The next morning we drove up to the state archives, a new, ecologically sensitive building tucked into a high bluff above Hilger's Gulch in the capitol complex. The letters written to Governor Farrar regarding Tom White Hawk's crime and punishment were stored in temperature-controlled vaults. We spent the morning reading them, sitting across from each other at a round table in the archives reading room. The letters became predictable, the arguments repetitive, after the first few readings. Whether for or against the death sentence, they cited deterrence, humanity, and the Bible as the basis of their arguments. A large majority were against the death penalty and in favor of a sentence reduction.

The tone of the letters was distinctly different. The anti-death-penalty letter writers knew the issue better, were rational, and were frustrated that their point of view was not universally accepted. The pro-death-penalty letters were filled with high emotion, most of it sincere, some of it Biblical righteousness they quoted from some pamphlet they had found on the subject. I was surprised to discover I knew one of the letter writers. He was a high school friend who was an undergraduate at UC Berkeley when he wrote his letter. He wrote that "an eye for an eye makes the whole world blind" and signed his name with the title "A Philosophy Student." I made a copy and sent it to him. He sent me an email a few days after receiving it, thanking me. He said he had plagiarized it from Gandhi but subscribed to the philosophy.

Leaving Pierre, we drove east again on I-90 and then south to Vermillion. I found Fred Barton's name and address online. Fred was no longer working in the mechanic's shop across from the courthouse. The address was an assisted living center on the east end of town. He would be close to ninety. I wanted to see him, though not to convince him that Tom was a victim of circumstances or that forgiveness would set Barton free of the bitter prison he lived in. I wanted him to know that he had a right to his anger and that those of us who worked for justice in Tom's case also understood the depth of his suffering. That may be the only consolation he needed, I thought. He deserved as much.

Gary was a good sport about it. He came in with me but asked that I identify him as a friend, not the man who had worked to release Tom from prison. No reason to upset the old man. We stood at the front desk, waiting for the aide to return from Fred's room, where she had gone to ask if he would see us. The aide, young but with defeat already in her eyes, her hair flat and tied in a bun, said Fred would see us. We followed the aide, her body already laboring under a bad diet and no exercise though she couldn't be thirty years old, down the hall-way to Fred's room.

Fred was sitting in a chair, holding a lunch tray on his lap. He had eaten very little of the food. The aide took the tray and left us alone with him.

"Do you remember me, Mr. Barton? Craig Peters. We sat in chairs on the driveway outside your mechanic's shop once, facing east toward the courthouse, watching people go in and out of the jail entrance."

"I've forgotten a lot, you know. The aide said something about Jim Yeado. Did we talk about Jim?" he asked, curious now, perking up. A few strands of hair were combed over his bare head, which was covered with liver spots. The place was too warm. The windows were fogged up with the nursing home's humid air.

"We did. I was writing a story about Mr. Yeado. We talked about him and the murderer."

"If only the Lord would spare me that memory."

"Tom White Hawk died the other day. Did you know that?"

"My daughter, Ellie, told me. My wife, she's gone," he said, pausing, trying to remember something. "Right to the end, that Indian boy was made out to be some kind of hero. Ellie said the newspapers ran long stories about him being a model prisoner and writing poetry and practicing Indian religion and all. Nothing about the man he killed in cold blood. What kind of justice is that?"

"That's why I came by, Mr. Barton. You have a right to those sentiments. I'm not here to talk you out of them."

"I feel the same about that murderer now as I did back then," he said, "and that's all I'm going to say."

We were back in the car and had driven several miles before Gary broke the silence.

"You don't really believe that, do you? That Barton's better off with the anger?"

"I didn't say that. I said he had a right to it. Big difference."

"You don't think forgiving Tom would be better for him?"

"Maybe. But forgiveness is a lie if one doesn't feel it. Fred knows that."

"The question was never who did it or whether the act itself was cruel. The question was why? That's what Jerry Vincent taught us. The war against the Lakota was a deliberate genocide. There weren't supposed to be any survivors. When some did survive, they were disinherited and put on reservations, fed and clothed and medically cared for but always with resentment and after some of the benefit had been skimmed off for the deliverer. Tom was one of those survivors. We didn't realize how damaged they were. We usually don't know until it's too late," he said.

"Tom's sins were greater than the misery he was raised in. He was a symbol but could have been so much more, a reconciling force, and in that sense, he betrayed his people. I know it's fucked up, but I can't seem to forgive him for that." I said.

We were silent for the last half hour of the trip, arriving at my apartment midafternoon. We—I was on my second marriage, this time for love, the first having been for ambition—lived in a historic department store building on Philips Avenue that had been converted into apartments. My editor had introduced me to Zoe, a new reporter then. Her long red hair, ivory skin, and reserved eastern cool had rocked the mostly male newsroom. She wrote like an angel, and when she showed interest in me, I fell hard. We married a year later.

Zoe was at work at the *Argus* when we arrived. Our apartment was empty. I helped Gary with his luggage, transferring it to the trunk of his car. Gary closed the trunk softly, not hard enough for it to catch, and opened and shut it again with greater force. The look on his face told me something was left undone, and he wouldn't leave without attending to it.

"There's something I've been meaning to ask you. The reason I wanted to ride with you to the funeral. What happened that day in the Yeado home? Tom was never clear about it, always vague and anxious to change the subject. I think he told you. Do you mind talking about it?"

"Let's go inside," I said. "I'll make some coffee."

We sat across from each other at the kitchen island. Gary, whose patient style had always set Jerry off, drank from his coffee cup and waited for me to begin. I had the impression he had waited a long time to hear this and was willing to wait a few more minutes if need be.

"I was tempted to ask many times but never found the right moment. It's not something you ask about to fill up the time, you know? After the parole board turned him down for the last time, he asked to see me. I went up there the same week. I thought he needed someone to talk to. He knew he was never getting out," I said.

"What did he say?"

"I should have known, but he wasn't feeling sorry for himself. He didn't bring up the fact that the parole board had closed the door to his freedom. He had a notebook in his hands. He handed it to me and told me to read what he had written in it."

"What was in it?" Gary asked.

"Here it is," I said, holding the notebook up and then pushing it across the smooth granite finish on the island. "Read it for yourself. There are quite a few different Toms. The one who wrote this confession is the editor of the prison literary magazine."

I pointed toward the living room. "Take a chair. The leather one is comfortable. It won't take long to read. A whole lot longer to forget."

On My Return
by Tom White Hawk

A long time ago, young Lakota men would go on a zuya, a journey. A zuya may last many days, months, or even years. They returned changed men after their many experiences in the world. They were more mature and ready to become responsible members of their tiospaye. If a young man had killed someone on his journey, they painted his face and took him to a sweat to cleanse him before he was admitted back into his tiospaye.

Tom White Hawk has returned from his long zuya in the white world of boarding schools, churches, and prison. He wishes to return to his relatives. He has taken a life during this journey. To cleanse that stain, he has written this record of the events of March 24, 1967.

Tom White Hawk is not proud of what he has done. He disgraced himself and his people. But he has paid a steep price and now asks that he be allowed to return to his tiospaye.

My Story

Why did I do it? I needed money for my wedding with Dottie and a lot of other things. I didn't intend on killing or raping anyone. We were two desperate Indian kids. But something took hold of me once we got to the house. It was like I was in a mirror box, watching myself and Willie in multiple images doing things that we never wanted or intended to do, sucked into a nightmare.

Dottie and I had a big fight that afternoon. I left Willie in the student union and went over to her auntie's place where she was staying. I hadn't seen her in several days. She was studying, in a serious mood, and wasn't interested in even kissing me. I asked her if she had another boyfriend and was maybe fucking him. That led to the fight. She told me I needed to grow up or something stupid like that, and I left but not before telling her that I was having second thoughts about getting married. I didn't really mean that, but I knew it would shake her up. I was really upset too and felt like hitting someone. I wanted to get in a fight, get hurt.

There was a weight room in Julian, down in the basement, old free weights and padded gym blankets on the floor. I went there after the fight and lifted for a while, getting some of the frustration out of my system. I took a shower and went back over to the union and found Willie with two other Indians from the Wapaha Club. I told Willie I was going down to Thorsten's, and he jumped up like a dog happy to hear it was going on a walk.

We played a lot of pool at Thorsten's that night. I let Willie win a few to keep him playing, drinking beer until they closed. Thorsten's closes at midnight, so we bought four quarts of Grain Belt in the big clear bottles to take with us. We both knew why we would need the beer but didn't talk about it. Leaving the bar, we started walking down the sidewalk and then stopped outside the jewelry store, which is right next to Thorsten's on Main Street. Willie peeked in through the large window at the display cases, which were dark but full of valuable jewelry pieces. I panicked for a second, worried that someone would see Willie looking in and maybe put two and two together after the robbery. But nobody was on the street. I looked in too. The safe was easy to see beyond the display cases at the far end.

I had to see Dottie again. I wanted to make up with her, and I was feeling very affectionate, thinking maybe something could happen. Dottie's auntie didn't like me much. She saw my tattoos, and nothing I said or did would change her mind after that. She was a boarding school grad too, Holy Rosary, but she bought all the propaganda and lived like a white. People who read this may be surprised to hear me say it, but

I was quite aware that I was being held up as
a model Indian, an Indian white people could
live with. It was all I knew. By the time I went to
college, that wasn't who I was, but that was what
people still wanted me to be.

Dottie and her auntie had bedrooms on the second floor. When we got to her place, I threw a
couple of dirt clods against her window to wake
her. She came down right away. She stood with
her arms crossed in her nightgown, staring at us
like we were two naughty kids, and I suppose we
were, swaying and slurring our words, drunk on
the beer we'd been drinking. I told Dottie I loved
her and apologized for what I said earlier that
afternoon. I really did love her. We had talked
many times about getting married that summer.
But we had a problem. We needed money, and
Willie and I were about to take care of that. I was
drunk and in my drunken logic thought Dottie
should appreciate that fact, but of course she
didn't know what was up. I put my arm around
her and tried to kiss her, but she pushed me
away and said I was pathetic. We got into another
fight, the kind where I explode inside and want
to hurt myself or somebody else. Dottie went
inside and locked the front door.

We could hear the lock turn, it was so quiet out.
And then I remembered the rifle. I ran up to
the door and knocked softly. She asked what
I wanted through the door, and I told her the

rifle. Phil had dropped off the rifle, my trusty old .22-caliber Winchester with a scope, the day before, and I had taken it over to Dottie's because I couldn't keep it in the dorm. I was going to show Dottie how to shoot the rifle and hunt with it. Phil showed me how to aim it using the scope. He wrapped his arms around me when I was aiming it, his lips brushing my neck, and patiently explained where to locate the crosshairs on the target, how to slowly pull the trigger. Writing about that rifle brings up a lot of memories, all bad.

Dottie opened the door and handed me the rifle. How stupid was it to give me that rifle after midnight, all drunked up? What could we possibly be doing with it at that time of the night?

When we got back to Julian, we went to my room. My roommates were gone, home on Easter vacation. I tried to sleep, but I was too hopped up, thinking about what we were going to do and about a lot of other things, mostly things that weren't going my way. I was depressed a lot in those days, a groove I couldn't climb out of. I'd felt like that before, but I always came out of it and felt better. I was locked into my obsessions, how certain people had made me what I was and I couldn't do anything about it anymore.

About five in the morning, I woke Willie up. He didn't want to get out of bed. I told him it was

time to go and then had to pull him out of bed.
At his trial, Willie tried to tell the judge and jury
he didn't know what we were about to do, but
he made that story up to save his own skin. He
knew what was going down. What did he think
we were about to do, go to church? We left Julian
and walked back to the construction site where
we hid the rifle and beer. Very warm for that
time of the year, and foggy. We walked down the
center of the street, shrouded in the fog. When
we got to the construction site, I chugged a quart
of the beer. I took a few phenobarbital pills. I
had a big-ass headache.

We didn't talk much. Willie was the original silent tongue, until he got on the stand, and then
he lied and repeated all the big words his lawyer stuffed into his head. I took a few big swigs
from my second quart, and then we left for the
jeweler's home, carrying the last two quarts of
beer and the rifle.

We walked down Dakota Street to Main and
kept going down the bluff to lower Vermillion,
following the low road that runs by the sewage
treatment pond, shooting bottles and cans in the
ditch. At University Street, we turned back up the
bluff. There were nice homes along both sides
of the street, one of them the jeweler's home.

We stood on the jeweler's front lawn, thinking about what to do next. I stared for a long

time at two trimmed evergreen trees, tall cones looking like guards protecting the entrance of their house. I guess that's when the hallucinations started, the feeling that I was in a mirror box with images moving in and out, especially my peripheral sight. Willie grabbed me by the shoulder and shook me, breaking the spell. He was getting nervous, asking me questions about the plan, as if I had drawn it up on the back of an envelope and knew exactly what to do next.

I didn't know, but I pretended like I did. I went over to the side of the house where the garage was and punched out a glass pane on the entrance with the butt of my rifle. It didn't sound like glass shattering, more like a light metal tinkling sound in some far-off corner of my mind. I reached through the broken pane, unlocked the door, and opened it. I asked Willie, "Shall we enter?" trying to make light of it since he was losing his nerve, ready to run. When he hesitated, I grabbed him by his shirt with my free hand and pulled him inside the house.

Inside, a stairway leads down to the basement, a furnace room with a concrete floor and fieldstone side walls. The kitchen was on the right as we entered, everything very neat. The place smelled like old people, stale but clean, very clean. We tiptoed down the hall and found the dining room, a table with hutches in two corners filled with fancy china. We sat down in the living room, Willie in what looked like the wife's chair and me in the jeweler's, as if we had been invited in. It felt natural to be there, expecting the wife to come in from the kitchen and ask if we wanted something to eat.

We heard, or thought we heard, someone walking on the floor above us in the bedrooms. I grabbed the rifle and walked up the steps. Once on the landing at the head of the stairs, I stopped to listen. At first all I could hear was the drip, drip, drip of a leaky faucet in the nearby bathroom, but then the jeweler shouted, "Who's there? What do you want?" and I went into the bedroom where his voice was coming from. He was getting out of his bed and so I lunged at him with the rifle, like they taught us in bayonet training at Shattuck. He clutched the rifle barrel, and I pulled the rifle back out of his grip. Just as Dr. Satten theorized at one of my court hearings, I was someone else. Shooting the jeweler seemed like self-defense. I shot him, and he fell back and collapsed on the floor. The bullet hit him above his heart.

The next thing I knew, his wife was pulling on my arm, screaming hysterically. I pushed her off, and the jeweler grabbed the rifle and I pulled the trigger, hitting him in the gut. Willie heard what was going on and came up the stairs. I handed him the rifle and pulled the wife back into her bedroom. She was shivering and trembling like a scared dog, like old Laddie before he died. I took some nylons hanging on a rack on her clothes closet door and stuffed one in her mouth. Willie helped me tie her down to the bedposts with more nylons. I noticed a diamond ring and some other jewelry on her dresser. I scooped it all up and put it in my pocket.

We went back into the jeweler's bedroom. He was groaning, in pain and mumbling something. I started to panic, feeling sorry for him one moment, and then that feeling changed and I didn't know why I was in this house, standing next to this dying man, like the outer edge of a dream you are about to wake from. I could see the blood seeping out of a bullet hole in his back, like spring water gurgling up from the ground, and that brought me to my senses, remembering why we were there. We rolled him over and asked him for the combination to the jewelry store safe. He wouldn't give it to us at first, but I nudged him in the back, and he finally gave in. A lot of numbers, I knew I'd better write them down, but there wasn't a pencil or pen in the bedroom. I went downstairs and found a knife on the kitchen counter and used that to carve the numbers on the wooden floor. Then we found his billfold on a bureau in his room, and so I opened it and split the cash with Willie. There wasn't much there, maybe thirty bucks.

We went back downstairs and sat around for a while, Willie in the old man's chair this time and me on the wife's. Willie thought we should call an ambulance, but that didn't make sense to me. Why would we call an ambulance if we were the ones who broke into the house and shot him? I decided to go back upstairs and see how he was doing. I still had the gloves I brought with me in my back pocket, and I stuck one of them in the bullet hole in the old man's back. He kept saying, "Let me live," and I heard a chorus sing the same refrain, "Let him live, let him live," and I couldn't get it out of my head. I patted him on his side, as if help were coming, hold on, old man, for a few more minutes. Back downstairs, we sat in the same chairs and said nothing for the longest time.

The house and neighborhood were dead quiet. I could hear the first bird singing with the morning light, a single note and then another and another, and soon enough all the birds were singing in chorus. I called Dottie from the jeweler's phone and tried to make up with her, but she was still pissed at me, after all I had done and was still willing to do for her. Maybe she did have another boyfriend and this was all a mistake. I told her as much, and she hung up on me.

I called Father Hubert at the Episcopal church, thinking he could help me out of this mess, but when he answered I pretended everything was hunky-dory. I asked him what time services were that afternoon, Good Friday. He invited me to come and said they were serving a meal after, biscuits and gravy and honey, one of my favorites. I told him I would be there. I called Dottie and we talked like a normal day, and when we were talking, I thought it was.

Willie started to get real antsy to leave. I told him someone would see him. There were kids shooting baskets in the school playground across the street. I told him we'd hide out all day and then leave when it got dark again, but he wouldn't listen to reason, or what I thought was reason at the time. Before Willie left we split up the money and jewelry I found on the bureau in the bedroom. I told him to call me at exactly ten o'clock when he got back to Julian.

After Willie left I started having hallucinations, imagining there were people outside waiting for me. I closed all the curtains and turned all the family pictures face-side to the wall or down on the coffee tables. The people in the pictures had grim, knowing smiles, judging me, condemning me. "Tommy White Hawk is a phony and a killer," they said. I felt so bad I went upstairs to check on the old man and the wife. They were okay. I went back downstairs and looked for something to drink, some beer, but there was nothing in their refrigerator, just a ham wrapped in netting, a green Jell-O salad with shaved carrots, and other stuff for their Easter weekend meals. No alcohol. I spotted a package of Oreos on the counter and ate two rows of them and drank some milk. I got real sick after that and puked in their kitchen sink.

Willie called at ten. We didn't talk much, just listened to each other breathe over the phone for several minutes, wanting to wake from this bad dream. Then Willie broke the spell and said he was hitching a ride. I found out later that Butch Artichoker saw Willie outside of Meckling, walking along the railroad tracks. Butch picked him up and gave him a ride to Mission.

When I hung up, I started thinking about Dottie again, that this was all for her and how ungrateful she was. I got more and more worked up and had this powerful urge to have sex. The next thing I knew I was standing over the wife, tied down on the bed. I slowly untied the nylons holding her legs. She knew what I wanted. I pulled out my cock, it had never been so hard, so hard it hurt. She didn't put up any struggle. She smiled and slid to the center of the bed and opened her legs. It wasn't easy entering her, and so I went to the bathroom and found some Vaseline. I slipped right in then and came right away. I went back downstairs, disgusted with her, and laid down on the couch and cried for a long time. I had the feeling that I was not really myself, that someone else was doing all this. This person,

Who Was Not Tom White Hawk, slept awhile and then woke up and went back upstairs and stood above her again at what must have been exactly noon, because the emergency siren was wailing. She didn't move a muscle this time. I went downstairs afterward and laid down on the couch, staring at the ceiling.

Later, I went back upstairs and checked on the old man. I thought he was dead. He didn't respond when I tried to stir him. I rolled him up in the rag rug on his bedroom floor and carried him down the stairs, through the living and dining room. At the top of the stairs leading down to the basement, he groaned again. I dropped him and found a skillet in the kitchen and clubbed him with it across the top of his head. I carried him down the stairs and laid him next to the fuel-oil furnace. An old coal furnace that once heated the house stood in the center of the basement, reminding me of when I used to shovel coal for the big furnace at the Hare Home. As I was about to go back upstairs, I felt real sorry for the old man and put a pillow under his head. Something was telling me from somewhere that the pillow was stupid and crazy, but I did it anyway.

Back upstairs in the kitchen, I found a big roasting pan and a mop. I filled the pan with some water and went back up to the jeweler's bedroom and cleaned up the blood on the floor. There was a lot of it. I took the roasting pan down to the kitchen and put it into the oven, thinking that was a good hiding place for the evidence.

The rest of the afternoon went by very slowly, like slow motion. I watched the twins next door in their bikinis sunbathing in the backyard. They laid out on striped beach towels and blankets. A strange scene with no leaves in the trees yet and the grass brown. I tried to read a story in one of the Catholic magazines, *America,* on the coffee table in the living room. The story was about Jesuit missions in Mexico, but I couldn't concentrate. I laid down on the couch and fell asleep, dreaming that I was a little boy again and Mom was consoling me and telling me that I had to give myself up, that I was going away for a long time.

The telephone woke me up, ringing and ringing. I didn't answer it. I knew whoever was calling would try to talk me into giving up. I thought about leaving, running as fast as I could—no one could catch me once I got going. But I decided to wait until it got dark again. And then I opened the curtains a crack and saw that a crowd had gathered on the front lawn. Time passed so slowly. I waited and waited, and then finally I heard someone knock at the side door and open it. A voice, I learned later the police chief's, asking if anyone was home. I panicked again. I ran upstairs, untied the old lady, and helped her put on her nightgown, a nice light-salmon-colored one with embroidered floral designs. I told her to go outside. I peeked through the curtains as she left the house and saw the police chief and sheriff greet her, and she started to talk to them, pointing back at the house. That's when I knew it was over, and I ran upstairs and into her bedroom. I crawled into her closet and hid under a pile of her clothes like I did at the Rosebud school when they came to cut my hair. I could hear the sheriff and the police chief downstairs, moving slowly through the dining and living room and climbing the stairs, their leather shoes sliding on the wood steps. They searched the jeweler's bedroom first, moving cautiously, and then came into the wife's bedroom. The sheriff saw my shoes sticking out from the pile of clothes and reached in and grabbed me with one hand by the hair. "Come out or I'll blow your fucking brains out," he said, the revolver in his other hand pointed at the side of my head.

The End

Gary held up his cup for more coffee. I filled it. He glanced at me while taking a sip.

"I know this is hard to believe," he said, setting the cup down. "Standing where you and I do, we can't fathom a shift into madness. It's too scary. We fear losing our own grip. But mostly it's a failure of our own imagination. That's why criminal insanity cases are so difficult. Juries often deadlock on this point. But Tom could no more walk away once he had unlocked that side door of the Yeado home than he could stop his own heart from beating. Something exploded in him. He lost control," Gary said.

"There was always someone in Tom's life he could rely on," I said. "Sure, many of them took advantage too. They got something in return. Some felt they had saved him and were satisfied with that reward, but others wanted more, and maybe they got what they wanted or needed from him. But most would give more than they took, and he knew that. At the murder scene, while two people forty years older than him were frozen in terror upstairs in their bedrooms, he called two people who loved him, Dottie and Father Hubert, hoping with some crazed logic that someone would yet again save him."

"You're asking more from Tom than he had to give. You've reduced it to something personal between the two of you. Don't do that. He was an incomplete person. He didn't know that. You remember how curious he was about his own mental health? He thought he could solve his problems by reading a textbook.

As if there were a formula explaining why he had destroyed two lives."

"So forget about the Yeados?"

"The victims deserve our pity and support, but Tom has a claim on our conscience. I know it's not popular now, but responsibility for his insane acts did not end with him."

"I've thought about that gesture, the placing of the pillow under his victim's head, a lot over the years. It's the only shred of empathy, to say nothing of remorse, he showed the entire time. He never apologized for what he did. Not to me, not on the stand, not in his statement before Judge Brady the day his death sentence was handed down," I said.

Gary shrugged.

"Why did he write this down?"

"He told you. It freed him. He's with his relatives now, the only place he ever wanted to be. Tom had no further use for the camouflage he wore all his life, the personas he assumed in each new environment. He might have been saying, 'I live in a cell, alone. I know who and what I am. Take it or leave it.'"

"But why did he give it to me?"

"Who knows? Perhaps you were the last person in his path who understood the context. Giving it to a guard or prison chaplain, even the warden, would not release him."

Gary was silent for a moment, thinking about what he had said.

"But I don't think that's the half of it," he continued.

"What is it, then?"

"Tom trusted you. Not that you would keep what he wrote a secret, but that it wouldn't change how you felt about him. That you would still love him for who he was, not the idealistic image others needed before they rushed to help him."

I walked Gary out to his car, teasing him about his Volvo, the predictable liberal status symbol. In the driver's seat, he buckled up and checked the rearview mirror. He pulled a pair of aviator sunglasses from his shirt pocket. The sunglasses looked out of place on the old man. We promised to keep in touch—a lot easier, we agreed, now that we had email. He backed his Volvo out of the parking space and stepped on it, disappearing into the five o'clock rush, for what it was worth. I went back inside and cleaned up the coffee cups, mindlessly wiping the kitchen island down with more care than I had ever taken. I felt tired, very tired, and I went to the bedroom and fell into the bed, wanting desperately to fall asleep, to be done with it all, but sleep would not come, even with pills. Like Tom, I now had to live with what I had done, and not done. With what I had become.

ACKNOWLEDGMENTS

The characters in this novel were imagined within the context of two infamous murder cases in South Dakota. The actions and dialogue of the characters, for the most part, were created by me.

Details of the murders, as presented in the novel, are true to the historical record. The sources listed below were researched and consulted during the writing of this novel. The primary sources listed here can be found in the Thomas White Hawk file in the Clerk of Courts Office, Clay County Courthouse, Vermillion, SD.

PRIMARY

Bandy, James. Letter to Nils Boe. January 15, 1968.

Hall, Douglas. Brief for postconviction hearing. June 6, 1969.

Leander, Dr. Richard B. Letter to Lee McCahren. October 16, 1967.

Leander, Dr. Richard B. Psychiatric report. October 16, 1967.

Mahoney, Dr. James D. Letter to Chuck Wolsky. October 10, 1967.

Mahoney, Dr. James D. Psychiatric report. October 10, 1967.

McCahren, Lee. Letter to Philip Zoubeck. October 11, 1967.

McCahren, Lee. Letter to Philip Zoubeck. November 3, 1967.

McCahren, Lee, and Arnold Nelson. Deposition for postconviction hearing. March 27, 1969.

Rumpf, C. W. Affidavit.. Physician, Shattuck School. Post-Conviction Hearing. April 30, 1969.

Rumpf, C. W. Letter to Lee McCahren. June 19, 1967.

Satten, Dr. Joseph. Psychiatric report. December 1968.

Shattuck Military Academy Clinic logs. Record of Thomas White Hawk's visits. 1963–1966.

Shattuck School. Grade reports. Thomas White Hawk. June 1964–June 1966.

Stands, William. Deposition for postconviction hearing. May 9, 1969.

Stein, Dr. Jacob. Psychological report. September 1967.

University of South Dakota. Grade reports. Thomas White Hawk. 1966–1967.

White Hawk, Thomas. Letter to Philip Zoubek. December 12, 1966.

White Hawk, Thomas, memoir. August 14 and 18, 1967.

Winans, Judge Fred R. Memorandum decision. Postconviction hearing. June 12, 1969.

Zoubeck, Philip. Letter to Lee McCahren. June 22, 1967.

Zoubeck, Philip. Letter to Lee McCahren. September 14, 1967.

Zoubeck, Philip. Letter to Lee McCahren. October 9, 1967.

Presentence Report. Thomas James White Hawk. United States District Court, District of South Dakota, Southern Division. January 12, 1967.

Transcript. Thomas White Hawk vs. The State of South Dakota. Sentencing. January 15, 1968.

Transcript. Thomas White Hawk vs. The State of South Dakota. Arraignment. October 2, 1967.

Transcript. Thomas White Hawk vs. The State of South Dakota. Hearing. May 5, 1967.

Transcript. Thomas White Hawk vs. The State of South Dakota. Plea of Guilty. November 13, 1967.

Transcript. Thomas White Hawk vs. The State of South Dakota. Arraignment. July 14, 18–19, 1967.

Transcript. Thomas White Hawk vs. The State of South Dakota. Pre-Sentence Hearing. November 16, 1967.

Transcript. William Winford Stands vs. State of South Dakota. December 6, 1967.

Transcript. Thomas James White Hawk v. State of South Dakota, Post-Conviction Hearing. May 12 -15, 1969.

Transcripts and Notes. Thomas White Hawk Interrogations. March 24, 1967.

MISCELLANEOUS

Clapp, Jim. Letter to Lyman Ogilby. February 13, 1969. Lyman Ogilby papers. Episcopal Church in South Dakota Archives, Center for Western Studies, Augustana University.

Newberg, G. Letter to John Milton. September 23, 1970. John Milton papers. Center for Western Studies, Augustana University.

Letters and Petitions. Frank Farrar Papers. State of South Dakota Archives. Pierre, SD.

Statement Concerning Thomas White Hawk Commutation. Frank Farrar Papers. State of South Dakota Archives. Pierre, SD.

White Hawk, Thomas. Application for Commutation of Sentence, transcript. South Dakota Board of Pardons and Paroles. January 15–17, 1969.

NEWSPAPERS

Andersen, Harl."White Hawk Says He 'Gave Up' In Court." *Sioux Falls Argus Leader*, May 14, 1969

Barnett, Mrs. Webster. Letter to the Editor. *Vermillion Plain Talk*, January 25, 1968.

————, "Director Tells Reasons Behind Petition on Capital Punishment." *Volante*, January, 1968.

————, "Tribune Says Stands Mistreated after Trial." *Volante*, March, 1968.

————, "White Hawk Sentenced to Complete Life Term." *Volante*, October 27, 1969.

Editorial. "Kill Capital Punishment?" *Minneapolis Tribune*, January 28, 1968.

Editorial. "Time of Decision" and "Blame Dakotans." *Vermillion Plain Talk*, January 25, 1968.

————, "White Hawk Gets Chair for James Yeado Murder." *Vermillion Plain Talk*, January 18, 1968.

———, "Armour Site of 2nd Trial." *Vermillion Plain Talk*, March, 1968.

———, "White Hawk Was Ready For Jail Break." *Vermillion Plain Talk*, January 25, 1968.

Eliason, Larry. "Death Penalty On 1970 Ballot?" *Volante*, February 25, 1969.

Erickson, Howard. "Many approve death for White Hawk." *Minneapolis Tribune*, January 17, 1968.

Grow, Doug. "S.D. Murderer ends up dying middle-aged death." *Minneapolis Tribune*, May 17, 1997.

Hansen, Gary. "Efforts Fail To Repeal Capital Punishment Law." *Sioux Falls Argus Leader*, February, 1968.

Hansen, Gary, "Mission Residents Shun White Hawk." *Sioux Falls Argus Leader*, December 12, 1968.

Hansen, Gary, "White Hawk's Only Home Was Hillside Log Cabin." *Sioux Falls Argus Leader*, December 13, 1968.

Hansen, Gary, "During White River Trial Berry Tells Of Shooting Little Brave." *Sioux Falls Argus Leader*, September 25, 1969.

Lawrence, Craig. "Stands Innocent On Two Charges." *Volante*, March, 1968,

Lawrence, Craig. "Stands' Verdict Ends 14-Hour Vigil." *Volante*, March, 1968.

Lawrence, Craig. "New Judge to Hear Further White Hawk Case Proceedings." *Volante*, February 4, 1968.

Lewis, Finlay. "Death Sentence on Guilty Plea Came As A Surprise." *Minneapolis Tribune*, January 21, 1968.

Lewis, Finlay. "ACLU Offers to Aid Condemned Youth." *Minneapolis Tribune*, January 18, 1968.

Lewis, Finlay. "Drive Launched for White Hawk." *Minneapolis Tribune*, August, 1968.

Lundquist, John. "Thomas White Hawk Knew Glory For Athletic Prowess." *Sioux Falls Argus Leader*, December 11, 1968.

Oberdorfer, Dan. "20 years after murder, S.D. Indian to seek possibility of parole." *Minneapolis Tribune*, August 3, 1987.

———, "Berry is Found Innocent in Ranch Shooting Death." *Minneapolis Tribune*, September 26, 1969.

Ripley, Anthony, "Death Sentence Against Indian Commuted By Dakota Governor." *The New York Times*, October 26, 1969.

Vizenor, Gerald. "ACLU and the Death Penalty." *Volante*, April 9, 1968.

———, "Director Tells Reasons Behind Petition on Capital Punishment." *Volante*, January, 1968.

———, "Tribune Says Stands Mistreated after Trial." *Volante*, March, 1968.

———, "White Hawk Sentenced to Complete Life Term." *Volante*, October 27, 1969.

Watson, James L. "The Yeados Are Gone: James Yeado Is Dead and Mrs. Yeado Moved." *Sioux Falls Argus Leader*, December 9, 1968.

Watson, James L. "'Officers Describe Death Scene; People Describe White Hawk'." *Sioux Falls Argus Leader*, December 10, 1968.

Watson, James L., "White Hawk Says He Wants To Live; Many People Trying To Assist Him." *Sioux Falls Argus Leader*, December 14, 1968.

Young, Steve. "After 20 years, can S.D. forgive White Hawk?" *Sioux Falls Argus Leader*, October 4, 1987.

Young, Steve. "White Hawk's death closes saga of brutal murder, rape." *Sioux Falls Argus Leader*, May 8, 1997.

———, "Farrar, Boe Decline Comment On White Hawk." *Sioux Falls Argus Leader*, December 20, 1968.

———, "Berry Is Found Innocent In Ranch Shooting Death." *Sioux Falls Argus Leader*, September 26 1969.

———, "USD Student Charged With Rape, Murder." *Sioux Falls Argus Leader*, March 25, 1967.

SECONDARY

Stevenson, Winona. "Studies in American Indian Literatures." *Suppressive Narrator and Multiple Narratees in Gerald Vizenor's Thomas White Hawk.* Vol. 5, Issue 3 (1993): 36–42.

Rodriguez, Jauna Maria. "Vizenor's Shadow Plays: Meditations and Multiplicities of Power." In *Native American Perspectives on Literature and History*, edited by Alan R. Velie, 107–115. Norman: University of Oklahoma Press, 1994.

Vizenor, Gerald. *Thomas White Hawk.* Mound, MN. The Four Winds. 1968.

Vizenor, Gerald. "Why Must Thomas White Hawk Die?" *Twin Citian Magazine.* June, 1968.

Vizenor, Gerald. "Thomas James White Hawk: Wrap-Up?" *Twin Citian Magazine.* January, 1970. p. 39–40.

Vizenor, Gerald. *Tribal Scenes and Ceremonies.* Minneapolis: The Nodin Press, 1976.

Vizenor, Gerald. *Woodarrows*. Minneapolis: University of Minnesota Press, 1978. Reprinted by University of Nebraska Press, 2003.

Vizenor, Gerald. *Crossbloods*. Minneapolis: University of Minnesota Press, 1990.

Vizenor, Gerald. *Postindian Conversations*. Lincoln: University of Nebraska Press,1999.

White Hat Sr., Albert. *Zuya*. Salt Lake City: The University of Utah Press, 2012.

Made in the USA
Middletown, DE
16 August 2023